D1524130

NORA

C.J. PETIT

C.J. PETIT

Printed in the United States of America

First Printing, 2017

ISBN: 9781081324186

TABLE OF CONTENTS

C.J. PETIT

PROLOGUE

Eureka, Colorado
April 18, 1875

Jake stood before the judge, his hands holding Laura's delicate fingers as he gazed into her perfect blue eyes. He could see the love behind her eyes as he knew she could see it in his.

He knew he was the luckiest man on the planet to have won her affections and he knew that every other man in Colorado was either insanely jealous that she had chosen him or simply hadn't seen her.

Jake was so overwhelmed as he stared at his bride that he almost missed some of his vows, but somehow managed to mumble his way through the ceremony. Laura recited hers perfectly, of course. He didn't believe that it was possible for her to be or do anything that wasn't perfect.

The judge intoned, "By the powers vested in me by the state of Colorado, I pronounce you man and wife," and Jake didn't need to hear the next line as he took Laura into his arms and kissed her for the first time as his wife.

After they signed all the necessary legal forms, Jake and Laura stopped at the bank and the land office to make his wife a full partner in the marriage.

Once all of the annoying paperwork was done, they stepped into their rented buggy and left Eureka to head to his ranch for a glorious wedding night, a wedding night that could hold no disappointments for either of them as they'd done full-dress rehearsals for the past week, although full-undressed rehearsals might be more accurate.

As the buggy rolled quickly south to the ranch, they would steal smiling glances, the occasional kiss, and more than the occasional anticipatory fondle. Jake never could have predicted it just a month before, but here it was. He had just married the most perfect woman he had ever met and was still in a state of disbelief. Why she had chosen him above all the others that must have begged for the first place in line was a mystery he knew he'd never understand, but she had. Just two and a half weeks after meeting Laura Jefferson at a church social, she was now Laura Fletcher, his wife. Jake knew he'd spend the rest of his life doing everything that he possibly could to make her happy, and it would begin when they reached his, now their, ranch.

Jake turned the buggy into the access road and after pulling it to a stop outside the barn, bounced out, hustled around the back of the buggy, and helped his beautiful bride from the seat.

"I'll go and get ready for our wedding night, my husband," Laura said as she gave him one of her dazzling, knee-weakening smiles.

"I'll be in as soon as I get the horse unharnessed, my wonderful wife," Jake said as he tried to match her smile but knew he never could.

Laura kept her smile as she floated away from the buggy and walked to the house with Jake's eyes hypnotized by her feminine features as she moved so gracefully and yet so enticingly away.

She gave him a come-hither look before entering the house, and Jake sighed, then turned to the mundane business of unharnessing the horse. He'd bring it back to the livery tomorrow. He had much more important things on his mind at the moment.

CHAPTER 1

May 13, 1875

Jake was leaving the house and walking to the barn to saddle his horse that morning when he spotted a rider trotting down the access road.

He changed direction and headed for the front yard, identifying the rider as Billy Miller, the butcher's son. Billy also served as one of the messenger boys for Western Union, and Jake assumed that he was bringing a telegram, which was always a momentous event. He hadn't received a telegram in over a year, and that one had brought him bad news and hoped that this one wasn't of similar ilk.

He waved at Billy who waved back and angled his rough-looking old horse towards him. It wasn't a true nag yet, but it was close.

"Morning, Billy. Can I guess you've got a telegram for me?"

Billy didn't smile but slowed his horse, then stopped and replied, "Yes, sir, Mister Fletcher," pulled a yellow sheet from his pocket, leaned over, and offered it to him.

He dug through his right pocket, found a nickel, and exchanged it for the message.

Jake opened the telegram and read:

JAKE FLETCHER JF CONN RANCH EUREKA COLO

MOTHER NOT WELL
MAY NOT LAST A WEEK
REQUESTS YOUR PRESENCE

HARVEY PIERCE MD KANSAS CITY MISSOURI

Jake simply stared at the sheet and tried to come to grips with what he was reading. His mother had been in the best of health when he had visited her last and couldn't imagine why she had suddenly taken ill.

He reached into his pocket, took out a nickel, and handed it to Billy as he said, "Thanks, Billy."

"Sorry to be bringin' bad news, Mister Fletcher."

"Never blame the messenger, Billy," Jake replied as he managed a weak smile for the boy.

Billy nodded, wheeled his poor mount, and rode back down the access road.

The telegram still in his hand, Jake trotted back to the front of the house, leapt over the front steps onto the porch, threw open the door, and entered.

"Laura!" he shouted as he passed through the front room and headed for the hallway.

"In here!" she replied loudly from the kitchen where she was baking an apple pie for him.

Jake's boot steps echoed through the house as he stepped quickly down the hallway and into the kitchen.

Laura turned to smile at him and saw his troubled face.

"What's wrong, Jake?"

Jake held the telegram out to her, and after she took it from his shaking hand, read it quickly, then looked up at him with deep concern in her eyes.

"This is terrible news, Jake. When will you be going?"

Jake replied, "How long will it take for you to get ready? The eastbound train leaves at 11:20."

"Jake, as much as I'd love to go with you and meet your mother, under these circumstances, I think this should be a private time between a mother and her son."

Jake took her hands in his and smiled at her, letting himself swim in those marvelous blue eyes before saying, "You're always so thoughtful, my love."

Laura sighed and kissed Jake before saying, "Not as much as I should be. Now, you go ahead and pack quickly, so you can catch that train."

Jake exhaled, let her hands go, turned, and stepped quickly to their bedroom, took out his travel bag from the closet, and began packing.

Two hours and forty minutes later, he was stepping onto the Atchison, Topeka, and Santa Fe's eastbound train to Kansas City. The eleven-hundred-mile trip would take almost two days, and he was worried that he might not make it home in time.

It was only when he was rolling eastward that he realized he should have sent a telegram to his father letting him know he was coming so he could tell his mother. It might have strengthened her will to live so he could say goodbye to her. It was too late now but thought that he might send one when they made one of their coaling stops along the way.

The train was making almost forty miles an hour as it crossed the plains, but it was going much too slowly for Jake.

Jake never did send the telegram because he figured it would only arrive a day before he did at the earliest. For that entire, forty-six hour and thirty-six-minute journey, all he did was absent-mindedly watch the boring landscape roll past and feel guilty for not visiting his parents more often. He hadn't even told them about Laura yet because he was a bit busy.

Jake didn't even wait for the train to stop as it pulled into Kansas City's large railway station. He was on the steel passenger car's platform as the large, wooden platform of the depot appeared and he jumped from the moving train onto the stable wood, stumbled, then regained his balance, and with his travel bag in hand quickly ran to the edge of the platform, hailed a cab and told the driver to take him to 118 Morgan Street.

He had this horrible sense of foreboding deep within him as the driver guided the carriage through the cobbled Kansas City streets. When the carriage halted in front of his parents' house, he handed the driver a Morgan silver dollar and didn't bother waiting for any change.

As the carriage rolled away, he raced up the long, bricked walkway, jumped the three stone steps to the porch, and stopped before the dark red door. He wanted to barge inside but was concerned that he may be interrupting a formal ceremony, so he pulled the doorbell cord, his heart pounding against his ribs.

The door swung open thirty seconds later, and he was stunned as he stared at his smiling mother.

"Jake! What a surprise! Come in!" she said cheerfully.

Jake stayed rooted in place and stammered, "Mama, you're…you're okay?"

She tilted her head and looked at him curiously but noticed the mixture of near-terror and absolute confusion on his face.

"Yes, dear, of course, I'm okay. Why would you ever think otherwise?"

Jake stuttered, "The…the telegram. You were sick. Doctor Pierce said you were deathly ill. I thought you might even be dead before I was able to arrive."

Now his mother was genuinely confused as she asked, "I'm fine. Who is Doctor Pierce?"

Jake's stomach plummeted as he walked inside, his mother closing the door behind him.

After he took a seat, he waited for his gloriously healthy mother to take a seat across from him.

"I received a telegram from someone named Doctor Harvey Pierce two days ago and he said you were ill, might not survive a week, and you had requested my presence."

"I have no idea who this Doctor Pierce is. You know Doctor Johnson is our family doctor."

"I thought maybe he was a specialist or something."

"You should have sent a telegram and I would have set your mind at ease."

Jake nodded, still in utter confusion as to the source and reason for the telegram, and said, "I should have. Maybe there was a mistake and it was sent to the wrong place. If it was sent from Kansas City, then the operator could have thought it was meant for Eureka, Kansas instead."

"That must be it. So, will you stay for a while and tell us how everything is going way out West?" she asked with a smile.

Jake returned her smile and said, "No, Mama. I need to get back to my wife as soon as I can."

"Wife?" she asked with wide eyes, "When did this happen?"

"Three weeks ago. Everything happened so fast. I met Laura at a church social and fell in love with her instantly. Mama, she's so perfect! I wanted to bring her home and surprise you, and we were getting ready to make the trip, but then this telegram arrived and threw that plan into the wastebasket."

"I'm somewhat disappointed that you didn't invite us to the wedding, Jake, but I can understand how you might be so excited that you'd want to get married quickly."

"I'm sorry about that, too, Mama. Laura wanted to get married as badly as I did," then, after a short pause, added, "You know, Mama, I'll admit that I was surprised that she fell in love with me, too. I mean, she's so beautiful that every man who saw her at that social, including the married ones, lined up to dance with her. But she only danced with me. I know I'm not the handsomest man around, so when she made it clear that she had chosen me, I was almost shocked."

"Now, Jake, don't go making yourself to be such a poor catch. I'm just surprised that you waited this long. There were other young ladies that set their caps for you. Did you know her very long?"

13

"Oh, no, Mama. She only moved into Eureka a few weeks ago. That's why she was at the social, to meet people."

His mother nodded, then said, "Well, you'll have to bring her to see us soon."

"I will, Mama. I'll go and send her a telegram that everything is all right and it was probably a misdelivered message and that I'll be returning to Eureka the day after tomorrow."

"Well, at least we'll have you here for two days."

"I'll tell you and Papa all about her."

He went to his old room, unpacked his travel bag, then left the house, walked to the nearest Western Union office, and sent the telegram to Laura to ease her worries. He knew she'd be concerned for him because she was just so compassionate and caring.

When he returned, his mother had a fresh pot of coffee made, so they sat in the kitchen and he talked about the ranch and other things, but mostly about Laura as she prepared dinner for his father, who arrived two hours later.

He was as surprised as his wife had been to see his son sitting in the kitchen and was even more stunned by the news that Jake had married.

Throughout dinner, Jake gladly repeated all of the Laura stories to his father that he had gushed to his mother all afternoon.

It wasn't until they were having coffee and apple pie after dinner that his father said, "So, tell me about this telegram."

"It showed up early in the morning, two days ago and was from a Doctor Pierce in Kansas City saying mama was really sick and wasn't likely to make it through the week."

His father sipped his coffee and sat back.

"I don't know of any doctors named Pierce in the city, and I thought I knew most of them, at least by name."

"Well, maybe he's just a specialist at the hospital or something."

His father closed his left eye, tilted his head, and said, "Did you ever wonder why a doctor would send you a telegram? Wouldn't you think that he'd just tell me, so I could send you the message? How would he even know your address? And if your mother was sick, you'd have to know that I'd send that wire as soon as I could."

Jake began to feel queasy as he replied, "I thought that you were so distraught that maybe you asked him to send it."

His father slowly shook his head, saying, "You know me better than that, Jake. How long would it take me to send a telegram?"

"But it was probably just misdirected and should have gone to Eureka, Kansas."

Again, his father shook his head.

"They don't make that kind of mistake. Besides, that would mean that there's a man named Jake Fletcher living on another C-F Connected ranch outside of Eureka, Kansas."

Jake slipped from queasy to downright nauseous. *How had he missed so many things that pointed to a deliberate attempt to get him away from his ranch? But why would anyone want to lure him away?*

Jake dropped his head and stared into his half-full coffee cup.

"How did I miss all this? I just read it, took it as gospel, and jumped on the train. I didn't even send a telegram saying I was on my way."

His mother replied, "It was because you were upset, Jake. You read the telegram and all you did was worry about me. You raced to the train station and hurried back to Kansas City not thinking about the telegram itself."

"But still, that doesn't mean I should have been so damned blind!" Jake exclaimed.

Then his father asked, "Why would someone want to get you away from the ranch?"

Jake's head snapped up and he replied, "Some jealous man wants my Laura for himself. You should have seen how they all looked at her at that social."

"He'd have to have a friend in Kansas City to send that telegram," his father said.

"There was enough time to send letters back and forth. Maybe his friend thought it was a prank or something."

His father shrugged as his mother said, "Are you staying the night? The first westbound train leaves at 6:15 tomorrow morning."

"Yes, Mama. There's no point in my sending another telegram either, is there?"

"No, Son," his father replied.

Jake closed his eyes and hoped that Laura was still safe.

———

After a horrible night of nightmares, Jake was up with the predawn, dressed, and walking through the early morning mist to the train depot by six o'clock. He bought his ticket and shortly after sunrise, was boarding the train for the interminable two-day train trip back to Eureka.

The train seemed to take forever as he thought of more and more horrible things that could have befallen his bride. *How could he have been such a fool as to not notice the absurdity of that telegram?* If anything happened to Laura as the result of his stupidity, he'd never forgive himself.

To make matters worse, the train was delayed outside of Dodge City when some valve failed, and they had to make a repair. He was furious as he waited for them to fix the damned locomotive and almost thought about buying a horse and riding the remaining two hundred miles.

It added almost seven hours to that already too-long trip and all he could do was wait. He'd had two meals in Dodge City as the train sat on the siding to allow eastbound trains to pass.

Finally, they re-boarded the functional train, regained the main track, and were rolling westward again.

The train finally pulled into the Eureka station late that afternoon. He'd been gone more than five days by the time he jogged into the livery, saddled his tan gelding, Sandy, and after paying Joe Phillips for keeping him, he mounted and walked him out of the livery. Once outside the big barn, he turned onto the main street, set him to a medium trot, and after leaving town, nudged Sandy into a canter to get to his ranch as soon as he could.

The southerly wind combined with his horse's speed was threatening to rip his Stetson from his head as he raced south, so he had to use one hand to hold it in place. He slowed slightly to make the turn into his access road and focused on the front of his house as he accelerated to a gallop the last quarter mile, then pulled to a sudden stop, letting Sandy sit on his haunches as a huge cloud of dust enveloped him and his rider. Jake leapt from the saddle, not even looping the reins around the hitching rail before he raced inside shouting, "Laura! Laura!"

But there was no response, and his heart sickened as his worst fears were realized. She was gone. *Someone must have taken her!* Jake was on the verge of panic as he searched the house looking for signs of struggle and found nothing. He began to believe that maybe she had been taken outside.

Before he left, he checked to see if anything else was missing, but after doing a quick inventory, found nothing gone. Whoever had taken Laura hadn't stolen anything else, but in his search, he found that most of her clothes were gone, which confirmed his fears. This had been a well-organized kidnapping, but the lack of signs of a struggle bothered him. He thought Laura would have put up a fight and tried to imagine a scenario where that wouldn't have happened. He finally concluded that the kidnappers must have held her under gunpoint, it was the only thing that made any sense.

He jogged out of the house and after more than thirty minutes of closely studying the dirt, found no evidence of struggles on the grounds either. He didn't see the hoofprints from the kidnappers' horses but figured they may have walked to the house quietly in the night. That mental image of the brutes

18

entering the bedroom and finding Laura in her nightdress almost made him vomit.

He returned to the back of the house, stepped onto the porch, and just stared out vacantly into the pastures, wondering where the kidnappers could have taken her. He tried not to think of what they were probably doing to her and how terrified she must be.

His wife, his beautiful, perfect Laura was probably huddled in some dark, damp room frightened out of her wits awaiting another visit from one of her kidnappers after having already been molested several times.

He began to imagine what the heartless bastard who had planned this crime would look like. He would be mean-looking and have cruel, emotionless eyes as he took her.

Jake clenched his fists as he wished he could find the man and kill him by just beating him to death.

His poor Laura was now in the clutches of some pitiless thugs and he felt lost. He could almost hear her voice as she told him how much she loved him almost hourly over those miraculous few weeks of their marriage, and not just in their frequent, impassioned beddings, either.

He stood there at the edge of the porch, imagining the sounds of her voice, his Laura's voice. As he listened, he suddenly became aware of something he *wasn't* hearing.

He shook off the memories for a moment and listened more carefully to the real world. He had almost three hundred head of cattle on the ranch, and it was rare to go more than a few seconds without hearing the low of one of the critters. Yet he hadn't heard any in over three minutes of listening on the porch, and now that he thought about it, he hadn't heard or seen any since he had arrived.

He trotted back around to the front of the house and mounted Sandy again to inspect the herd, riding east to the pastures where the main herd usually stayed. He crossed a gentle rise and stopped. He didn't have to be talented in arithmetic to do a head count of the herd. There were eleven cattle grazing peacefully… just eleven.

Jake just sat, looking at his eviscerated herd. *How could almost three hundred head be stolen in just five days?* The stunning discovery drove him to immediately rethink the whole kidnapping theory. With that many cattle gone missing, it would take a group of rustlers to move that many. Maybe Laura had tried to stop them, and they'd taken her as a hostage. *But why had they taken her clothes?*

He sat on Sandy and continued to stare at the tiny group of cattle that didn't even qualify to be called a herd and tried to come up with a possible solution that made any sense.

After his debacle with the telegram, he finally threw away the emotional aspect of the disaster and just examined the facts.

He'd been lured away from his ranch by a fake telegram. While he was gone, his new wife whom he'd only really known for less than two months disappears along with most of his herd of cattle.

As the gray clouds of his mind finally parted, he felt a lot worse than he had when he had first believed that someone had sent him from Eureka to steal his wife. He began to believe that his wife had been part of a bigger scheme to take everything he owned.

There was a simple way to either prove or disprove his new theory waiting for him in Eureka, and he desperately hoped that his new theory was just hogwash. He turned Sandy from the pastures, exited his ranch, and headed north. There was just enough time in the day to get his answers, and ten minutes later, when he entered Eureka, he rode directly to the Colorado State Bank. Once outside the building, he stopped and stepped down, tossed Sandy's reins over the hitching post, hopped onto the boardwalk, and entered the bank. His stomach was doing flips as he approached Mike Christensen, one of the bank's three clerks.

"Howdy, Jake. What can I do for you?" he asked.

Jake sat down in the chair next to his desk and as he began to nervously massage his Stetson's brim, asked, "Mike, has Laura made any withdrawals in the past few days?"

"Sure. She came in Friday and said that you needed to buy some cattle, including a prize bull over on the Kansas side. She took out two thousand dollars. I thought that was a pretty bold move on your part."

Jake didn't want to appear to be the fool that he suddenly realized he was, so he asked, "So, what's my balance?"

Mike stood, walked to the teller's window, pulled out a ledger, copied the balance to a sheet of paper, and returned to his desk.

Laura had left him $378.45. How generous. It probably would have been too suspicious to close the account.

"So, did you get those cattle?" Mike asked with a big smile.

Jake finally swallowed his pride as he replied, "No, Mike. I didn't go to buy any cattle. I got a phony telegram saying my mother was near death and ran off to Kansas City. When I arrived, I found out that my mother was fine and I'm pretty sure that my new wife not only cleaned out the bank account but sold almost all my cattle, too."

Mike grimaced and replied, "I wish there was something we could do to help, Jake."

"Not unless you can set back time and smack some sense into me," Jake replied, then added, "I was gonna go and see the sheriff, but I know there's nothing he can do because she was legally entitled to the money and the ranch, too."

Mike just nodded as Jake stood, turned, and walked slowly out of the bank torn between extraordinary anger at himself and Laura and almost as an incredible emptiness for the colossal betrayal.

He rode more slowly back to the ranch torturing himself for being such a fool. She had married him for the money, taking almost all of it, including his cattle herd.

He ran the numbers in his head. If she'd been a whore, he'd have paid her about a hundred dollars for each of the nights that they'd been together, but that was just for the cash that she had taken. Then he recalculated the amount including the sale of the cattle. In the five days, he was gone, Laura had arranged to sell almost the entire herd. That should have been another five thousand dollars, which meant that her whore price had risen significantly. And that's how he was beginning to see her. Laura was no longer a compassionate, loving wife, she was a manipulative, outrageously costly whore.

In less than a week, he had gone from a reasonably successful small rancher to almost nothing. He'd check with the land office in the morning, knowing that she could sell the ranch without his signature, but he wouldn't doubt anything anymore.

He trotted Sandy back to the barn, unsaddled him, and brushed him down. His head was racing about how to find Laura and make her pay for what she had done.

How could he have been such an idiot?

He knew why but didn't want to admit it because it was so obvious. He had been so smitten with Laura, he let the obvious facts stay locked in the back of his mind.

He knew he wasn't the best-looking man in Eureka, and at best, he was average-looking. But when he had met Laura in April at that church social, he let his own pride get in the way of common sense.

Laura was the complete package. She was absolutely beautiful. Her blonde hair and blue eyes alone could make grown men's knees wobble. Her figure was stunning. She had a soft, melodious voice that flowed through your ears and captured your soul. When she smiled at him for the first time, he knew he was totally smitten. If he had just stepped back and asked, "why me?", and provided himself with an honest answer, then maybe, just maybe, he would have been more distrusting. But he threw all his native common sense out the door, down the road, and out of Colorado. Laura was smiling at him and that was all that mattered.

She must have done her homework well, too. Jake was a lifelong bachelor with an unmortgaged ranch that had been left to him by his mother's older brother, his Uncle Ernest, six years earlier. Jake had visited his Uncle Ernest every summer when he was in school and had worked for him after he had graduated. When Uncle Ernie had succumbed to his advanced case of tuberculosis, there was never any doubt who would be named his heir.

He could have sold it and pocketed the cash, but he had always loved the ranch. Running a ranch seemed to be his calling and everything simply made sense to him. He had hired just a single permanent hand and had worked hard, rarely taking a day off. But the hard work had paid off and he had put away a comfortable nest egg. His hand had quit just two weeks before the telegram, without giving a reason. Looking back now, he wondered how Laura was able to get him to leave.

He remembered how she had smiled at him as she signed her name as Laura Fletcher on the bank account, giving her access. That same smile was present when she signed the deed of the land, which gave her the right to sell cattle carrying the C-F connected brand.

Jake wanted to kick himself in the butt for being such a moron but found it physically impossible. They hadn't even had a month of wedded bliss before that telegram had arrived. But even now, he had to admit, it had been a hell of a month.

She must have operated quickly to empty the bank account and move and sell the cattle. *How could she move almost three hundred head of cattle so fast?* The railroad stockyards were only eight miles away, so it would have only taken a few hours to get them there, so she must have hired some cowhands. That took a lot of planning, no matter what, and it was only then that Jake began to understand the scope of the operation that had left him in ruin.

Two hours later, he was lying on his bed thinking of how he could find her to try to reclaim as much of the seven thousand dollars of his money as he could.

His only clue was that telegram, and there were over a dozen Western Union offices in Kansas City, so it would be difficult to track. He could ask Sam Harper at the train station which direction she had gone, but it was just as likely that whoever was helping her had simply picked her up in a carriage and driven her to Denver.

Her name probably didn't make any difference, either. Laura Jefferson was the name she had signed on the marriage certificate, but he doubted if it was her real name. So, he'd make some inquiries tomorrow, but he was already beginning to feel defeated.

As he lay there, letting his self-pity take control, he closed his eyes and saw those big blue eyes looking into his as she told him how much she loved him. It was that image, the memory of the total dishonesty that had led him to this and changed his whole demeanor. Yes, he'd been foolish. Yes, he lost almost everything he had, but he still had the ranch and he still had Sandy. And he still had enough money to find Laura, or whatever her name is, then make her and her partners pay for what they did to him. He let his anger fill him and it was much better than the wallowing self-pity it replaced. Never again. He'd never be fooled again, and he'd make sure that she and her friends never fooled anyone else.

It was getting dark outside when a driven Jake got out of bed, determined to chase her and her cohorts to hell if he had to. He'd sell those last eleven cattle to fund his search. That would give him a couple of hundred dollars, plus the ninety-two dollars he still had after that unnecessary trip to Kansas City. If he had to, he'd use the remaining money in the bank account and even sell the ranch, but he was now single-minded in his mission to stop her.

As he stormed down the hallway to the kitchen, he suddenly froze and banged his forehead with the heel of his hand. *The cache!* He couldn't recall if he'd shown Laura the secret cache that he'd put away in case the bank failed.

He turned and trotted quickly into the second bedroom, slid the bed four feet across the floor, and stuck his finger through a small knot hole. He pulled the board loose and was gratified to see the pouch still there. He pulled it out and poured the fifteen double eagles into his hand. Thank God, that he hadn't told her about the money. It was another three hundred dollars to add to his search for his pseudo-wife, so he'd leave the greatly reduced savings in the bank as a backstop.

He'd have to limit his expenses, though. He returned the board to the floor and put the bed back in position before walking out to the kitchen and doing an inventory of what he could take with him.

There was enough food for a week at least, so that was good. Then he left the kitchen and the house, and walked out to the barn, hoping that Coffee was still there. The horses in his small remuda, all six of them must have been sold with the cattle, but he hoped that they hadn't sold Coffee.

He was pleased to see that the dark brown gelding was still there, so Jake could use him as his pack horse. He didn't have a pack saddle but could probably trade the second riding saddle for one. The third horse that usually was kept in the barn was a handsome palomino mare that he had bought for Laura after she had accepted his proposal was gone, of course.

Time to come up with a plan. He knew that this would be an almost impossible task because, in the end, he didn't know anything about the woman he had married. His only clue might be in those intimate moments they shared when she talked about growing up in a small town in Kansas. He had a hard time remembering the name of the town though, because she only said it once, and then had almost seemed embarrassed for having told him. The more he thought about it, the more distant it became, so he dropped the subject and would try to remember it later. It might all be a fabrication anyway.

Jake fixed himself dinner. He may have had a limited menu, but what he could cook, he cooked well. He laughed when he first saw Laura trying to prepare a meal. She was lost in the kitchen and anything she tried to make was a disaster. He was glad he hadn't had to eat the apple pie she was making when he left for Kansas City. He wound up doing the cooking during their brief marriage, which should have been a clue, but at the time, he thought it was cute.

He'd have almost six hundred dollars to mount the search. He'd have to buy some more supplies and have to do better on the weapon side as well. He only had his old Colt Walker for a sidearm, but he did have a good shotgun, so that was a plus. But he'd have to buy a new pistol, probably a rifle too, and the ammunition for the new guns. That would take a good sixty dollars out of the kitty.

Before he set out, though, he'd stop over at the United States Marshal's office in Denver and see if they had any reports of similar scams. It would be embarrassing to admit how he'd been hornswoggled, but he'd have to suffer through it. He'd probably have to confess his stupidity a lot more than once as he made his long and difficult search. He'd need a way to hide his cash, too, so a good money belt would be the best solution.

As he lay in bed that night, it finally occurred to him that if this was a recurring scam, then Laura Jefferson, or whatever her real name was, had probably married other foolish men and made off with their bank accounts. Most women, even if they weren't nearly as pretty as Laura, could get a man to do some pretty foolish things. A woman as incredible as Laura could get a man to put a ring around her finger in a matter of hours if she flashed him one of those smiles while she was wearing a revealing outfit. She hadn't dressed provocatively when she had been with him, but after he'd seen her without clothes, he could only imagine how tempting she could have been with the right choice of bodice.

As he drifted off to sleep, he wondered if he should bother to get the marriage annulled.

———

After fixing himself a big breakfast the next morning and cleaning the house, Jake saddled Sandy and Coffee, mounted Sandy, and trailing the darker brown gelding, rode to Eureka.

First, he'd stop in at the sheriff's office to add to his reputation as being the biggest fool in town, if not Colorado.

"Mornin', Jake," Sheriff Ed Barnes said cheerfully as he walked into the office, "Heard that wife of yours kinda stole you blind."

Jake, despite his embarrassment, had to laugh as he replied, "Yup. She took me for damn near everything. Almost emptied the bank account, left me eleven head of cattle, and took off. I'm pretty sure that I'm not the only one that she hornswoggled, either. It sounds like a real flim-flam operation and I aim to track her down and get my money back, or at least most of it."

"Well, good luck with that. You know that there's nothin' I can do unless you can prove it was fraud, and that means you need to find some other feller she married."

"Do you think I can get the marriage annulled based on what happened, Ed?"

"I'm not a lawyer, but I bet it's about the same rules. Find some other feller she married first, and then you could."

Jake nodded, then the sheriff said, "You might want to head to Denver and ask the U.S. Marshal if there were any more cases like yours. If she was marryin' other fellers, they wouldn't be near each other."

"That's where I was headed for next, Ed. Thanks," Jake said as he gave him a short wave, turned, and left the office.

He mounted Sandy, then headed back to the livery to see about getting a pack saddle for Coffee. Three minutes later, he stepped down in front of the barn, tied Sandy off at the hitchrail, and walked inside.

When he had gone to Kansas City, he had used the livery near the train depot, but as he entered Wally Tilton's livery, he was stunned to see Laura's palomino mare standing in a stall staring at him.

Wally saw him enter and said loudly, "There you are. I was wonderin' when you'd show up. I heard that that new blonde bride of yours left you hangin'."

Jake shook his head in disbelief at the speed and depth of the rumor mill as he replied, "She did. I'm surprised she left the palomino, though."

"When she dropped her off, she said she didn't deserve to ride such a beautiful horse."

Jake was surprised and asked, "Did she say anything else?"

"Nope. Just that you'd pay for the boarding fee when you picked her up."

"How much do I owe you, Wally?"

"Two dollars."

Before Jake handed him the cash, he said, "I need to do some dickering with you first, Wally. Coffee over there has a good saddle right now, but I need him to have a pack saddle. I'll trade you that saddle for a pack saddle, new shoes for all three animals, and that two-dollar fee."

Wally scratched the side of his stubbled chin and said, "That's a mighty hard bargain, Jake. I was kinda lookin' forward to the cash so I could buy myself a new razor."

Jake laughed lightly and said, "That sounds fair, Wally. I'll give you the two dollars if I can walk out of here with three newly-shot horses and Coffee wearing a pack saddle instead of his riding saddle, assuming it has four panniers already attached."

Wally grinned, shook Jake's hand, and said, "I'll have 'em ready to go in an hour."

"Okay. I need to go over to the land office and the bank anyway."

"Gotta take that lady's name off a few things?"

"That's the idea," Jake said before leaving the livery, walking out to the street, and then leading Sandy and Coffee into the big barn.

The stops at the bank and the land office didn't take long, and he wasn't the least bit surprised to find that the land office clerk had already pulled his deed and was waiting for him to arrive to have Laura's name removed. The gossip mill hadn't missed any corners.

His next stop was to the gun shop, where he traded his old Colt Walker for a new Colt Model 1873 that they were already calling the Peacemaker. There was only one that was chambered for the same .44 cartridge that the repeater would use, so he was glad to buy it and a gunbelt that could hold eight spare cartridges. He only got two dollars on the trade-in and was happy to get that. He bought a new Winchester '73 and six boxes of .44 cartridges as well, then added two boxes of buckshot for the shotgun.

Then he headed to the dry goods store for his additional supplies. He didn't need much food, but he bought a new cooking grate, four more shirts and two pairs of denim trousers, four pair of underpants, and two more Union suits. He had to get a new scabbard for the Winchester, too. He bought five pounds of jerky and a large sack of crackers for the trail and added a reel of ever-useful cord and four boxes of matches. He finalized his purchases with a new pocketknife.

That cost him $23.75, which wasn't too bad. He then had the order set aside, except for the pocketknife that he slid into his pocket because, well, it was a pocketknife. He then left the store, walked down the street, and picked up his three horses. He shook Wally's hand, mounted Sandy, led the other two down the street to the mercantile, and brought two of the panniers into the store where he and the proprietor loaded them. He lugged the panniers one at a time out the door and hung them onto the pack saddle, lashed them down, and after mounting, headed out of Eureka and back to the ranch.

Once there, he rode directly into the barn and stripped all of the horses. The palomino still had her new saddle, and Jake wasn't sure what to do with her, but that was a decision he'd have to make before he left.

If she hadn't been such a pretty horse, he would have just had Wally make an offer for her, but even though she'd remind him of Laura, he couldn't give the mare up.

He returned to the house with his new weapons, and after he had a quick lunch, took the Winchester and Colt out to the pastures for some target practice.

His Colt Walker, like most pistols before the 1873 Model, used percussion caps and had to have each cylinder loaded manually. Even an experienced hand took almost two minutes to load a percussion revolver using the paper loads, and Jake wasn't that experienced. It also made target practice a bit annoying, so he hadn't done nearly enough to remain proficient.

But the cartridge-loading Colt Model 1873 and the other new revolvers eliminated those problems. Reloading was much faster, carrying spare ammunition was much cleaner and there wasn't the problem of dropping the tiny percussion caps when trying to put them on the nipples, either. The only downside, as far as Jake was concerned, was the ability to add a little extra powder when filling a chamber for that added punch. Of course, the other side was true as well, too much added powder and the pistol could blow up in your hand.

Jake toted his new repeater and had his Colt at his waist as he reached his target range. The target was set at sixty feet, which was silly for the Winchester, so he'd have to walk back another sixty or seventy yards to make it a challenge.

He dry-fired the Colt for a while to get adjusted to the new weight and feel of the pistol which was lighter and better balanced than his old one, then loaded the Colt with six cartridges. He worked slowly at first to get a feel for the new pistol with the added weight from the cartridges, but it still felt light in his hand as if it were a toy. The Walker was a heavy pistol and very robust. This model weighed just over half as much but seemed just as solidly built.

By the time he had emptied the chambers, and the cloud of gunsmoke had cleared, he was impressed with his new sidearm's accuracy. It hadn't lost any power from his old Walker and seemed to be more precise in its ability to deliver the .44 caliber bullets on target.

He fired another six rounds with the pistol, and after examining the damage and the location of the hits, he was very happy to have bought the weapon and thought he should have bought one when they first arrived on the market almost two years ago.

He slipped the empty pistol into his holster, then carried the Winchester and the half-empty box of ammunition another hundred paces to the south, away from the target.

The Winchester wasn't his first repeating rifle as he'd owned a Henry for six years, but after the long spring in the loading tube had snapped and a cartridge had jammed in the loading mechanism two years ago, he'd never had it repaired because he wasn't overly fond of the design anyway. He'd meant to buy one of the Winchester '66 Yellowboys to replace it but hadn't gotten around to it. Now, he was happy to have waited as he examined the '73 more closely. He knew it was essentially the same design as the '66 but seemed more solid.

He began sliding cartridges into the side loading gate until he'd filled the magazine tube with fifteen rounds. Then he levered a cartridge into the chamber and brought the sights into alignment on the target about a hundred and twenty yards downrange.

He made his mental adjustments for the breeze coming out of the northwest and the altitude and then squeezed the trigger.

The butt popped against his shoulder, then he waited for the smoke to clear to examine the second target to the left of the one he'd just filled with holes from the Colt. He was off to the right and low, but not by much.

He made his adjustments and his second shot was much better. By the time he'd fired the last cartridge, the target's eight-inch center had been obliterated.

He returned to the house, cleaned and reloaded both weapons, satisfied with his purchases.

———

The next day, Jake drove his eleven head of cattle to the stock pens. The purchaser was expecting trouble when Jake arrived but was relieved when Jake admitted it was his fault for trusting a woman, not his for buying the critters. He had asked the purchasing agent who had driven the cattle into the pens, hoping that he'd at least get an idea of who had helped her, but the agent told him the cattle were already in the pens that morning when he arrived.

He was able to get twenty-two dollars and fifteen cents a head for his cattle, adding $243.65 to his new money belt. Now the ranch was empty. If he didn't find Laura, or whatever her name is, and get at least some of his money back, he'd probably have to sell the ranch, although he really would rather not. Uncle Ernie had entrusted the ranch to him, and he'd already lost the cattle because of his foolishness. He didn't want to disappoint him even more.

When he returned that afternoon, he began to pack his panniers for the extended time he'd be on the trail. His first stop would be in Denver, and he knew it would be much faster if he took the train, but he didn't want to spend his money on transportation if he didn't have to. Besides, he felt he needed to become more acclimated to life under the open sky.

CHAPTER 2

At dawn the next morning, Jake rose as if it was a normal day, but it was far from that. After washing and shaving, he made himself a large breakfast, eating the last of the eggs in the house. He'd pick up more on his way out of Eureka.

After cleaning the dishes and making sure the house was locked, he carried his food panniers out to the barn, saddled all three horses and loaded Coffee with the panniers, and tied them down.

He had his new Winchester in Sandy's scabbard and the shotgun in the palomino's. Most of the ammunition was in one of the panniers.

The palomino had a name that she'd been given by Laura, and even then, Jake had hated it. She called the handsome mare Sugar, and Jake was now determined to come up with a new name when he thought about it. But for now, she was just the palomino and not Sugar.

He rode into Eureka, bought some more eggs, and just because he wanted to do some more practice shooting, four more boxes of .44 cartridges.

At 10:18 on the bright Saturday morning of May 22nd, 1875, Jake Fletcher rode out of Eureka, Colorado heading northwest to Denver, uncertain of when or if he would return.

The trip to Denver took him three days of hard riding, but the weather had been kind and he'd only run into one long spring shower that had actually been refreshing. He had eaten all his eggs on the short trip, which surprised him, and he'd need some more things before he left Denver, including even more cartridges. He'd spent almost an hour each day practicing with his new guns, expecting he'd need to be ready to use them if it came to that. He made sure to keep them clean and well oiled as they were his protection against highwaymen. He knew he was a good target with his pack horse of supplies and two nice horses with full sets of tack. He was alone as well, so he would be an easy target.

But he reached the big city without any issues, and before he did any shopping in Denver, he had to visit the United States Marshal.

He arrived in Denver around ten o'clock in the morning and it took him some time to find the smallish office of the United States Marshals Service in the rapidly growing city. He had expected it to be some grand, brick building, but was surprised to find it tucked in across the street from the state offices.

He reined in, stepped down, and tied off Sandy before entering the office and spotting a deputy marshal at the desk.

He looked up at a dust-covered Jake, smiled, and asked, "Can I help you?"

Jake removed his Stetson, and replied, "I'd like to report that you're looking at the biggest fool in the state of Colorado. I was just hornswoggled by a woman that I had recently married. We'd been married four weeks before she cleaned out my bank account of two thousand dollars and sold all my cattle for almost six thousand more. I have no idea what her real name is or where to find her, but I know she had an accomplice in Kansas

City. I was just wondering if you'd heard of anyone else who had been a victim of this kind of scam."

The deputy smiled and Jake thought he was going to laugh at him and was ready to accept his humiliation.

"You'll want to see Deputy Marshal Hank Jenkins. He worked a case in February that sounds a lot like yours. Blonde woman, with blue eyes, about five and a half feet tall? A real looker, from what I heard. She married a well-to-do banker in Beaver Creek before taking his money and running off. She must have liked you though because she was only married to him for a week. He got a telegram saying his father had died and he left for Wichita. She cleaned him out of over four thousand dollars. I don't have the details, but if you want to wait around, Hank will be back shortly. He's over at the livery getting his horse checked."

"Thanks. It sounds like her. I'm surprised that she operated so quickly. I would have thought they'd lay low for a while."

"When con artists run a scam like this, they hit as often as they can in one area before they move on. If they do it once, word gets out pretty fast, so they have to operate quickly. My guess is they've already left the area. They probably went either north or east. There are a lot more targets in Kansas, so that would be my guess as to where they went after they took your money."

Jake nodded, then sat down and waited for Deputy Jenkins.

He was just looking at posted wanted posters on the bulletin board when it hit him.

"Chaffee!" he exclaimed, startling the deputy marshal.

He turned to the lawman and said, "Chaffee. She said she grew up in Chaffee, Kansas. It may have been just a story she made up, but I'm not so sure. When she mentioned it, she seemed embarrassed as if she made a mistake. I think I'll head that way after I leave here. Maybe I'll stop in Beaver Creek and talk to the banker on the way."

"Good luck with that. My impression from Hank was that he didn't want anyone else to know about it."

Just then, United States Deputy Marshal Hank Jenkins walked into the office.

"Hank, this gentleman just dropped in. Seems that your blonde scam artist has another victim."

Hank looked over at Jake and said, "Come with me to our office in the back. I'll take down your story and I'll fill you in on what I found in Beaver Creek."

Jake followed the tall man into a small room that looked like its sole purpose was for talking to suspects or witnesses.

"Have a seat. What's your name, by the way?"

"Jake Fletcher," he answered as he pulled out the chair and sat down.

"Call me Hank."

Hank sat opposite Jake, took out a sheet of paper and a pencil, then said, "Now, tell me your story."

Jake spent ten minutes going over all the aspects of his fleecing, from meeting the enchanting Laura Jefferson at the social to his discoveries when he returned from Kansas City. When he had finished, Hank wrote for another two minutes, then laid the pencil down on top of the paper.

"Yours is fairly close to the banker's story in Beaver Creek. The difference was that he met her at the church itself. She said she was new to the area and needed some help with her money. The banker was older than you. How old are you?"

"Twenty-six."

"He's thirty-seven, and not as good-looking as you, either."

"Hank, I may not be homely, but I'm not exactly handsome, either."

The deputy smiled and replied, "I didn't say that you were. The banker was not a handsome man at all. Even I look better than he does. That's what made it so surprising to me. How could a man approaching forty who looked like a tired weasel ever think that a young, very attractive woman would fall for him?"

"I felt the same way. I couldn't figure it out, but when you're smitten, you forget the obvious things."

"That's what he said, too. Anyway, she became Mrs. Claude Liston just twelve days after she arrived in town. Four days later, he gets a telegram from Wichita saying his father was dying and off he goes. The next day, she tells a clerk that he had wired her to bring the money to pay off his father's debts. She took the cash and left. She got away with over four thousand dollars and left him with just over five hundred."

"She left me with less than four hundred. But if she married him in February, how could she marry me in March?"

"What name did she use?"

"Laura Jefferson."

"She was Lydia Jenkins in Beaver Creek, which makes it somewhat interesting. She used a name with the same initials. No relation, by the way."

"Did he mention anything about a hometown? She told me that she grew up in Chaffee, Kansas, almost as if it was a mistake that leaked out."

"No. They didn't share many quiet moments. She seemed to have a lot of headaches or some other malady. I think he bedded her once in four days, just to consummate the marriage."

"That's another difference. We were very busy on that front. I gotta tell you, Hank, if she had only taken a thousand dollars and left the cattle, it would have been worth it."

"That is interesting. There is something else, too. I think she operates with a man, probably her real husband, but that's pure guesswork on my part. He's probably the one who sends the telegrams. So, what are your plans?"

"I'm going to try and get my money back. I'll ride over to Chaffee and, even though it's a long shot, I'll see if she really was from the area. Then, I'll have to wait and see if I can track them down. It's not going to be easy, but it's all I can do."

"Well, I'll tell you what. You send me a telegram every now and then and I'll let you know if I hear anything else."

"I appreciate the help. I've got to get moving. It's a long ride to Chaffee."

"About a week, I'd reckon."

"Yup. That's what I'm thinking."

They shook hands and Jake headed out of the office to his waiting horses. It was going to be a long ride, but he began to have a small glimmer of hope that he might be able to find his elusive faux bride.

———

First, he headed to a huge store that only sold groceries. He filled up his panniers, and in addition to his planned purchase of more eggs and bacon and coffee, added some unusual tins of foods that he hadn't seen before. He also bought some peppercorns and a small grinder. If he was going to have to stay under the stars, he'd at least eat well.

He also made one more stop at a hardware store and bought a small tent as well as more eating utensils. That one day of rain had made him recognize the need for a basic piece of shelter.

He rode east out of Denver just after eating a good lunch.

By three-thirty, he was already twenty miles out of the city.

———

Fifty miles southeast of Chaffee, Nora Graham sat in darkness in her own body waste. She was hungry, and her parched lips were the only external signs of her incredible thirst. She alternated between anger and despair. *Why had Chet done this to her?* It had been almost two days since she had been locked in the closet. She knew that there was heavy furniture against the door because she had exerted every bit of her strength after the first few hours to try and push it open. She knew then that she had no way to get out and in a few more days, she would die here.

Nora never shed a single tear after realizing that morbid fact. She had cried for hours after Chet had locked her in the closet, but once she knew she was doomed, she hadn't cried at all. *What good would that do?* Besides, it was moisture she couldn't afford to lose.

As she sat in her own filth, the foul odor not even noticeable any longer, she thought about how much different she had felt just a few days earlier. After years of understanding that she was destined to be an old maid, her life changed, and she had gotten married.

Some marriage this had turned out to be, she laughed to herself. Locked in a closet, forgotten, and still a virgin.

"*What a fool I am*!" she thought.

She was sliding into a deeper level of hopelessness when she heard a door slam, then footsteps walking down the hallway. Her heart began to race as she heard the chifforobe being moved away from the door. *She was being rescued!*

She tried to get up from her sitting position, but she was too weak to stand, her muscles wound tight from having to sit for so long.

Finally, the door opened. and the sunlight poured in. She was almost blinded by the bright light and put her hands in front of her eyes as she felt two hands pulling her to her feet. When she was finally able to focus, she saw her new husband Chet looking at her.

He scrunched up his face and said, "Nora, you stink!"

Nora tried to ask why he had locked her away, but her mouth was too dry. But he was back and maybe there was a reason he had locked her in the closet, as impossible as it seemed.

She tried to walk but was frozen in place as she looked at him with pleading eyes to make things right.

But Chet finally just laughed and said, "You'd better go and take a bath and clean out that closet. At least now I can't be arrested for murder."

Nora was stunned. *Murder?*

She stood there dumbfounded as Chet said, "And don't bother trying to get the law involved, either. You gave me the rights to everything, and I took what I could. Good luck with the rest of your life. Sorry I didn't consummate the marriage, but I do have my standards."

Then he began to lean forward as if he were going to kiss her goodbye, but then crinkled his nose again, whistled, turned and walked down the hallway and out the door, slamming it behind him.

Nora stood frozen in place for another minute before trying to move her feet but collapsed to the floor. At least she could now stretch her legs for the first time in two days.

Chet was gone, and she knew he wouldn't be back, but didn't care. She was going to die an old maid, but at least she wouldn't die in that closet, and not in a few days.

But even as she lay on the floor, she had a sinking feeling that although she hadn't met his standards for taking her to his bed, what did meet his standards was her bank account.

———

When Jake began to ride that day, it was a bright, mild spring morning, but by noon, the weather began to take a dip into the other extreme. The clouds began building from the west and the wind picked up dramatically. Jake pulled his slicker on over his heavy jacket, not wanting it to get soaked with the impending rain.

When the precipitation finally began falling it wasn't rain. The temperature had dropped to near freezing and the moisture first began falling as ice pellets. With the wind from the northwest, it wasn't too bad as the pellets were being driven into his back. Then, after a few more minutes, the ice pellets gave way to snow.

Jake looked for someplace to set up his camp. He was only thirty-eight miles out of Denver, and he was nearing the town of Box Elder but was determined not to get into the habit of using hotels. He saw an entrance road to a farm or a ranch and turned.

When he approached the farmhouse, he pulled to a stop fifty feet before the porch and announced his presence using the accepted method.

"Hello, the house!" he shouted to make his voice heard over the wind.

The door opened and the man of the house, about mid-thirties and heavy-set with beetling brows stared out at him.

"What do you want?"

"I was wondering if I could put up in your barn for the night."

"Go ahead."

"I appreciate it."

The man didn't reply, but simply closed the door before Jake turned Sandy toward the barn, and once there, stepped down, opened one door, and led his horses inside, closing it behind him, grateful to be out of the wind and snow. Jake gave the place a quick perusal and thought that it was a well-maintained barn, then began unsaddling the three horses. Once that was done, he brushed them down as they drank from the trough, then set them into three of the empty stalls, leaving just one free between his three animals and the two draft horses in the last two.

He was debating about what to make for dinner when the door opened, and the farmer's wife entered carrying a bowl. She was bundled in a heavy jacket with a scarf over her hair, and her pleasant face and smiling eyes shone from inside the scarf's frame.

She held out the bowl and said, "We've already eaten, and I thought you'd like to have something warm."

Jake thankfully accepted the still steaming bowl and replied, "Thank you, ma'am. I really appreciate it. I'm sure your cooking is better than mine."

She smiled and said, "It's a terrible day to travel. Are you heading for Box Elder?"

Jake had already begun spooning the very tasty stew as he answered, "I'll just be passing through town heading east. I'm going to Chaffee, Kansas."

"Where is that? I've never heard of it."

"It's a small town about another hundred and seventy miles away."

"Do you have family there?"

"No, ma'am. I'm looking for a woman that I married last month before she cleaned me out of my savings and sold all my cattle. I was a fool and she let me know it."

"That's a shameful thing for her to have done."

"I think the shame is all on me, ma'am. It turns out that she had done the same thing to a banker in Beaver Creek the month before. Pretty faces can do a lot more than just turn heads. They empty wallets if the man is stupid enough."

"If you find her, what will you do?"

Jake put the spoon back into the bowl, looked at her, and answered, "That's a good question. I guess I'll just take her to the local law and try to get my money back."

"Well, good luck with that."

"Thank you, ma'am," Jake said before he quickly finished the stew, and handed her the bowl before adding, "The stew was really tasty ma'am. I really do appreciate your consideration."

"Well, I hope you find her and get back what she stole."

"So, do I, ma'am."

She smiled, then turned, opened the door, and returned to the nasty weather as Jake quickly closed it behind her.

Jake looked at the closed door and the foolishness of marrying Laura struck him even harder. *Why couldn't he have found a sweet and considerate woman like that to marry instead of the pretty, but selfish one he had married?* Or thought he married, as he suddenly realized that if she had married the banker, he wasn't married in the first place, and could get his sham marriage annulled. That alone would make the legal issue of regaining his stolen property easier.

He set up his bedroll then took off his slicker and heavy jacket, hung them on a nearby peg, then removed his new gunbelt and hung it up as well. He then slipped off his boots, slid into the bedroll, and finally gained some much-needed heat after a few minutes.

As he lay on his back with his hands behind his head, he thought about the farmer's wife again. He had always sought out the pretty girls, as most men did. He knew that he wasn't the most handsome sort, but at the same time, women seemed to like him. Maybe because he wasn't as crude as most of his contemporaries and spent time listening to them. Whatever the reason, he had more than his fair number of lady friends.

He'd had some dalliances with the pretty girls, but nothing ever took hold until he met Laura, and look how that had turned out. Jake then vowed that he'd start paying attention to those other qualities that he'd previously neglected. He'd never make that mistake again, that is if he ever married at all. The one he'd tried sure left a sour taste in his mouth.

————

He woke early and had all the horses saddled and ready to go by six o'clock. He had opened the barn door a crack and found snow, but no clouds or wind. The temperature seemed to be moderating already as well.

He opened the door all the way, led his small entourage from the barn, then closed the door and mounted Sandy. He had left a silver dollar on the barn floor where he had slept, knowing that they wouldn't have expected it but knew it would be appreciated.

He was on the road and making good time as he entered Box Elder an hour later. The town was beginning to stir as he stopped at the local café, ingeniously called the Box Lunch, where he had a hot, filling, and quite tasty breakfast. It was worth the twenty cents, plus the nickel tip, then as the sun was blasting into his eyes, he mounted and left Box Elder still wondering if he should stop at the bank at Beaver Creek eighteen miles away. He thought about it for the next hour as the temperature passed freezing and the snow began to melt.

———

When he entered Beaver Creek around ten o'clock, he decided he had nothing to lose, so he stopped at the bank and tied up. He entered the lobby and asked a clerk for Mister Liston. It turned out that Mister Liston was the bank president and was shown to his office.

Jake entered the office with his Stetson in his hands and met the eyes of Claude Liston and had to agree with U.S. Deputy Marshal Jenkins that he had a strong resemblance to a weasel.

"What can I do for you, sir?" he asked with a warm smile.

Jake asked, "Mister Liston, could I speak to you for a few minutes about your recent marriage?"

Claude Liston assumed a totally different attitude as his brows furrowed making him appear even more like a weasel, and an angry weasel at that.

"I'll ask you to leave my office, sir. I do not speak of that. Ever," he snapped.

Jake replied, "Mister Liston, I'm only asking because I was married to that woman last month. She took me for almost eight thousand dollars."

His attitude reversed again as he calmed and said, "Close the door and have a seat."

Jake closed the door, then took a seat in one of the two chairs on the customer side of his desk.

"How did you find out about me?" he asked.

"I went to file a complaint with the U.S. Marshal's office. They said that you had experienced a similar situation earlier this year. I thought I'd stop by to see if you could give me any more information than I already have. I'm going after her, Mister Liston, and I'm not going to rest until I find her."

"You want her back? After what she did?" he asked incredulously.

"No, sir. I want her in jail, and I want my money back. I'll try and get yours back as well."

"I really would appreciate that. I would have chased after her, but I have a business to run."

"I have nothing but an empty ranch after she sold all my cattle. I just need to find out if you know anything else about her. She mentioned that she grew up in a small town in Kansas named Chaffee, but she only mentioned it once."

"She didn't talk to me much. She did mention once that she had a brother, though. Looking back, I'm wondering if she wasn't referring to her real husband."

"I'm sure she has at least one accomplice. The deputy marshal in Denver thought it was her husband, but that would mean that he would have been in Kansas City when I was duped a week ago."

"He must have been in Wichita when I got the telegram."

"Do you still have it?"

"No, she took it."

"She used the name Laura Jefferson with me, and the deputy said she used Lydia Jenkins with you. I find it odd that she used the same initials. I'd guess it was because her original name used those same two letters."

"She had a travel bag with L.J. on it, so that would make sense."

"I never noticed that. I saw the travel bag, but I didn't notice the initials."

"Can I ask you a very personal question?" Claude asked.

"This is all very personal, so go ahead."

"Did you have issues consummating the marriage?"

Jake paused then replied, "No, it was just the opposite. It seemed as if we spent all of our time in bed."

"Oh. I suppose I needed that one last confirmation about what an idiot I was in that whole scam," he said before he leaned back and sighed.

Jake thought he'd make the banker feel better by saying, "It doesn't really matter, does it? She didn't care one bit about either of us. She just whispered all those words of love and desire into our ears and didn't mean one word. I guess every time she said, 'I love you', she must have been laughing inside."

"She told you that? She never did to me, not once."

Jake was surprised, but said, "Different approaches for different victims, I think. She knew I wanted to hear it, so she told me. Maybe she thought she didn't have to with you."

"I told her many times, but every time I did, she'd just smile and give me a peck on the cheek."

"We learn, Mister Liston. I'll never make that mistake again."

"I should have known better. My Matilda was nothing like Lydia. She was so kind and caring. She wasn't anywhere near as pretty as Lydia, few women are. But she had an honest, smiling face and I miss her a lot. I guess being lonely had a lot to do with it, but you're right, neither of us should ever make that mistake again. I doubt if I'll ever remarry."

"Same here. Of course, for me, I was never married in the first place, and I doubt if you were married to her, either. Mister Liston, I vow that I'll do everything I can to bring her to justice and return what she stole from you."

"Thank you. But she'll never be able to return my dignity or my trust in people. I never did get your name."

"Jake Fletcher."

"Well, good luck, Mister Fletcher."

They both stood and shook hands before Jake turned and left his office and strode across the lobby.

Jake left the bank with as many new questions as answers. *Why had Laura, or Lydia, or whatever her real name was, treat him so differently than Mister Liston?* He assumed it was because of his physical appearance and doubted if she meant a single word of affection.

He mounted Sandy and led the two horses out of Beaver Creek toward Kansas, still about another hundred miles further east. Then he'd have to find Chaffee and hope that she had made an honest slip of the tongue and mentioned her real hometown. If she had, then maybe he'd learn a lot more about the woman who had almost ruined his life but taught him a valuable lesson.

CHAPTER 3

Three days later, Jake entered Kansas. It was 10:15 in the morning when he crossed the invisible line, but he had no idea that he'd exited Colorado. The road he was using paralleled the railroad, and he wondered which was there first, the road or the railroad.

He passed through the towns of Horace, Tribune, and Selkirk before he broke for a late lunch at two o'clock. He had his horses drinking in a stream off to the south of the road about a hundred and fifty yards when he noticed three men riding west. They didn't have a lot of supplies with them and only one of them had a coil of rope looped around his saddle, so they probably weren't ranch hands. They surely didn't have the look of farmers, either.

He knew the town of Leoti was just a few miles up the road, so he didn't pay them any special attention for a while. But as they got close to where he had turned off, he noticed that they all turned to look in his direction. It wasn't a quick glance, but a continued stare, which set off warning bells. He pulled the shotgun from its scabbard but kept eating his jerky as he watched them ride past, expecting them to suddenly turn in his direction.

But they stayed on the road as Jake washed down the jerky with some metallic-tasting water from his canteen while they passed and continued west. Jake watched until they crossed a low rise and disappeared from sight a half mile down the road. Maybe it was nothing, or maybe they were just scared off by his shotgun.

After returning the shotgun to its scabbard on Coffee, he climbed back into the saddle and got his horses moving again, angling toward the road. He picked up the pace a bit to increase any gap and checked behind him every minute or so.

He reached Leoti twenty minutes later and felt safer once he entered town, but quickly passed through the little burg, and three hours later was looking for a campsite.

He had continued to check his backtrail, only not as often after leaving Leoti, when he found a decent location that was a couple of hundred yards south of the roadway. It was probably the same creek he had stopped at earlier, as it snaked alongside the rails and the road.

The new campsite was sheltered by some cottonwoods, so he led the animals into the trees and began unsaddling and unpacking Coffee. He decided on a cold camp as those three men still had him spooked. If they had smiles on their faces, he wouldn't have paid them a second thought, but they all seemed to be weighing his value as a potential victim.

Once his cold camp was done, he took out his reel of cord and wrapped it around one of the trees, and walked around the other trees, making a loop around each one, keeping the cord taut and about six inches from the ground. He finally completed the semicircle and tied off the cord. It wasn't perfect, but he felt better knowing he'd have warning of any stealthy approach after the sun disappeared below the western horizon and its distant Rocky Mountains. He couldn't trust his horses to let him know of any nighttime visitors.

He had some cold beans and washed them down with cold creek water, then laid his bedroll down. He slid his shotgun from its scabbard, walked to one of the big cottonwoods, and sat down, leaning against the thick trunk. He kept the horses near the creek so they could graze and drink and at the same time, keep out of the line of fire should it be necessary. It was the first time he felt threatened during the entire trip and he didn't like not knowing what their intention was, if any. He knew that it was more likely that they were just innocent cowhands, but that didn't match their appearance or their location, and he expected trouble.

The sun had set, and Jake just chewed jerky and sat on a log about thirty feet from his bedroll and packs, which wasn't as cold as sitting on the ground near the tree trunk. He was beginning to relax after the two hours of peace and quiet and figured those three men were probably thirty miles away by now. No one could see him in the dark and without a campfire, they wouldn't find his camp, or so he believed.

The almost full moon rose a half hour later. It was a bright moon and no clouds diminished the light as it reached the earth. He checked on his simple cord booby trap and was gratified that it was still difficult to see. The moon was bright, but the leaves on the trees blocked the moonlight from illuminating the white cord effectively. He walked toward the edge of the trees, then looked back toward the road and almost stopped breathing.

They had returned after all. The three men were riding slowly along the road, obviously searching for where he'd left the hard-packed surface. Jake backed into the trees a few feet, his eyes never leaving the approaching riders.

One of them suddenly pointed at the ground where he had left the road, but Jake couldn't hear what he said. He must have barely spoken, or they had just used hand signals. These three men were experienced highwaymen and his level of worry just ratcheted up a few notches.

They knew he hadn't stayed in town and must have spotted his tracks, then he glanced back at the horses, and noticed that the light coat of the palomino stuck out like a beacon, so they must have seen her or soon would.

They all stood in their stirrups and began scanning in his direction and soon, Jake heard their excited, but hushed chatter. They must have spotted the palomino.

As they guided their mounts off the road heading toward his location, Jake cocked both hammers on his shotgun and stepped backward toward the campsite, keeping them in sight as long as he could. Then he quickly turned and walked behind two trees at the corner of the small copse and waited behind what was no longer a warning device, but his booby trap.

Jake could hear the three horses approach his camp as he waited behind one of the cottonwoods. They suddenly stopped about a hundred feet from the horses, dismounted, and he heard three pistol hammers being pulled back into position.

Jake was scared, bordering on terrified. He had never had to do this kind of thing before, and his heart was pounding so loudly he thought it would give his position away as they walked closer.

His ears heard the pounding of his blood that his heart was pulsing through him as he drew the shotgun level but kept his finger away from the trigger to prevent an accidental discharge. There would be a time when they were close.

And they were getting closer with each carefully measured step. They tried to be quiet, but two of the three were wearing spurs, and the slight jingle they made was a great way to keep them located. Jake also noticed that they were all staying together, which he felt was their first serious mistake. He slipped off his Colt's hammer loop to have it ready as a backup. He was as ready as he could be.

"Hello, the camp!" shouted one, startling Jake, but not enough to get him to react.

Jake could see all three of their pistols pointing in the direction of the heavy packs in the center of his camp. With their light gray canvas, they reflected what little light there was in the trees. Without hearing a response, they continued forward more hesitantly.

"Hey! Mister! We just need to talk to you," he shouted again.

Jake didn't want to give away his position off to their right, so he said nothing. He was even beginning to wonder if he had the nerve to pull the trigger at all. He was about to kill three men, and he gave serious thought to warning them.

The shouter was going to yell again when he and his partner to the left both tripped over the cord and their pistols both discharged into the dirt. The third man, recognizing the cord, stepped over it and quickly scanned for Jake.

"Drop the pistols! I got two barrels loaded with buckshot pointed at you!" Jake yelled, making his position known.

The only upright man swiveled in his direction and fired, the flame from his pistol illuminating his position.

Jake didn't hesitate as he pulled the trigger and the night was lit up as the two barrels exploded, sending dozens of heavy lead pellets spraying across the campsite.

The three men all took significant hits from the discharge. The standing man was no longer standing, and the two men who had begun to rise when Jake yelled were back down.

Jake was shaking as he set down the shotgun, pulled his pistol, cocked the hammer, and stepped forward.

The standing man was dead having taken at least a dozen of the lead balls in his lower chest. The shouter was also dead, with eight missiles embedded in his neck and head.

The third man was still alive, but barely as his life's blood was squirting from his right carotid artery as Jake stood over him.

"Why did you come in here like that?" Jake shouted in a quivering voice.

The third man looked up at him, opened his mouth as if to answer, then just collapsed and died without saying a word.

Jake was lost for a little while. After slowly holstering his pistol, he unsteadily walked to the log he had been sitting on, careful not to trip over his own booby trap, and sat down. His hands were still shaking as he lowered his head and stared at the ground as the gunsmoke still hung over his camp in the still air. He stayed unmoving for ten minutes before he took a deep breath, stood, and walked back over to where the three bodies lay. At least he hadn't vomited.

He began to gather wood to build a campfire because he needed the heat and more light to examine the three men. Fifteen minutes later, when it was bright enough, he went over to the first man on the left. He went through his pockets looking for identification, found $12.35 in his pocket, and shoved it into his own pocket, then took off the man's gunbelt, picked up his pistol, shoved it into the holster, and hung it on a nearby branch. He checked the second man. He had $24.10, which also was pushed into his pocket before he stripped the gunbelt from the body and added it to the branch. The last man who died was also the last man he checked. He only had $10.55 on him, but he wouldn't need it anymore.

When he was finished with all three, he walked out to their horses, led them to the campsite, and after he tied them on some of the cottonwood branches, pulled their saddlebags. All of them had Winchesters in their scabbards, too, but he'd check them out later.

He walked the saddlebags back to the campfire and one by one, dumped their contents onto the ground. He found clothes, some cans of beans, and some ammunition, but nothing at all to identify who they were. He knew that rigor mortis would prevent him from getting them on the saddles after an hour or so, so he loaded each one onto a horse. He removed the cord from the trees and after using some of it to tie the bodies down, wrapped the rest around the reel.

When everything was done, he sat down before the fire, feeling the heat on his face, and wondered what was wrong with him. He had just killed three men, and he should feel guilty, but he didn't. They were going to kill him, but he had been lucky enough to get them first. Maybe that was why he didn't feel shame or remorse. Whatever the reason, he knew that he'd need to leave early in the morning and decided to head east to Scott to deliver the bodies. It was larger and it was also on his way to Chaffee. He didn't want to lose those miles.

After cleaning all of the guns that had been fired, Jake didn't bother sliding into his bedroll but just used it as a mattress after pulling his blanket over him for warmth. He didn't want to be trapped inside.

———

It was still just predawn when Jake left his campsite because he hadn't slept at all. He had a long string of horses now, and the last three were all loaded with dead men. He had skipped breakfast to get on the road and figured he'd eat after he talked to the sheriff.

He arrived in Scott just after eight o'clock, stopped before the sheriff's office, and stepped down. Residents were gawking at the sight, but Jake paid them no mind as he entered the office.

"Morning!" greeted a cheerful deputy. "What can I do for you?"

Jake calmly replied, "I have three bodies outside. They came to my camp with pistols drawn last night. I heard them coming, so I had my shotgun on them. I told them to drop their guns and they fired. I fired and they all took enough buckshot to put an end to them."

The deputy's demeanor shifted as he said, "Just a minute. I'll go and get the sheriff."

He hustled back to an office inside and the sheriff walked out with the deputy in tow.

"You said you have three dead men outside?" he asked.

"Yes, sir."

"Let's go and look at 'em," he said before they all exited the office, stepped onto the boardwalk, and approached the horse train.

The sheriff walked up to the first man and pulled his head back, then did the same for the other two.

"Come inside and tell me what happened," he said, then turned and entered the jail.

Jake followed him into the main office with the deputy walking behind him. The deputy then walked around the desk and stood behind the sheriff as he sat in the chair at the desk while Jake took the chair facing the desk.

Jake began his story, saying, "I was traveling east on the road yesterday around two o'clock...", and finished just three minutes later. There really wasn't much to tell.

The sheriff exhaled sharply and said, "You're one lucky man, mister. The middle guy on those three horses is Walt Hollister, and he's a nasty piece of work. The first one is Oscar Davis. He's not as bad, but still not a nice man. I don't know who the third man is, but if he's riding with those two, I can't imagine he's a good churchgoer. Now, I'm going to go out and check some things and you need to come along."

They all walked outside again where a dozen people had already gathered, standing around watching the rare show. The sheriff pulled each of their Colts and checked them before returning them to their holsters.

"You got your shotgun?" he asked.

Jake stepped to Coffee, slid the shotgun from its scabbard, and handed it to the lawman. He broke it open and ejected the two spent shells.

"Everything backs your story, not that it mattered much. I'm going to go through the wanted posters to see if I can identify that third man."

He turned to his deputy and said, "Ed, go ahead and walk those three bodies down to Joshua. Bring the horses back."

"Will do, boss."

Jake followed the sheriff back inside and sat down as the sheriff began thumbing through wanted posters. He pulled one, then a second, and finally a third.

"Well, it turns out that the third man may have been worse than Walt. Altogether, they have rewards of five hundred and fifty dollars, and it looks like you did everybody a favor. You wanna see 'em?"

Jake nodded, and the sheriff slid the three posters across the desk. He was a bit shaken as he read that the third man, Amos Bixby, had been wanted for three counts of murder. Walt Hollister was wanted for murder, robbery, and rape. Oscar Davis was just wanted for robbery and assault.

"You can do what you want with the horses and weapons. I assume you already went through their pockets, and don't be embarrassed if you did. You're entitled."

Jake nodded and said, "I've never even shot at anyone before. I was hoping that they'd just ride on."

"Well, that may be, but a lot of folks will sleep better with that bunch gone. What's your name, anyway?"

"Jake Fletcher."

"Well, Jake. I'll go ahead and wire the ones who posted the rewards. They'll wire back and authorize payment. It probably won't show up until later today or early tomorrow. You gonna hang around?"

"I suppose. I'm heading to Chaffee and I'd like to get there as soon as possible."

"What do you have to do over in Chaffee? That's kind of off the beaten path."

"I was swindled by a woman that I think came from there. I need to get more information and hopefully track her down."

"Good luck with that. You might want to get some breakfast right now, though. Ed won't be back for a while."

"Thanks, I'll do that."

Jake left the office and walked three doors down to the run-of-the-mill small-town diner with a sign proclaiming GOOD FOOD. At least it wasn't false advertising, so he enjoyed a very nice breakfast before heading back to the sheriff's office. Before he made it to the jail, he spotted Deputy Ed leading the three horses down the street, and the deputy waved him over.

"What are you going to do with these?" he asked.

"I don't know. I guess I'll take them down to the livery and see if the liveryman will buy them."

"I'll buy this big bay, here. He's a lot better than the old nag they assigned me when I took the job."

"You keep him, then. I'll take the other two."

"I gotta give you something to keep me honest. How about ten bucks."

"That's fine."

Ed reached into his pocket and handed him a gold eagle, tickled about his great buy. The horse and saddle would have set him back a good hundred dollars if he had to buy them normally.

Jake and Ed walked the other two horses down to the livery, and once they were inside, Ed explained the situation to the liveryman and Jake wound up selling both horses and saddles for a hundred and twenty dollars but kept all three Winchesters and Colts. He wasn't sure what he'd do with them, but for now, they'd all be on Coffee or ex-Sugar somewhere. He returned to the sheriff's office with a sizeable amount of cash added to his pockets but would move most of it to his money belt when he went to the hotel.

He and the deputy entered, and Ed took his accustomed seat behind the desk while Jake plopped down in the same one that he'd used before.

"You gonna hang around for a while?" Ed asked.

"Until the reward money comes in, I guess."

"The boss said you were headed to Chaffee. What for?"

Jake sat and explained what had happened to him as Ed sat back, intrigued by the story, yet still wore a poorly suppressed smile on his face.

When Jake finished, Ed said, "So, technically, even though you ain't married to her, you at least got to enjoy her favors for a month."

"You know, Ed, I figured at one point that if she had walked off with a thousand dollars from my bank account, I'd have been pissed, but I'd have let it go. It was a momentous, incredible month, but she got greedy and took almost all of it."

"Now I married a nice girl. She really watches the money, too. She'll be happy as can be that I bought the horse for only ten dollars because she's a sweetheart. She isn't really pretty, but I think she's cute."

"That's all that matters, isn't it? That she cares about you and you care about her?"

"I guess that's right. What do I care what everyone else thinks of her, as long as I like her?"

"I was too wrapped up in what Laura looked like to pay any attention to the rest. But never again, Ed. If I ever get married again, it'll be for the right reason. I know it's not gonna be anytime soon, though."

"Well, I hope you find out more when you get to Chaffee. You gonna stay at the hotel?"

"I think so. A bed would be nice for a change, right now I'm gonna take my horses down to the livery. I need to have their shoes checked, too. I had them shod before I left on this trip, but they put a lot of miles behind them already."

He rose, waved goodbye to Ed, and stepped back outside, untied Sandy, mounted, then led the other two down the street to the livery where he had them boarded and asked to have the shoes checked and replaced if necessary.

The liveryman was happy to get some of his money back, despite the bargain he'd gotten when he bought the two horses from Jake.

It was only a dollar and a half for the stay and if they needed shoes, it would be another three dollars per set. Jake paid the buck and a half, then headed for the hotel with his saddlebags over his shoulder, carrying his Winchester.

He paid two dollars for the room and got his room key, went inside, and sat the saddlebags in the corner with his rifle. He now had four Winchesters and four Colts in his possession along with nine full boxes of cartridges and four opened boxes, giving him a lot of firepower. Why he decided to hang onto them, he hadn't a clue. After that confrontation with those highwaymen, more guns seemed safer. He may get rid of them later after he'd calmed down. Another problem was that he would now have over a thousand dollars in his possession, and it made him nervous. He'd keep enough cash in his pockets for any needs and to satisfy any potential robber, but he'd keep almost all of it in his money belt.

He headed back out of the lobby and walked to the dry goods store across the street and over a block. It was quite large and had a variety of items that he hadn't seen since he left Eureka. In addition to some supplies, he indulged in a personal vice and bought some penny candy, not a lot, but a nickel's worth wasn't exactly a small bag, either.

———

The next morning, his first stop was to the livery where he had to pay for three sets of new shoes but asked that the horses be saddled while he had his breakfast. He wasn't sure the new shoes were completely necessary, but he'd rather have them replaced than have one of the horses throw a shoe before he reached Chafee. He left the horses in the barn and as he headed to the diner for some breakfast, he was stopped on the way by the sheriff, who was headed to the hotel to find him.

"Your rewards all came in, Jake," he said as he handed him a short stack of paper that didn't look like currency.

Jake asked, "What are these?"

"I guess you haven't seen 'em before, but they're Western Union vouchers. You can cash 'em at any bank."

"That makes sense," Jake said as he read the top voucher for a hundred and fifty dollars, "I'd rather have them this way, too. It's a lot safer than carrying all that cash."

"Yup. So, you'll be heading for Chaffee soon?"

"Yes, sir. I'll have my breakfast and then ride east."

He shook Jake's hand and said, "Good luck, Jake."

Jake nodded, then after the sheriff turned to go back to his jail, he slid the vouchers into his pocket for the time being, then headed for the diner.

After he had his breakfast, he returned to the hotel, handed in his key to the desk clerk, and returned to the livery, where he found his equine trio saddled, his four Winchesters and the shotgun in their scabbards.

He led his newly shod horses out of the barn, mounted Sandy, then rode out of town, taking the northeast fork of the road toward Chaffee, richer and much more heavily armed.

As he rode, just as he had every day since he had started, he thought about his future beyond Laura Whomever. He had nothing else to occupy his time as he passed the miles. He couldn't chat with the horses, although it may come to that in a few more days. He always kept coming back to the blindness he had when he met Laura. He had been so infatuated that he had ignored all of the warning signs. He kept returning to one word…stupid. Looking back, he even recalled his friends commenting that Laura must have been blind to have chosen him. They weren't right about her being blind, he was the one who had been blind, blind and stupid.

By the end of the day, he had passed through the towns of Manning, Farnsworth, and Shields and made camp about ten miles before Ransom. He hadn't seen anyone who looked suspicious on the road since he left Shields, so he picked a nice site with lots of water and grass, but no trees. The road traffic between the towns had dried up considerably once the railroads had come through. If he'd taken a north-south road to go to one of the towns away from the tracks, he would find more traffic.

But that wasn't the direction he was headed yet. Soon, though, he'd have to diverge from the rails.

He took his time setting up his new campsite, getting the horses stripped and settled, digging a firepit, and setting up his cooking grate on top, and once he was satisfied, he finally made himself a good, hot supper. Once he'd finished his last sip of coffee, he extinguished the flames. It wasn't going to be that cold tonight, and there was no sense in announcing his presence to the world. He was still jumpy over the shooting incident.

———

When he woke up the next morning, he was already anxious. He should reach Chaffee in the early afternoon if he kept a decent pace, so after sliding from his bedroll and answering nature's call, he set about breaking camp. He didn't make a real breakfast because his stomach was queasy, so he calmed it down with a heavy dose of crackers.

Shortly after sunrise, he was back in Sandy's saddle and on the road with the sun bright in his eyes. He looked back at the palomino and wondered why he still kept the horse with him. She wasn't carrying anything other than the nice saddle that he'd bought for Laura with a Winchester and two of the Colts in the saddlebags. Non-Sugar was just an expense now and he should really just sell her at the next stop, but she was just too pretty to let go.

He patted Sandy's neck and said, "Sorry that you have to carry me around all the time, Sandy, while your girlfriend back there has it so easy, but I'll make it up to you some time."

Sandy didn't reply, so he continued his northeasterly heading at a medium trot.

Before the sun reached its zenith, he had passed through McCracken, then shifted to a smaller, more northerly road toward Chaffee which was now only two hours away.

The closer he got to the town, the more he began to doubt that he would find anything to help him, and began to feel as if he were just tilting at windmills like that Don guy. He started to believe that he was falling for one last Laura lie.

Jake finally arrived in Chaffee, Kansas early in the afternoon, and even though he had chewed on some jerky as he rode, he decided he'd celebrate his arrival with a hot lunch. So, he dismounted before Mama's Diner, tied off the three horses at the hitching rail, and went inside. It was a nice place for such a small town, then took a seat at an empty table, removed his hat, and waited to be served. The normal lunch crowd had already gone, so it wasn't long before a short, but cute waitress stepped up to his table.

"What can I get for you, sir?" she asked with a big smile.

"What's the special?"

"Baked chicken and mashed potatoes with biscuits."

"Sounds good. Coffee?"

"Of course, sir. I'll be back in a moment."

She returned with his entire order in less than a minute. It paid to order the special. As he was probably going to be the last customer ordering the special that day, there seemed to be extra helpings of the chicken and potatoes. There was also a small mug of butter, too.

"Thank you, miss," Jake said as he reached for his cup of coffee.

"You're welcome, sir," she replied with a smile, then turned and left him to his feast.

He almost couldn't eat the vast amount of food but felt almost obligated to finish it because it was so good. He finally finished the last bite, avoided the pending belch, paid his bill, and left a heavy tip.

Now it was finally time to do his long-anticipated information gathering. Since he'd started the extended ride to Chaffee, Jake had been formulating the questions he'd ask and those that would be the most likely to provide any answers.

First, he dropped off his horses at the livery, and it was there where he would ask his first questions. The liveryman's eyebrows rose at the sight of two Winchester stocks pointing up from the pannier along with the other two in Sandy's and the palomino's scabbards but said nothing.

Jake's questions didn't find pay dirt, so he paid for two days and then walked to the Chaffee House hotel. He registered, paid for a night, then took his key and left the hotel to head to the town marshal's office for his first real stop, not knowing what to expect when he arrived. Small-town marshals ran the gamut from men who couldn't spell law to truly good lawmen. Even then, a stranger asking about a local usually wasn't well received. He hoped that the tale of his own stupidity would loosen the marshal's tongue.

He entered the office and found the marshal behind his desk, writing a report of some form, so maybe there was hope.

"Good afternoon, Marshal," he said as he stepped closer to the desk.

"Afternoon. I've never seen you before. Are you passing through?"

"Sort of. I came to Chaffee to find some information about a woman that may be from here."

"Oh?" he asked, a hint of distrust already in his voice.

Jake then launched his 'I'm stupid' narrative, saying, "My name is Jake Fletcher, and I have a ranch near Eureka, Colorado. I used to have about three hundred head of prime cattle on the place. It wasn't a big ranch, but it was mine and I took care of it. About a month ago, I met a girl at a social in town whom I hadn't seen before. She was nothing less than spectacular, the complete package with a very pretty face and an exceptional figure. We had a whirlwind romance and she married me, which even at the time, astounded me.

"Anyway, everything was fine for a few weeks until I got a telegram saying my mother was ill. I left for Kansas City and when I arrived, I found she was in perfect health. The telegram was a fake, and so was my marriage. When I got back home, I found that my new wife had sold all my cattle and emptied my bank account. I since discovered that she had done the same thing to a banker in Beaver Creek the month before she showed up in Eureka. The problem I had at the time was because I had married her, she was entitled to take the money, so there wasn't a crime until they found out she was a fake herself."

The marshal's attitude shifted remarkably as he exclaimed, "Damn! That will set a man's blood to boiling. How can I help?"

"She once told me that she was from Chaffee. I'm not sure if it was true, but it's all I have to go on. She was blonde with blue eyes and was very well shaped with an incredible face and smile. I think her name had the initials L. J. because she used the same initials for both of the marriages and her other victim told me that she had them on her travel bag."

The marshal leaned back in his chair, smiled, and said, "That sounds like Lucy Johnson. She was an only child and was spoiled from the time she was knee-high. She wasn't blonde when she lived here, but she had blue eyes and was, as you said, very well shaped. Every man in town would stop and watch her walk by since she was fourteen. She knew it, too. She had a way about her and learned how to use what God gave her. She was able to say anything and make it sound like the God-blessed truth even if it was a pack of lies. Yes, sir, I'm pretty sure that you found our Lucy."

"What became of Lucy? I mean, why did she leave Chaffee?"

"She finally met her match in Charlie Haskins. He was as good-lookin' to the ladies as she was to the men. He showed up in town looking for his cousin, Ralph Haskins. Charlie was older than she was, by about five years, I think. When he showed up, Lucy had just turned eighteen and was looking to get away from Chaffee to a more exciting life. She made no bones about how she hated livin' in this town. She married Charlie after just two weeks of courtship, and he took her away with him. That was the last we ever saw either of 'em."

"Can you describe Charlie Haskins?"

"Sure, but you have to remember that I haven't seen him for seven years. When he was here, he was about two inches shorter than you are and about a hundred and sixty pounds, I'd guess. He had black hair and brown eyes. Like I mentioned before he was a real handsome man and that's why he's easy to remember. He kind of swept into town like a tornado. He was left-handed, too. Aside from that, there weren't any marks or scars."

"Could I borrow a pencil and paper and write this all down?"

"Sure."

The marshal pulled the pencil out of his drawer and yanked a wanted poster off the stack, flipped it upside down, and began writing.

Charlie Haskins, 5' 8", 160, black/brown, left-handed, age: 30. Lucy Johnson, dyed blonde, blue, 5' 5" 120, age: 25.

He slid the wanted poster across the desk to Jake, who folded it and slipped it into his pocket.

"Thanks, Marshal. This helps a lot. I'll wire the U.S, deputy marshal in Denver who's working the case in a few minutes. I'll be leaving in the morning. I just have to figure out where to go from here."

"Good luck," the marshal said as he stood and shook Jake's hand.

Jake nodded, then turned, left the jail, and walked to the Western Union office at the end of the street. The operator was napping as he entered but snapped awake when the door closed.

"Afternoon," he said, rubbing his eyes.

Jake smiled and pulled a sheet to write his message.

US DEPUTY MARSHAL HANK JENKINS DENVER COL

**MY LAURA WAS LUCY JOHNSON FROM CHAFFEE
LEFT SEVEN YEARS AGO
MARRIED CHARLIE HASKINS NOW AGE THIRTY
FIVE FOOT EIGHT ONE SIXTY BLACK BROWN LEFTY
BOTH VERY HANDSOME
ANY NEWS**

JAKE FLETCHER CHAFFEE KANSAS

He paid the sixty cents fee and told him if there was a response, he'd be in the hotel, then left the office and returned to his hotel room. He was tired and stretched out on the bed to think for a while. At least that was the plan until he soon drifted off into a well-deserved nap.

He woke up forty minutes later, confused, but after a few minutes, he recalled where he was, but stayed put on the bed to do the thinking he'd expected to do when he'd first laid down. Once he was fully awake, he began to wonder how to use the information he'd just been given.

It had been an incredibly valuable trip after all, and he'd have to sift through the different aspects of Lucy Johnson's life. He had a more accurate picture of the woman he'd known as Laura Jefferson, and it made him feel even more foolish. At least he knew who her partner was, then quickly amended that to he knew who her husband was.

He decided to go and get dinner, so he rose from the bed, stretched, and grinned when he realized he'd been snoozing with his Colt still strapped to his waist. He left the room and as he walked through the lobby, the lady at the desk called to him.

When he reached the small counter, she said, "You have a telegram, Mister Fletcher."

As she handed him the message, he said, "That was fast. I only sent it an hour ago."

He walked away from the counter, took a seat then unfolded the yellow sheet and read:

JAKE FLETCHER CHAFFEE KANSAS

GO TO ALBERT KANSAS
SEE SHERIFF
ANOTHER CASE
GOOD LUCK

US DEPUTY MARSHAL HANK JENKINS DENVER COL

Jake was stunned as he thought, "Another one already?"

He practically danced to the diner where he ordered a steak with all of the fixings to celebrate the news, even though it would have meant misery for some other poor guy. He wondered how Lucy could have had some man picked out, get him to woo her, and marry her in just two weeks. She was good, but he didn't know she was that good. Then again, he would have married her in a day if he'd had the nerve to ask.

He returned to his room and had to look at his map of Kansas to find Albert and was surprised to find that it was only about thirty miles southeast of Chafee. So, she was close and so near to her hometown, too. He wondered if it was intentional or just happenstance. It also made him wonder again how she could have gotten this far, found a sucker, and reeled him in so quickly. He figured if she had taken the train, she'd have had the time, but it still would have been difficult to pull off.

———

He was on the road by eight o'clock the next morning, having had a last meal at the memorable café. He kept a quick pace until he arrived in Albert just before noon.

He didn't delay for lunch or even a stop at the livery but rode directly to the sheriff's office, stepped down, tied off Sandy, entered the office, and found a deputy at the desk.

The deputy looked up as he said, "Howdy, Deputy. My name's Jake Fletcher and U.S. Deputy Marshal Hank Jenkins said to stop by to see the sheriff because you had a case similar to mine."

The deputy smiled and replied, "So, you're the guy who got hooked. Yup, just happened last week. Sheriff Holcomb sent out a telegram to the marshal's office about it."

"So, what's this guy's story?"

He laughed and replied, "It wasn't a guy. She's a woman named Nora Graham. Some handsome dude named Chet Holden swept her off her feet and married her five days later. He sticks around for three days and then locks her in a closet and sells off her herd and almost empties her bank account. Then he returns to her ranch, lets her out, and waves her goodbye. He took her only horse after selling the draft horses and rode off. She was so weak she had to stay put for two days before she could walk to the neighbors."

"Could I talk to her?"

"You could try. She's a little mad right now. But if you want to try, her ranch is the Rocking G southeast of town about six miles."

"Do you know which way the bastard left?"

"He took the train east and disappeared."

"Thanks. I'll head down to her ranch and hope she doesn't shoot me."

"I wouldn't put it past her. Now, if you were a woman, maybe you'd be safe."

"I'm not going that far," Jake said with a grin, then saluted, turned, and headed for the door.

The deputy was still snickering as Jake left.

Jake stepped out onto the boardwalk, mounted Sandy, and headed east out of town until he caught the road heading southeast.

A little over half an hour later, he found the access road to the Rocking G, turned toward the house, and really hoped he didn't get shot. He kept it slow and non-threatening as he approached the quiet house and stopped about fifty feet from the door.

"Hello, the house!" he shouted, then sat there hoping a shotgun didn't pop out of a window.

After he had waited almost a minute, he was about to shout again when the door opened, and Jake assumed he was looking at Nora Graham. She was average height for a woman, about five and a half feet, and not noticeable for any other reason. She had long brown hair and big brown eyes, and her face wasn't bad, it just wasn't what he would classify as pretty.

"What do you want?" she asked with a snarl.

"Ma'am, my name is Jake Fletcher. I have a ranch south of Eureka, Colorado…an empty ranch. I was married last month to a woman whose name I have since learned was Lucy Johnson. She sold off my cattle and emptied my bank account. I've been trying to find her to get my money back."

"That hasn't got anything to do with me. You may not have noticed, but I'm a woman."

"I understand that, ma'am. But she was married to a man named Charlie Haskins. Unless I'm wrong, that's who caused your problem. He's about two inches shorter than me, has black hair and brown eyes, He's left-handed and the marshal described him as very good-looking."

Her eyes went through a rapid sequence of anger, regret, and even a bit of sadness as Jake waited for her reply.

Finally, she sighed and said, "Go ahead and step down, then come inside and we'll talk."

Jake dismounted, looped Sandy's reins over the hitching post, climbed the three steps onto the porch, and then passed through the open doorway and into the main room where Nora was already sitting in a chair with a stern face.

"When did this happen?" she asked, not offering him a seat.

Jake removed his hat, and as he remained standing, replied, "Two weeks ago was when I found out about it. We were married on April 6th and I was sent a bogus telegram saying my mother was ill. I took the train to Kansas City, but by the time I was able to get back, five days had passed, and she had sold my herd and cleaned out my bank account. The total was almost eight thousand dollars."

Nora's stern visage softened as she said, "Would you please sit down? My neck is hurting from looking up at you."

Jake suppressed a smile, then quickly took a seat across from her and waited for her to talk.

Nora exhaled and then said, "I met Chet Holden at church. I had never seen him before, but I found it hard to keep from staring at him because he was very handsome and kept stealing glances at me as if he was interested. After church, he introduced himself and we talked for a while. He seemed to like me, and just two days later, he asked if he could call on me. I was so incredibly overwhelmed by his attention because it was all so alien to me.

"I had pretty much expected to die an old maid, but here was this handsome man telling me that he loved me. I never even so much as asked him where he was from, I was so much in love, or what I thought was love. We were married just eleven days after I first met him. I was so excited and didn't pay any attention to my normal good sense. I should have known better. No man would be interested in me, especially one as good-looking as he was. I was nothing but a smitten, stupid fool.

"The first thing he did after we were married was to fire my only full-time hand and said that he'd handle the cattle. I should have argued with him about it, but I didn't. I was so taken by his charm and good looks that I had lost any semblance of common sense. He could get me to do anything with just a smile. Ever since he left, I've kicked myself for not seeing the obvious indications that everything he did or said was just about stealing what I had.

Jake nodded as he looked into those sad, hurt brown eyes and said, "Your story sounds like mine, with one obvious difference. I decided that I wasn't going to just sit around and let her get away with it. Now that I know who she is and who her partner is, I'm going to find this pair if it's the last thing I do. How much did he take from you?"

"Just over five thousand dollars, including the cattle. I don't know how he moved the cattle, though. He couldn't have done it himself. I don't think he even knew the difference between a bull and a steer."

"I asked that question of the purchasing agent who bought my cattle back in Eureka. He said the cattle were already in the pens when he arrived. If I had to guess, they hired some drovers to move them and then paid them enough to make them disappear afterward. It wouldn't cost much. Pay them twenty-five dollars and there would be a number of volunteers, and I'm pretty sure they gave the drovers my remuda horses as well."

"He didn't leave me any horses or cattle," Nora said, before asking, "How can you find them?"

"I know that Charlie Haskins went east after taking your money. Lucy Johnson, the woman I married, also went east. I don't think they'd stay in a small town because they have all that money and it would be hard not to notice them in a small town so I'm thinking either Wichita or Kansas City. If I find them, I'll notify the local law officers and have them arrested. They couldn't have spent that much of the money yet, and I already promised a banker in Beaver Creek Lucy married before she married me that I'd get his money back, so I should be able to get yours back for you, too."

Nora looked down at her hands and softly said, "This was my father's ranch. When he died, I should have sold it, but I stayed because it was all I had and really had no place else to go, even if I did have the money. We were down to two hundred head, but I wouldn't give up. Now, I lost it all and I'm sick about it. That bastard may have taken my cattle, my horses, my money, and what little dignity I had, but I'm not losing this ranch because of him. I want to see them punished, so I'm coming with you."

Her response startled Jake who said quickly, "Ma'am, I'm not taking the train or a stagecoach. I'm riding because I don't want to depend on any coach line or railroad's schedule. I can't sit around waiting for a train."

"I understand that, and it doesn't affect my decision. I'm not exactly a debutante or a sweet, innocent girl. I know what I am, and if I'd been honest enough with myself before he arrived, then I wouldn't have found myself in this situation. I was a plain, ordinary woman headed for spinsterhood. Now, I'm a married woman without a husband headed for whatever term you can think of."

Jake shook his head slowly and said, "You're not married, ma'am. The woman who did what she did to me is married to the man who married you. They've probably been married a dozen times each, so neither one of us is married."

She sat back, laughed sarcastically, then said, "Now, that's a relief. I'm back to just being a spinster again."

"Ma'am, at the risk of sounding personal, there's another reason you can't come along. What if you're pregnant?"

Nora stared at him for a few seconds, then started laughing even harder.

Jake had no idea what she thought was so funny about possibly being pregnant until finally, she stopped and looked at him.

"You don't have to worry about that possibility, mister. You see, he never got that far. He made one excuse after another until he locked me away. He even told me before he left that I wasn't up to his standards. Why would he lower himself to consummate the fake marriage? So, you see, I'm still very much a virgin, and your concern about a possible pregnancy is without substance."

Jake blushed and tried to talk but couldn't as she just looked at him with those big brown eyes, almost mocking his embarrassment.

Finally, he said, "That may be, ma'am, but you still can't come along. You're a woman and I'm not bringing a chaperone with us. I don't believe the horses qualify, either."

Nora glared at him and snapped, *"Do you think I care about a chaperone?* If you come near me, I'll cut you with my knife."

Jake then shook his head and firmly replied, "Then I'm definitely not taking you along. Why should I risk getting sliced if I bump into you? No, ma'am. I'm leaving now and if I catch up with them, I'll wire your money to you."

Before she could reply, he quickly stood, turned, and walked out the door, leaving a surprised Nora Graham sitting on her chair.

He quickly stepped across the porch, leapt to the ground, then hurriedly untied and mounted Sandy, then turned all three horses and began walking them away from the house.

He was a hundred feet down the access road when he heard Nora shouting, "Wait! Please!"

He pulled Sandy to a stop, twisted in the saddle, and witnessed a sight that he'd never forget.

Nora Graham had hiked her skirt up to her hips and was racing behind him and actually leaving a dust cloud in her wake.

Jake was torn with indecision. He really should press on, but he just watched the woman racing toward him. She may be annoying and a woman, but she had been victimized as he had.

She reached him after ten more seconds of flat-out running, pulled up, and bent over at the waist, gulping for air.

He looked down at her, waiting for her to make any argument that was worthwhile but had to sit in the saddle for another full minute before she could talk.

She finally stood straight, looked at him with her pleading deep brown eyes, and begged, "Please take me with you. That was a horrible thing for me to say. I don't even have a knife except for my kitchen knives. I have just had it with men after what Chet did to me. Please understand that. I'll be as little bother as possible, but I need to go, I want to make that bastard pay for what he did, and you are my only chance to do that. I can be helpful, too, because I can go into places that you can't if you're looking for a woman."

Jake heard her and realized she was right. There was a logical reason to bring her along, but still, it was going to slow him down.

Jake looked down at her and said, "Let's go back to your house and we can talk some more."

She exhaled as Jake dismounted, then took Sandy's reins and walked beside Nora as they headed back to the house. He didn't say anything as she was finally able to get enough air to breathe normally when they reached the porch.

He hitched Sandy again and figured that the horses must think all humans were nuts. They stepped onto the porch and entered the house through the still open door, then returned to the main room, where he sat while she walked into the kitchen, probably to get something to drink. She returned after a minute with two glasses of water, handed one to Jake, and sat down.

"I apologize for being such a shrew, but I'm still so angry about what happened. For a week, I was so happy and then reality crashed down on me like a tornado," she said before taking a long drink of water.

"I can understand, ma'am, because I was in exactly the same situation. I was in ecstasy when the judge pronounced us man and wife, and then the first three weeks were extraordinary, followed by that crushing discovery."

Nora's eyebrows peaked as she asked in surprise, "Did you say three weeks? You actually were together for three weeks?"

"Three weeks and two days, actually. I wasn't surprised by it until I met the banker in Beaver Creek who she had married the month earlier and stole four thousand dollars. He just got to consummate the marriage, but nothing more, and said that she barely let him do that."

"But you did?"

Jake flushed a light pink as he replied, "Yes, ma'am. Like I said, it was an amazing three weeks. It made the end a lot worse, I think."

"I'm sorry, but I forgot your name."

"Jake Fletcher. Call me Jake."

"Call me Nora. Are you hungry, Jake?"

"Not yet. I'd rather get some details worked out if you don't mind."

"That's a good idea. I promise I won't cut you, or even scratch you if you bring me along."

Jake couldn't stop a smile from forming on his lips as he replied, "That's something. Now, do you have a horse?"

"No. I had my one horse, but he sold that, too."

"Oddly enough, I have a spare one. It was the one I bought for her because I wanted to go riding with her. She's a pretty palomino mare. You can have her if you'd like."

"What's her name?"

"Laura called her Sugar, but I hated the name. I was going to give her a new name, but now that she's yours, you can do that."

"You mean you're giving her to me? I thought you just meant I could ride her."

"Nora, you seem like an honest woman, as opposed to the one I gave the horse to originally. It would help erase that."

"Thank you very much, then. I'll come up with a name that suits her when I ride her. How are you with food?"

"I'm pretty good. I'll need to get some more in town."

"I had just stocked up before this all happened, so I have plenty. I may not be much to look at, but I can cook."

Jake laughed and said, "You're fine to look at, Nora. I'm fed up with gorgeous women anyway. I let my own pride get in the way. I've felt like a real idiot ever since I uncovered the truth. Do you know I actually spent hours trying to come up with a possible explanation for her disappearance, the missing clothes, and rustled cattle? Even after the phony telegram, I was trying to come up with some excuse so I wouldn't have to admit how stupid I'd been."

Nora tilted her head slightly and replied, "You're all right to look at, too, Jake. Don't sell yourself short. What else do we need?"

"You'll need a bedroll and a slicker. Do you have a heavy jacket? It still gets kind of cold out there, especially after the sun goes down."

"I have the jacket, but not the other two."

"Can you shoot a gun?"

"I have my rifle."

"What is it?"

"I don't know the model, but it shoots a .31 caliber ball. I have a good amount of powder and caps as well."

"We can leave that here, and I'll give you a Winchester. How about a handgun? Have you ever shot one?"

"No, but I won't mind learning."

"It just so happens that I have three extra Winchesters and Colt revolvers with me and nine boxes of ammunition. So, I'll give you the best of each of them and I'll let you practice as we move."

"Why so many guns?" she asked.

"I was jumped a few nights ago by three highwaymen. They came into my camp with their pistols cocked. I told them to drop the guns because I had my shotgun pointed at them. One started firing, so I pulled the trigger. They all took a bunch of buckshot at close range and died. It turned out they were all wanted men, so the sheriff gave me their guns. I sold their horses, though."

Nora sat with her eyes wide and asked, "Have you been in a lot of gunfights?"

"Never before that one, and I'd rather not do it again, either."

"So, when do we leave?" she asked.

"This afternoon, we can go into town, and you can do some shopping. How much money did he leave you?"

"Not much. He left me $65.70 in the bank, and I have $12.25 on me."

"Don't worry about it. I have almost a thousand dollars on me right now, so I'll buy whatever you need. You'll need to take more riding clothes with you, and you might find britches more suitable for cross-country riding. But when we get into cities like Hutchinson and Wichita, you'll probably want to be wearing riding skirts."

Nora was stunned that he had that much money with him after losing so much to that woman, but simply replied, "Alright."

"All of the horses have been recently shod, so we shouldn't have any issues along those lines. Two of the panniers will be for your use. So, after lunch, we'll go to town and you can pick up what you need. I'm pretty much all set, although I might see if I can get some field glasses."

"I'll cook some lunch first."

"Would you like some help?" he asked.

She laughed, then smiled at him before replying, "No. I think I can do that."

Jake was startled by how much Nora's face changed when she smiled. She wasn't beautiful by any stretch of the imagination, but she was cute, and those big brown eyes were incredibly expressive.

After she walked down the hallway to the kitchen, Jake sat back and pulled out his map of Kansas, and checked the route. From here to Hutchinson was just about fifty miles, so they could make it in one day if they pushed it, but he'd hold back so they could arrive in the daytime. He also thought it might be a wise idea to see if he could buy a separate tent for Nora to use. It would keep her concerns to a minimum and probably be better for both of them.

A short time later, Jake found out just how good a cook Nora really was. In just twenty minutes, she had put together a quick lunch of small steaks covered in onions and some beans with bacon and molasses.

As he sat at the kitchen table, looking at the food, he said, "Nora, this is very good, and on such short notice, too."

"I was already making lunch when you stopped by. All I did was add another steak."

"Still, it all looks very tasty," he said as he cut into the steak.

She smiled at the compliment, having never received a single bit of praise since her father had died. Maybe the trip wasn't going to be too uncomfortable after all.

After lunch and quick cleanup, Jake brought two panniers into the house and set them down, then returned, picked out the best of the three other Winchesters, and checked its load.

Then he and Nora left the house, Jake slipped the Winchester into the palomino's scabbard, then they mounted, trailing a lightened Coffee behind them as they rode into Albert.

After five minutes of riding, Nora turned to Jake and said, "I have a name for her now. I'll call her Satin because she's so smooth. What did your make-believe wife think of her?"

"She never rode her, except when she left. She looked at her, smiled, named her Sugar and we put her into the barn."

Nora patted Satin's neck and said, "Good. Because I like her."

Jake smiled, happy that Laura hadn't ridden the mare now. It would have tainted her somehow, and the horse was too pretty to have that stain. He could see a new Nora already emerging as she sat in the saddle and was pleased with his decision to bring her along. At least he wouldn't have to talk to the horses now.

They arrived at the mercantile, dismounted, and as soon as they entered the store, Jake sent Nora off to get her clothes. He had thought of some other things that they might need now that there was a female along. He bought two new toothbrushes and tooth powder, some scented soap, a nice hairbrush, some privacy papers, and four towels, then he added the small tent, as well as her slicker and bedroll. He took his order to the counter, set them down, and asked the storekeeper if he had any field glasses.

He replied, "Got one old Army set that I've had for a while. They'll only cost you two dollars."

After rummaging under his counter, pulled them out and handed them to Jake.

Jake slid the glasses from their shabby case and found that the optics were still quite clean and sharp, despite the scratched and rubbed metal housing.

"Add these to my order and you can package the rest of this until Miss Graham gets her things," Jake said as he laid the field glasses onto the counter.

"Sure enough," he replied before he began sliding the purchases into a large bag, not even raising an eyebrow about his comment about buying things for Nora.

As he was stuffing the bag, Jake added to the order when he grabbed another pocketknife and set it onto the counter. His had come in very handy and thought Nora would find a good use for it. He smiled when he recalled her threat just a few hours ago and knew that Nora was probably the last person on the planet who would stick him with the blade now.

Nora waddled to the front of the store with her selections in one massive bundle in her outstretched arms. As bulky as it appeared, Jake noticed at least two omissions.

He stepped past Nora, walked back to the rear of the store, picked up a small light gray Stetson, then returned and set it on the counter.

Nora looked at him as he said, "You'll need some good riding boots, too. The ones you are wearing are all right for just working around the house, but not for what we have waiting ahead of us."

Jake was expecting some form of protest, but Nora simply replied, "Okay," then headed back to the shoe section.

After she returned with her acceptable set of boots, Jake paid for the order then he and the proprietor loaded everything into the panniers. Jake lugged them outside, loaded them onto Coffee then lashed them down for the short return trip.

"What else did you buy? That was more than a pair of field glasses," Nora asked as she mounted Satin.

"I'll show you when we get back. It's not much, but I thought you could use this," he said as he handed her the pocketknife.

She laughed again then smiled as she slid it into her pocket as she replied, "You're taking a real chance, mister."

"I already took a much bigger chance a couple of months ago, and that one didn't turn out so well."

"Neither did mine," she said as they began riding south.

They reached the ranch house less than an hour later, and Jake set the panniers with the new orders in the kitchen near the others so he could redistribute the load later.

Jake then said, "I'll get the horses put away and brushed down. Feel free to go through the panniers. There's no secret stuff in there."

He left Nora unpacking the panniers as he left the house, then led the three horses into the barn. He unsaddled them, then brushed them down before returning them to their stalls.

When he returned to the main room, he was surprised to find Nora sitting in a chair brushing her long brown hair with the new hairbrush.

She looked up at him, smiled, and said, "I'm sorry. It's just been so long since I've used a hairbrush. I have a comb, but this is so much nicer. I just never thought about it."

"I didn't see one in the house and figured with all the riding we'd be doing your hair would be a tangled mess when we stopped for the night. It's probably less painful than a comb, I would think."

"Much. That was very thoughtful. Thank you. I also noticed you remembered other things to make me more comfortable. You are a very considerate man, Jake."

Jake was surprised when he found himself blushing.

Nora noticed and smiled but didn't laugh.

Jake then said, "Traveling with a woman is new to me. I needed to make sure you had everything you needed."

"It's still very considerate. Now, about the guns."

"Yes. That's a more comfortable conversation area for me. I went through the Colts and found a rig that is in very good condition. It looks almost new in fact. Did you want to try it on?"

"Sure."

Jake retrieved the gun belt he had selected, removed the pistol, and handed her the belt.

Nora wrapped it around her waist and pushed it down snugly over her hips.

She looked at the gunbelt, then back at Jake, and said with a smile, "That's a surprise. I thought they'd fall right to the floor with nothing to hold them up."

Jake was trying not to stare at the aforementioned hips or to lapse into another round of blushing when he said, "The gunbelt fits you very well. I'll tell you what's funny about gunbelts. I've seen some men who insist on wearing their gunbelts really tight around their waists just like regular belts and their bellies hang over the top. One chubby man I knew was so flabby that he couldn't get to his pistol if he wanted to. That grip was buried under his love handles, and if he needed to pull his pistol, he'd have to unbuckle his belt and let it fall to the floor, just to find out if it was still there."

A smile formed on Nora's face as Jake continued his tale.

"And that presented one of two problems for the big man. The heavy roll of fat that hid that pistol handle could hold the gun in place if he turned the wrong way, so it could be stuck right there. Now that would have been funny, seeing him standing there with a loaded pistol hung under his gut. Then, if the gun did fall to the floor with the gunbelt, he couldn't bend over to pick it up. He'd have to have the man he was trying to shoot come over and hand him his own pistol."

Jake mimicked a man staring down at the floor as he said, "Uh…excuse me, feller, would you be as so kind as to pick up my Colt down there and give it to me so I could shoot ya?"

Nora was heavily into laughter as she let the image fill her mind.

Jake continued his acting as he looked back up and said, "On second thought, why don't you just save us both some time, pick up my pistol and shoot yourself, then I'll just say I done it."

Nora was laughing and holding her sides as Jake pressed on.

"You know it could all be worse, too. If he unbuckled his regular buckle by mistake, his big old britches could hit the floor with his gun. Of course, we'd all have to shoot ourselves after seeing what was left uncovered when his pantaloon curtain dropped."

Nora had been reduced to tears that rolled down her face as she almost collapsed from laughing.

Jake was just grinning at her, pleased with himself for giving her the simple gift of laughter after what she had been through. It took her a good five minutes to get control of herself.

When she finally calmed down enough to talk, she was wiping the moisture from her eyes and said, "I haven't laughed that hard in years. It does put certain images into your mind."

"None that you should let stay there, Nora. It could give you nightmares," he said, then turned the Colt butt first as he handed it to her and added, "So, here's your pistol. Once it's in the holster, keep the hammer loop in place so it doesn't get jostled and fall out."

She slipped it into its holster and pulled the strip of leather over the hammer without asking what the hammer loop was.

"It's kind of heavy," Nora said as she rotated her hips slightly.

"It is, but once you're used to it, it'll be all right. That gun is loaded, so I'll take out the cartridges and show you how to load it. But then I'll empty it again, so you can dry fire it."

"Okay," she replied, obviously understanding what dry fire was as well.

"Go ahead and give me the pistol," Jake said, curious if she'd do that right, too.

Nora pulled off the hammer loop, grasped the gun's grips, then rotated it in her hand and handed it to Jake butt first, as he had.

Jake smiled as he accepted the pistol, then said, "Now, this is a single-action revolver, so it can only do one thing at a time. You cock the hammer all the way back and it's ready to shoot. When you pull the trigger, it releases the hammer and that smashes the firing pin into the cartridge firing the bullet."

He pulled the hammer back a click to release the cylinder before opening the gate, then turned it on its end and rotated the cylinder to let the four full cartridges and one empty casing drop from the pistol without having to use the extractor rod.

"Why is one empty?" she asked.

"You only load five rounds to be sure you don't shoot yourself by accident."

"No, I understand that. What I meant was why is there an empty casing?"

"Oh. That one was aimed at me, I think."

She looked at him, and after a short pause, asked, "Were you afraid?"

"I was scared out of my wits."

She smiled and said, "Not many men would have admitted to that."

"Not too many get put into that situation, either."

"Jake, why do I need to know how to use guns? I thought the plan was to have them arrested."

"It is. I was more concerned with the amount of travel we'll be doing. After that last incident, I don't want you to be unprotected. Things are a lot worse for a woman than a man if she's alone."

"I know, and again, I appreciate the consideration. Alright, show me how to shoot this monster piece of metal."

"You should have seen my Colt Walker that I traded for this one. It weighed more than twice as much and felt even heavier."

"I probably couldn't use that one, could I?"

He smiled at her and replied, "Nora, with what I've seen of you already, I wouldn't be a bit surprised if you could handle a blunderbuss."

C.J. PETIT

Nora laughed and was more than just a bit pleased about the almost constant praise, knowing that none of it was phony or had an ulterior motive. The man who had said those words was the polar opposite of Chet Holden.

Jake then walked with Nora to the kitchen where they sat at the table and he spent almost half an hour showing Nora how to load and unload the Colt, how to draw and hold the pistol using a two-handed grip, and even gave her a short lesson on the ballistics of the bullet after it left the muzzle.

She was a quick learner, had the technique down quickly, and was soon drawing and cocking the Colt in one motion and sliding her left hand to the pistol's butt with confidence. But the real test would come when she used live ammunition.

Satisfied that Nora was ready, Jake said, "We still have some daylight left. Do you want to try some target shooting?"

"I was hoping you'd ask, Jake. I'm kind of excited."

Jake smiled at her enthusiasm and said, "Alright. I'll bring your Winchester so you can fire a few rounds from it as well. Loading and operating the repeater is very simple."

As Nora waited, Jake picked up the Winchester that he had chosen for Nora, then walked out of the kitchen to the porch and stopped while Jake looked for an appropriate target range. It was mostly Kansas flatland as expected, but he found a small bump more than a hill about two hundred yards out.

"Okay, Nora, let's get a target from the barn and walk out to that small hill."

She nodded, then they trotted down from the porch, then entered the open barn and while Nora patted Satin on her neck to renew her acquaintance, Jake hunted around and found a suitable one-by-eight board that had been cut to less than five feet.

He held it out to Nora and asked, "Do you mind if we use this for our target, miss?"

Nora laughed lightly and replied, "I don't care if we used the barn, but I don't think the horses would appreciate it."

"Let's go, then," he said as he began to leave the barn and Nora hurried to catch up as her shorter legs had to double time to match his much longer strides.

They walked out to the small hill, then he handed Nora her Winchester before he used his big knife to break the soil and then wedge the end of the board a good eight inches into the ground. Once it was reasonably solid, he found two good-sized rocks, then rammed one onto each long side to add extra support.

After giving it one more shove to make sure it would stay in place, he turned and said, "Okay, Nora, let's head about twenty of my paces away from our target."

Nora replied, "Not my paces, Jake?"

Jake laughed as he began stepping off the distance and said, "No, ma'am. I think ten feet is too close."

Nora laughed herself and replied, "I'm not that short, Mister Fletcher. It would be at least twelve or thirteen feet."

Jake was still smiling as he counted off his strides, then when he hit twenty, turned and looked downrange as Nora stepped beside him.

"This is a bit further than you should ever have to shoot, Nora. Now, when you pick up the target, don't waste time aiming using that iron sight on the front. It'll just make you hesitate, then you'll take time wiggling the barrel to make it perfect. Just look at what you want to hit and point the gun at the target. When your brain says it's right, squeeze the trigger softly. It should surprise you when it fires. Are you ready?"

She smiled and nodded.

Jake loaded the pistol with five rounds and handed it to Nora, who slid it into her holster and stared at the offending pine board sixty-six feet away.

Jake stepped back to give her room, unsure what to expect. She'd done very well with the dryfire exercise, but this was totally different, and he hoped that she didn't have the trigger already pulled when she cocked the hammer. He'd seen that happen once almost six years ago when one of his two ranch hands was practicing a quick draw and shot three of his toes off of his right foot.

Nora blew out her breath, rolled her shoulders, then smoothly pulled the pistol from its holster, cocked the hammer with her left hand as it arced upwards, then slid the hand to the pistol's butt to add the stability she'd need. She followed Jake's instructions to the letter as she aimed, picked up the board, and as she squeezed the trigger, was surprised when the Colt bucked in her hands, sending the bullet downrange. Jake was so busy watching her technique that he hadn't paid too much attention to the target, so just after the muzzle flared, he whipped his eyes to the left, spotted the board, and saw light streaming through a new hole in the wood. It was just an inch from the right edge, but it was three feet from the base and for a first shot, it was exceptional.

He turned his smiling face to her and exclaimed, "Wow! Nora, that's outstanding! Do you want to shoot the other four rounds?"

Nora quickly nodded as her brown eyes danced and her face was filled with her sense of accomplishment.

Jake couldn't believe the even more extraordinary transformation in her face and wondered how on earth she had developed such a poor opinion of herself. Then he recalled his first opinion of Nora when he'd seen her sad, hurt, and angry. That Nora wasn't plain, either, she just wasn't pleasing to the eye.

As he continued to watch her, Nora repeated the motion four more times, and less than a minute later, the board had four new holes. She had missed once, on her third shot, probably because she had rushed it.

Jake looked down at Nora and said, "Nora, that is exceptional. There aren't many gunfighters that can shoot that accurately, and you just started. Do you want to try the Winchester now?"

He could tell she was excited at the opportunity after such a positive experience with the Colt. Because she had shot a rifle before, Jake just pointed out the differences, showing her the action and how the lever cocked the hammer and cycled a new round into position. He also warned her of the added kick of the bigger round but didn't think it would be very much of a change.

"Okay, Miss Sharpshooter, let's head a bit further downrange for the Winchester."

Nora walked beside him as he stepped off another hundred and fifty feet, so they were around seventy yards from the target, which should be pretty easy for her.

"Now, for the Winchester," he said as he held out the repeater in front of her, "use the iron sights but focus on the target more. Don't waste time, though. As soon as you get the target aligned, take the shot."

She nodded as she accepted the Winchester, then levered a new round into position, ejecting a cartridge, which Jake caught in midair. She aimed, fired, and surprised both of them when she missed. She was a bit disappointed but recovered when she had two hits with her next two shots. She fired a total of ten before stopping, having hit the target seven times.

"Great job, Nora. We'll take the guns back inside and I'll clean them."

"I'll make dinner as compensation. Is that a deal?"

"The best I'll get today," he said as he smiled at her.

They returned to the house and Jake cleaned both guns before washing up, then wandered into the kitchen as Nora was still cooking and took a seat at the kitchen table.

"So, what do we do tomorrow?" she asked.

"We leave early and head toward Hutchinson. If we pushed it, we could get there in a day, but the horses would be too tired to go far the next day. I think we'll go more than halfway, but we'll play it by ear. When we get to Hutchinson, we'll act like any other couple. We'll walk around and go to stores and shops. How long we stay will depend on how we think we're doing. If we think we've seen a lot of people, but none match our pair, then we can go to Wichita. Now, Hutchinson is about half the size of Wichita, so we may need to stay in Wichita a bit longer. It's also where the banker's telegram came from."

"Where will we stay in the cities?"

"In a hotel. I'll get you your own room, so don't worry."

"No, that's not what I meant. I mean, do we stay in the commercial districts or do we stay near the residential areas?"

Jake was blushing again as he replied, "I was thinking commercial. If we stayed in the residential areas, then we'd look out of place. Something else I was thinking of doing was growing a beard so Lucy wouldn't recognize me."

Nora looked at him, then tilted her head before saying, "I don't think it would make any difference, Jake. She'd still pick you out easily. Besides, you wouldn't look good in a beard."

"I don't look good without one, either, but I'll hold off on the beard. I never did like them, anyway because it makes dinner dangerous. All that food gets caught in there and pretty soon you have all sorts of annoying creatures that want to be your good friend and take up residence on your face."

Nora laughed and turned back to the stove where she finished making her Mexican concoction with beef, beans, and onions with some spices that gave it a real tang.

She filled two bowls, added a plate of cornbread, then set them all on the table with two tall glasses of water before taking a seat.

After his first bite, Jake smiled and looked up at Nora as he said, "This is amazing, Nora. I've never had anything like it before, and I've had plenty of Mexican food."

"I made up the recipe myself. I just added spices until I liked it. Now I have it pretty often."

"I agree with your tastes. It would take a while to get tired of this, too. You are a great cook, Nora."

"Thank you, Jake," she answered with a big smile.

Jake couldn't help but notice how well they got along after just a few hours.

Nora had noticed as well, but neither of them expected anything else to happen.

After dinner, Jake helped her clean up after he told her he was used to it after all the years as a bachelor.

"How old are you, Jake?" she asked as she washed a plate.

"Twenty-six."

"I'm twenty-seven, so you don't have to ask."

"I wasn't going to. Age stopped being important after I was nine. It's funny. When we're kids, we can't wait to be grownups. Then once, we're adults, we wish we could be kids again sometimes. No worries other than the bully in the schoolyard or if we passed arithmetic."

She smiled sadly and said, "When I was in school, my biggest worry was the other girls. Boys think they're tough because they get into fights, but girls are vicious. They'll gang up and point out the one who's different because she's not pretty or has freckles, or big teeth. They call you names and laugh at you. Add that to being perpetually skinny, and it can be a difficult time growing up. I wanted to be an adult from the time I was six and never wanted to go back."

Jake dried the plate she handed him and said, "It's one of the problems with being a boy. We never paid any attention to the girls until we really started paying attention to the girls. We never noticed what they did, even then. We just, well, noticed. In my group, I was usually one of the big kids, so the bullies tended to leave me alone. But they would be merciless to the small kids."

"Did you ever do anything bad to the small boys?"

"No, but I wish I had stuck up for them more, though. I didn't help them until I was fifteen. Then, I just snapped one day when the biggest bully in the school, Joe Marston, who was also the biggest kid in the school, was picking on an eight-year-old. He was out of my vision when I heard a loud smack and turned to see Joe standing over little Andy Winston. He was laughing, and Andy had a bloody nose.

"It just rubbed me the wrong way, so I walked up to Joe, tapped him on the shoulder, and when he turned, I sucker punched him right in the face. He collapsed to the ground in a heap right next to Andy. His nose was bleeding, too. So, I helped Andy to his feet and everybody in the school noticed that Andy was standing there with blood running down his nose with a smile on his face while Joe was on the ground bleeding from his nose and was crying. I suppose I shouldn't have sucker punched him, but after that, I was determined never to let one of the big kids try to have their way with a little kid. If they wanted to fight among themselves, I couldn't care less."

"Good for you, Jake."

"You know, Nora. I've never told anyone that story before, not even my parents."

"Well, then I consider myself fortunate."

When the cleanup was done, they went to the main room to start packing.

As they carefully placed the different items into the panniers to keep the weight balanced yet the daily items accessible, Nora asked, "Are we taking any more of the guns with us, Jake?"

"I don't think so. We'll have two pistols, two Winchesters, and a shotgun. I think we're good. The rest will just be added weight, so we'll just leave them here."

"Okay."

Once Jake's supplies were stored, Nora brought some more food, including some spices and some jars of peppers, onions, and tomatoes, then some flour, sugar, and some baking powder, too. She then added some smoked beef that smelled good as she put it away along with a small ham.

Once it was all packed, Jake set them alongside the front wall and asked, "Can you lock the house after we're gone, Nora?"

"I can. I never have before, though."

"What was the longest you've been away from the house?"

"I went to Kansas City once when I was eleven and was amazed at how big it was."

"It's a lot bigger now. I was just there a couple of weeks ago when I saw my parents. If we have to go that far, we can stay with them. It's a large house and they have plenty of spare bedrooms."

"Are you sure? Wouldn't it be a bit awkward bringing home a strange woman who's not married to you?"

"How much stranger can it be than when I was almost bankrupted by my make-believe wife?"

She shook her head and then murmured under her breath, "At least she was closer to a wife than Chet was to being my husband."

"I heard that, ma'am," Jake said quietly.

"Well, it's true. All I got out of the marriage was a shove into a closet."

"How bad was that, Nora? You never did tell me what happened. I only got the gist of it from the deputy."

Nora sighed, then replied, "As you can imagine, I was really confused at first, wondering why he'd shoved me into the closet. Then I heard him moving heavy furniture against the door and began yelling at him to ask what he was doing. He never replied and I heard him walk away, but still thought it was some kind of a joke. After being in that dark closet for a few hours, I knew it was as far removed from a joke as you can imagine.

"By the time I realized he wasn't coming back, I was still more emotionally hurt, but that soon changed. I had to go to the privy something terrible after just a few hours, so you can imagine what the result was. He kept me in there for more than two days and I thought I was going to die, alone and unfound. I was actually more worried about the embarrassment of someone finding my body in the state I was in. Can you believe that?

"After those two days, and he had moved and sold my cattle and raped my bank account, he returned. He moved the blocking furniture, opened the closet, and pulled me to my feet. I could barely stand and the closet and I both reeked like an overfull privy in July. Once he had me standing before him, he told me that I smelled really bad and had to clean myself and the mess before he left. Then…then he smiled at me, Jake! After all he had done, he smiled at me! Then, I thought he was going to actually kiss me goodbye, but made a face, pulled back and said…he said that I wasn't up to his standards anyway."

Jake saw the immense pain in her brown eyes and said softly, "I'm so sorry, Nora. My experience was nothing like yours at all. I had three joyful weeks. Everything was so perfect except she couldn't cook and even then, I thought it was cute. How's that for being blind? But even when I found out, I never came close to what you had gone through. We'll make him pay for what he did to you, Nora."

Nora wiped the two tears that had slipped onto her cheeks and whispered, "Thank you, Jake."

Jake smiled at Nora and knew a topic change was in order, so he said, "I was thinking of something else, Nora. It's been nagging me ever since I started my search. The timing was too exact for just two people. The messages coming from Kansas City and Wichita don't leave a lot of spare time for your Chet to come and do what he did to you. I think there's at least one more involved. He may not go out and scam the folks like Chet and Laura, but he's there to provide support. They must send him a telegram and advise him what to do."

Nora looked down at her feet as she said, "That makes it harder, doesn't it?"

"No, it might make it easier, I think."

Her head jerked up as she asked, "Easier?"

"Who would you trust to do such a thing? It would have to be someone you really trusted. Who could you trust that much?"

"A brother?"

"Maybe not a brother, but it could be. I think it might be his cousin. Your fake husband had gone to Chaffee to meet his cousin, Ralph. Ralph must have known Lucy or Laura. I think when Lucy went off with Charlie Haskins, he might have brought Ralph with them or come back and gotten him later. So, if we go to Wichita, we see if anyone knows a Ralph Haskins. If we find him, we can watch him for a while and see if anyone shows up to meet him. We'll do the same thing in Hutchinson. It's smaller, so we should get an answer faster."

Nora saw the logic, nodded, and replied, "At least that's a real way to find them rather than just searching."

"I have one other ace up my sleeve. When we get to Hutchinson, I'll wire United States Deputy Marshal Hank Jenkins in Denver. He'll advise me of any recent scams that they've run. That's how I found out about you."

The happier Nora returned as she said, "I'm actually excited, Jake. We may be able to catch them."

"I know that Laura or Lucy wasn't armed when I knew her, but was Chet armed?"

"He had a handgun, and I think it was a Colt."

"So, it's possible that he would put up a fight. What was your read on him? I know it's difficult because you were enamored of him like I was with Lucy, but do you think he was capable of a shootout?"

"Oh, I'm sure he was. He was so cold and indifferent when he let me out of the closet. I think that was the real man, not the phony man that swept me off my feet."

"That's good to know, so I'll keep that in mind. We're all set for tomorrow, Nora. I'm going to get some sleep now and I'll see you in the morning."

"I'll be ready," she said with a smile.

Jake smiled back at her, stood, and left the main room. He had just stepped down from the porch heading for the barn when he heard, "Where are you going?"

He turned to Nora and replied, "The barn. I've already got my bedroll set up. I'll be back in the morning."

"Jake, you can sleep in the house."

"Nora, it's okay. I don't want you to feel uncomfortable. I'll see you early in the morning."

Nora was going to argue, but let it go as she returned to her house and closed the door behind her.

Jake watched her leave, walked into the barn, slipped off his gunbelt, then pulled off his boots and slid into his bedroll. He'd been surprised by Nora's offer after listening to that horrible story about what that bastard had done to her, but knew she'd be a lot more comfortable sleeping in a locked house.

Nora put on her nightdress and slid into her bed with many things on her mind. Her sudden offer to Jake had surprised her even as the words left her mouth. She'd only known him for a few hours, yet she felt so safe with him nearby. She felt a kinship and believed that he felt the same thing. They had each fallen victim to the false lie of needed love and had been kicked in the face by the truth. Unlike Jake, though, Nora believed that she was still plain and unattractive and there was no future for her. Spinsterhood was still waiting for her arrival and even if they found those two charlatans, she knew that she'd be back in her ranch house alone.

But each of them knew that things would change for them tomorrow night after they hit the road to begin their search.

CHAPTER 4

Jake was up early the next morning, but he didn't want to surprise Nora, so after leaving the barn and answering nature's call, he washed and shaved at the pump near the trough, then saddled all three horses and led them outside. He tied them in the front of the house and looked at the kitchen stove pipe to see if Nora was up yet, saw smoke, then walked around to the back of the house, stepped onto the porch, and knocked on the kitchen door. The door didn't open, but he heard Nora shout for him to come in, so he entered the kitchen and found Nora dressed for riding in her new clothes.

She was wearing some denim pants rather than a riding skirt, and he had to admit that they fit nicely. He looked at her very nice bottom for a few seconds without realizing it and thought that for someone who claimed to be so skinny, she didn't seem to earn that adjective from his vantage point.

She noticed that he looked at her differently and felt a bit of a rush when she realized that he was staring at her behind. Chet had never looked at her that way, and as she recalled, no other man had before, either.

Jake didn't notice that she had seen him as he had only stared for a few seconds before he brought his eyes level and smiled at Nora.

"Eggs and bacon, Jake?" she asked, with a slight pink flush.

Jake didn't see it in the bright morning sun that streamed through the window and replied, "We may as well enjoy our last one until we get to Hutchinson."

He walked close to the cookstove and helped Nora load up the plates, then after they each had a full cup of coffee, they walked to the table and sat down.

Nora was still a bit flustered as she ate but was able to eat her breakfast as she and Jake talked about the upcoming ride.

After they finished their filling breakfast, Jake let Nora clean up as he started to load the panniers onto Coffee. They were all loaded after fifteen minutes and it was time to leave.

In addition to her new denim pants, Nora was wearing her new boots, her Stetson, and had her Colt on her right hip. Her long brown hair hung down her back and was tied with a piece of old shoelace to keep it from getting too tangled, even with her new hairbrush. As she mounted Satin, Jake could see the look of determination on her face and contrasted it with the way she'd looked just yesterday. He believed that Nora had changed, and not just in her appearance.

They headed down the access road, then turned east, riding side-by-side trailing Coffee as the pack horse. It was like a Sunday ride except for all the weapons and it was a Wednesday.

There wasn't a lot of chatter between them as they rode, each thinking private, but not dissimilar thoughts. They passed Great Bend before noon and reached Ellinwood forty minutes later.

As they approached the town, Jake turned and asked, "Lunch, Nora?"

"I was hoping," Nora replied with a smile.

They let the horses drink at the trough before walking them to a café called Wilma's, dismounted, and tied them to the hitching rail. They stepped up onto the boardwalk before the café and Jake held the door for Nora as they entered. After they found a table and then placed their order, Jake looked at Nora and smiled.

"How are you holding up, Nora?"

"I'm fine. Are we making good time?"

"Right on schedule. I'm going to be disappointed in our lunch after eating your cooking, Nora."

Nora smiled again and pushed some loose strands of her long brown hair behind her right ear.

After they had eaten their satisfactory but not spectacular lunch, they mounted and soon left the town behind.

Jake kept the pace a bit slower, and they only rode another four hours before Jake called it a day when he noticed that Nora kept shifting in her saddle.

"We'll stop over there for the night," he said, pointing to a nice campsite about three hundred yards from the roadway.

"Why are we stopping so early?" she asked.

"We're only about twenty miles out of Hutchinson and I'd rather arrive in the morning to have a full day for our search. At our current pace, we'd arrive late in the evening. Besides, you're looking mighty uncomfortable."

She laughed and said, "I have to tell you, Jake. My backside is not used to such long rides."

"You're doing fine. It should get better by tomorrow, especially after a decent rest."

"I'll hold you to that."

They pulled over to the campsite and Jake watched as Nora gingerly stepped down, then rubbed her sore backside as she tried to walk off the effects of eight hours aboard a rocking horse.

Jake dismounted, then looked at Nora and asked, "Still want to call her Satin? How about Bricks?"

She laughed and replied, "I was thinking Nails."

Nora unsaddled Satin, or whatever her new name may be, while Jake unsaddled Sandy and Coffee. There were no trees nearby, but there was a healthy growth of bushes that would serve the purpose of providing her with some privacy.

After the horses were tended to, Jake dug a fire pit but held off building a fire. There wasn't enough wood for a long burning fire and it wasn't cold yet. He put up the smaller tent that he bought for Nora for the first time. He hadn't set one up before, so it took a little longer to figure out.

As he struggled with the tent construction, Nora was collecting food from the panniers for their dinner.

The sun was setting by the time their campsite was done and Jake started the fire, then set the cooking grate in place. He filled the coffeepot and set it on the grate before Nora took over.

"Have you ever done much camping, Nora?" he asked as he watched her set the frypan onto the grate.

"I used to go out with my father sometimes, but my mother would stay at home because she never wanted to sleep outside. How about you?"

"I don't think either of my parents spent much time outdoors after they were married. They were married in St. Louis and moved to Kansas City when I was eight. Then I spent all my summers with my Uncle Ernie at the ranch until I finished school and went there to live. He died when I was nineteen. We didn't camp out on the road very often because the railroad stockyards made cattle drives unnecessary. We'd get the cattle there in a few hours. but we'd spend some nights out in the pastures sometimes just to get out. Uncle Ernie was a good man."

"You said your parents are still in Kansas City?"

"They're in good health, too. My father is a vice president of a tool company. That's why they moved. His company decided to expand to Kansas City, and they sent him over to get it up and running. It's a thriving business with all the new factories and buildings going up. My mother is a very sweet lady. She and my father get along very well, and I can't recall them ever getting into a serious argument. I usually take the train once a year to visit since I took over the ranch."

Nora stared ahead as she said, "My parents both died when I was twenty from diphtheria. I never even got sick. My uncle and aunt told me to sell the ranch and move in with them, but I think they just wanted to get their hands on the money. I kept the only ranch hand we had, and he showed me how to run the ranch. I was doing pretty well until Chet showed up. He fired my one hand, Bob Witherspoon because he convinced me it was a waste of money now that he was there. If I had paid attention, I would have noticed how soft his hands were. But I was in love, so it didn't matter that Bob had worked for us for twelve years. He never said a word about it, either. He just collected his pay and left. I felt almost as bad about that as I did for losing the money and the cattle."

While she talked, Nora was cooking, almost absent-mindedly tossing in ingredients and spices.

Without looking up, Nora asked, "Have you had much of a social life?"

"When I was in school, I had a girlfriend named Martha Knickerbocker. She was a year older than I was and more familiar with the whole boy-girl thing. After I started living at the ranch, Uncle Ernie encouraged me to go to church socials and barn dances to meet young women. I think he knew his days were numbered long before the diagnosis and wanted to see me married and settled before he died. I disappointed him in that, I'm afraid. I still went to the socials and dances, but nothing ever came of it. I had a few dalliances with some of the girls, but that was all."

She stopped cooking for a moment and looked past the fire.

"I never went to anything like that. In school, the girls savaged me for the way I looked, and the boys ignored me. I hated the feeling, so after school, I never wanted to go to any place where they could do that again. That was why it was so unusual meeting Chet. He kept glancing at me in church like I was pretty or something.

"Then we talked afterward, and he acted as if he liked me, which was a whole new experience, especially because he was so handsome. He just smiled at me. No one ever smiled at me before, so I was overwhelmed. Before I knew it, we were married. You know what happened after that. And that is the complete story of my social life."

"I don't understand why you avoided socials, Nora. Surely you knew that you weren't the same skinny, freckle-faced, big-toothed girl from school anymore."

"Maybe not, but once you have that hung around your neck by your peers, it's hard to remove. Those girls in school were now wives and mothers. I was just a rancher. I didn't even own any real nice dresses. Why should I?"

"Didn't you buy one for your wedding?"

"No. Chet said it was frivolous, and that I looked fine the way I was. It was just another one of his lies."

Jake could see the pain in those brown eyes and said softly, "I think you look fine the way you are, Nora."

When she suddenly turned and looked at him, he quickly added, "He just probably didn't want you to spend any of your money."

She paused, then said, "That's more than likely. It was just another six dollars for his wallet."

Jake felt as if he'd said something that might have made Nora upset and regretted that it had slipped out. He had to watch those kinds of things.

Nora tasted her mix, was satisfied that it was ready, then dished out the food onto two plates before sliding the frypan from the grate.

Jake poured two cups of coffee and set them down near the plates, then they each picked up the coffee cups to warm their hands as they let the hot food cool just a bit.

Jake asked, "Nora, what are you going to do when we get the money back?"

"I don't know. Buy some more cattle, I guess, and see if I can find Bob and hire him back."

Jake nodded as he began eating the now much-anticipated food, then after swallowing his first bite, said, "This is outstanding again, Nora. I'm happy you came along, and not just for your cooking, either. I really enjoy talking to you."

She smiled and said, "Thank you, Jake. You're going to give me a swollen head with all of these compliments."

He returned her smile and replied, "I don't think that's possible, Nora."

She nodded and continued eating.

They finished their dinner and Jake let the fire die because there simply was no more wood for fuel.

Jake rolled out his bedroll and then rolled Nora's out in the tent before she asked, "How come one bedroll is outside and one is inside the tent?"

"Because you are sleeping in the tent and I'll sleep outside."

"That's silly, Jake. There's enough room for two in the tent."

"I'll stay out here where I'll be able to hear any visitors that might come by."

She ran his response through her mind and thought it was logical, but still asked, "Then why have the tent at all?"

"You need your privacy, especially in the morning when you need to change into a riding outfit for Hutchinson."

"Is that all? I don't care what I look like. It doesn't matter," she said quickly and with a touch of bitterness.

Jake knew he'd struck a nerve somehow and quickly replied, "I just want us to blend in as much as possible, Nora."

"Oh? And a woman in a riding outfit with a Stetson and a Colt won't stick out?" she quickly asked, still obviously displeased.

Jake continued bailing as he quickly explained, "Yes, Nora, that would be almost as bad because the gun would make you noticeable, too, which is what we don't need. But you can put that in the saddlebag until we leave. You can keep the Stetson on, though. It looks natural."

Nora's unexpected display of irritation dissipated as she replied, "Okay, then it's alright. I'm sorry that I was so touchy," then to move on, she asked, "So, where do you think they are?"

"Hopefully, they'll be together when we find them, and I'm about even on either Kansas City or Wichita. Hutchinson will probably just be a practice run for us. I don't think we'll find anything there."

"I wonder what they're doing right now," she added.

"That's a good question, Nora," Jake said.

———

At that moment, Lucy was in her room in Wichita, and she was seriously worried. *How could she have let this happen?* Charlie would be really angry when he found out, but she could still hold off telling him until she had to, maybe another month or two, but by then, even he'd notice. It was partly his own fault, too.

After they'd married, Charlie had proven to be surprisingly lackluster in the bedroom. His good looks and smooth demeanor hadn't translated well into his abilities as a lover. Lucy had done all she could to inspire him too, but he almost didn't seem interested after a few months, which had shocked her after all those years of men practically drooling over her.

Once he came up with the marriage scam, it became much worse for her as he told her that to make it work, she had to avoid pregnancy at all costs and had pushed her even further away.

She had grown hungry for attention, and the marriage scam had created an environment that lent itself to a way of fulfilling her unsatisfied urges.

She had been able to do as Charlie had asked to avoid any chance of conception until she met that rancher in Colorado, Jake Fletcher. Then she made the mistake of giving in to her desires and not only let him consummate the marriage but stayed with him for more than three weeks, enjoying every minute of their almost endless beddings. She couldn't get enough of Jake Fletcher as he satisfied her as no other man had. She was so taken by the experience that she almost wanted to stay but knew the consequences if she had.

She had stretched the time with Jake much longer than necessary until Charlie had arrived in Eureka one day and asked what the holdup was. She had come up with the excuse that he was getting a bank draft from his parents any day, which calmed Charlie, but she knew they'd have to end the sham marriage soon. She had regretted taking his money and cattle, but it was her job and her only concession was leaving the palomino.

And now this was her just reward. She was pregnant from that month of almost constant baby-making activity. Over the years with Charlie, she had begun to think that she was barren. She had been married to Charlie for over five years and nothing had happened, so, in her mind, she thought she was safe from this problem. She had never missed her monthlies, but she had now and that was the cause of her concern. Maybe she wasn't pregnant, and the long romps she had with Jake Fletcher had disrupted her timing, but she could only hope that was the case. She wouldn't tell Charlie until she missed a second, and then she'd have no choice.

Then there was Ralph, which was a totally different issue. As much as she hated having to tell Charlie, she was scared to death if Ralph discovered her secret. She had known Ralph Haskins for most of her life and had quickly categorized him as a witless bully. When she and Charlie had been married, Charlie knew that Ralph was not only angry just by leaving Chaffee; he was jealous that he had wooed and married Lucy. He, like many other young men in Chaffee, had a crush on Lucy, but Ralph's had bordered on obsession.

They hadn't seen Ralph for four years after they had married and left town until Charlie needed a third member to find targets and to send telegrams to set things up. It was then that he'd brought Ralph on board.

Since he had arrived, he made no secret about his cravings for Lucy, and even Charlie had a hard time keeping him under control. Only the promise of more money from the marriage scam kept him at bay when he explained to Ralph that Lucy couldn't afford to get pregnant.

Now, if Ralph found out she was pregnant, Lucy knew that the chains holding him back would be severed. Right now, he was in Kansas City, their normal residence, while she and Charlie were staying in the three-room apartment in Wichita that served as a secondary location for them to run their scams.

There was one other problem that Lucy saw on the horizon when she discovered that Charlie had ventured into her arena. Ralph had convinced him that he was like a Lucy for women and that he had found a potential target in Albert when he was passing through the town, a woman rancher who had never been married and was ripe for the plucking.

Charlie tried his luck and was in and married in less than a week and then back out with her money in ten days. Even Lucy had never worked that fast, especially with Jake Fletcher. Lucy was becoming expendable, and she knew it, so the pregnancy was going to compound the issue.

She just had no idea how to deal with it. The money was all controlled by Charlie since they'd started the lucrative scam. She had skimmed off a few hundred dollars, but not enough to get by. They had over fifty thousand dollars in the bank and Charlie was the only signature on the account. He doled out money as needed, and Ralph actually had more money than she did.

So, Lucy sat in her room and worried about what was going to happen in the next month or two.

———

Nora wasn't worried about any of those things but was very concerned about just the opposite as she stretched out in her bedroll in the tent with Jake outside. She felt safe from marauders sneaking into their camp at night but found herself in a quandary, a quandary that had set off her inexplicable reaction to Jake's innocent recommendation that she wear the more acceptable riding clothes when they arrived in Hutchinson.

She had known Jake for thirty-six hours and was already feeling foolish. It wasn't the same as it had been with Chet. That had been like a lightning strike. She had been blinded by the flash and glare and had no idea who he was or what he was. He was just a handsome man who had paid attention to her.

Jake was the complete opposite of Charlie. He wasn't handsome, not like Charlie, anyway. But he had something about him that she found extremely attractive. He had a rugged, honest face that made her want to trust him. And, unlike Charlie, he talked to her and listened. They even laughed together. She smiled as she recalled the fat man with a pistol story.

Nora enjoyed being with Jake. Maybe she was just going through an infatuation again, it had happened before.

The worst was in school when she was eight years old and had suffered the worst humiliation of her life up to that point. She had liked a boy named Johnny Doorman when she made the cardinal sin of telling him that she liked him. He had laughed at her and told the other boys that goofy little Nora liked him. It quickly spread among the students and they all laughed, especially the girls. For the rest of the day, she had been subjected to snickers, giggles, and hurtful barbs, and with each one, slipped deeper into depression. It was so crushing that she had left school without asking permission, walked home crying, and just hid in her room.

Then, after she was alone on the ranch, she thought that their only ranch hand Bob Witherspoon liked her. He was fourteen years older than she was, but he was the only male around. At least she hadn't made a fool of herself then. She had pined over Bob for six months before finding out that he didn't like girls at all. The only good thing about that infatuation was that she hadn't thrown herself at him.

Now, there was Jake, and he was so different from any other boy or man she'd ever known. He said he had several 'dalliances' with other girls but hadn't married any of them. If they weren't good enough, she knew she didn't have a prayer.

But he did like her, of that she was sure, and she had seen him looking at her like a man looks at a woman. She just didn't know enough about such things and was so inexperienced. Maybe he was nice to everyone and looked at all women that way. She just had no idea.

What she did know was that she really liked Jake and was enjoying being with him. If it was an infatuation that would end when he left for Colorado, she'd enjoy it while she could. But she knew, the longer it went on, the harder it would be when he left.

When he suggested that she wear the blouse and riding skirt, she knew that she'd look like all the other women and suffer the comparison. She wasn't ready for the stab of pain when she saw Jake look at a more comely or attractive woman, which to Nora, was all of them.

Jake was harboring no doubts at all about the slightly older woman in the nearby tent. He enjoyed being with Nora more than he had been with anyone else since Uncle Ernie died. She had substance, wit, and a way about her that was hard to describe.

She wasn't a raving beauty with a full figure like Laura/Lucy, but he'd finally learned that lesson. Nora was far from homely, or even plain, and her figure was more than acceptable. Plain could describe her face when she was angry or passive but when she was animated, that plain face transformed into an animated, expressive visage with sparkling eyes and a bright smile that was anything but plain. He would still categorize her as cute, rather than pretty, though. Pretty now seemed to describe something shallow, so skin deep. And shallow was something that could never be ascribed to Nora. He accepted 'cute' as more honest and soul-warming.

The only thing that concerned Jake was that she had been so hurt by Charlie that she might not trust any man. Added to that short-lived, hideous episode, there were her painfully long years among her acquaintances who could never be categorized as friends. He'd have to be careful not to hurt Nora. She was simply too good a person.

So, as the couple slept just four feet apart under the moonlit Kansas sky, each had concerns about the other that could have been solved by a few simple questions and honest answers. But the nature of those concerns was what prevented those questions from ever being asked.

———

The next morning, Jake was already up and functioning while Nora slept in the tent. The sun was sneaking above the horizon as he took care of his private issues and then washed and shaved in the stream. He decided to hunt for some dry wood for a fire, so he walked upstream, looking along the bank for some dry wood. He had his eyes focused on the ground as he stepped away from the camp adding to his armload of dead branches and twigs. By the time he had enough for a good-sized fire, he had walked almost a mile without realizing it. When he turned and looked back, he couldn't even see the camp because of the morning mist and quickly began retracing his steps back to the camp. It was still early, so no one would be on the road, but he was still nervous about leaving Nora alone.

Normally, he would be right about no one being on the road at this time of the morning, but he hadn't counted on Jerome Blankenship.

Jerome was a ne'er-do-well who had been staying at a nearby ranch, just two miles west of their campsite. He had stayed at the ranch to do some odd jobs in exchange for sleeping in the bunkhouse and hot food. Jerome had worn out his welcome after two days when he took a pie from the kitchen windowsill and ate most of it before being discovered. The irate ranch owner had given him until dawn to be off the ranch and had ensured that he did just that by having him ejected by two ranch hands.

Jerome had been walking since dawn and had spied the horses just about the time when Jake had begun his return to the campsite. He didn't even notice the tent, but the sight of three horses attracted his interest.

———

Nora was awake but had stayed snuggled in her warm bedroll for as long as she could. But nature called and she knew she had to leave her cocoon, so she slid out of the bedroll before stepping out of her tent. Once outside, she felt the stiffness from yesterday's long ride, so she spent a full minute stretching and rubbing her still aching muscles before she knew she had to answer nature's call.

She didn't look for Jake as she snatched up a bar of soap and a towel, then hustled behind the bushes. After her immediate needs had been satisfied, she walked directly to the nearby stream to wash.

———

Jerome had been startled when he spotted Nora exit the tent, then stopped to watch as she stretched and rubbed herself. He couldn't believe his luck. He'd seen the horses and the supplies, which were already a major temptation, but now there was a woman, too. *But where was the man?* Surely, the woman wasn't traveling alone. There were two riding saddles on the ground.

Jerome didn't have a pistol, or anything else either, so he had nothing to lose and a lot to gain as he turned off the road and walked quickly toward the camp. He was two hundred yards away when he left the road while Jake was still about eight hundred yards east of the camp.

―――

Nora had her face lathered in soap and was rinsing when she heard the snap of a twig in the distance behind her. She knew that it had to be Jake, so she continued to wash.

Jerome stood in their camp scanning for any signs of the man. The woman was washing at the stream just fifty feet away and hadn't noticed him. There were lots of supplies and Winchesters along with those three horses.

He was beginning to believe that the woman was traveling alone after all and was undecided about what to do with her after he used her. She wasn't that big, so maybe he should just toss her into the stream rather than bury her. Maybe he should keep her with him for a few days to keep him warm at night, he thought with a slight snicker.

―――

Jake was about four hundred yards out of the camp when the mist from the stream cleared enough for him to see Jerome standing in the middle of the camp. He didn't see Nora yet and assumed that she was still in the tent, but knew he had to get to the camp fast before the stranger found her.

He dropped the wood he was carrying, pulled his revolver, and began to run. He had decided not to shout a warning because he was too far away, and the stranger was already in the camp. If he yelled, then the man might take Nora for a hostage.

———

Nora had rinsed away the soap suds, slipped the towel from her shoulder, and then dried her face and neck. With her eyes now clear, she turned and smiled to say good morning to Jake but was stunned when she saw the leering face of Jerome Blankenship just four feet away.

"Howdy, lady. What you doin' out here all alone?" he asked with a menacing grin on his face.

Nora's eyes were wide as she quickly replied, "I'm…I'm not alone. My husband is here, so you'd better leave now, or he'll be angry and make you wish you were never born."

"I think you're lyin'. I don't think you got a husband or anybody else, but you're about to have me," he snarled as he took one long stride forward and reached to grab her.

Nora knew the creek was behind her, but still quickly stepped backward into the cold water as her eyes searched the misty landscape. *Where was Jake?*

"No sense in getting cold in that creek, filly. I'll warm you up some," Jerome said in a gruff voice as he stepped close again.

He suddenly lunged at Nora, grabbed her left arm with a powerful grip then yanked her out of the creek easily and dragged her toward Jake's bedroll as she struggled to get free, not even wondering why there would be a bedroll if she had just left the tent.

He threw her onto the bedroll, then sat on her knees, pinning her to the bedroll.

As he began to rip at her shirt, she finally found her voice and in a wild panic, screamed, "Jake!"

Jake hadn't needed to hear her desperate cry. He had seen Jerome grab Nora but needed to get closer without that bastard hurting her.

Jerome thought she was bluffing and he was too excited to tear his eyes from Nora anyway.

Jake was getting winded as he finally got within effective pistol range. He knew he had to take the shot now as he dropped to one knee and had to calm his breathing even as he cocked his hammer and brought it level.

It was a few horrifying seconds as he watched the stranger paw at Nora, but he couldn't fire until his muzzle stopped dancing.

Jerome had been concentrating on the struggling Nora so much, that he hadn't heard Jake approach, but didn't have to wait much longer.

Jake felt he couldn't wait another second as he squeezed his Colt's trigger from thirty yards away.

Jerome heard the pistol's report echo across the plain at the same moment that he felt the .44 slam into the left side of his butt. The force of that punch was enough to make him roll off of Nora to his right as the pain from the bullet's passage through his left butt cheek reached his brain making him scream in agony.

Nora was still shaken and wide-eyed as Jerome flew off of her but quickly turned to the sound and spotted Jake as he sprang from the ground and began to race towards her.

Jake pulled to a stop and looked at the screaming and rolling stranger as Nora scrambled to her feet, then, without concern for her immodest dress, she ran the fifteen feet to Jake, threw her arms around him, and latched on as tightly as possible.

"Nora, are you all right?" he asked as he looked down at the top of her head.

She wasn't crying, but she was shaking as she replied, "Yes, I think so. I'm just scared out of my mind. Is he going to die?"

Jake had his still-smoking Colt in his right hand and his left arm around Nora's shoulders as he replied, "Not unless there's something vital in his fat ass. That was the safest shot I could take to avoid hitting you."

Nora lifted her head from Jake's chest and turned to look back at the writhing Jerome and saw that the entire seat of his britches was already soaked in blood.

She returned her brown eyes back to Jake and gazed up as she asked, "Where were you, Jake?"

"I'm sorry, Nora. I was picking up driftwood along the stream and didn't realize how far I'd gone. Let's pack up now and leave. I'll buy you breakfast in Sterling."

"What about him?" Nora asked, still holding tightly onto Jake.

"He'll be a hurting son-of-a-bitch for a while. If I were him, I'd sit in the creek for a while. He'll be able to walk, but it'll hurt like hell."

It sounded like the demons from hell coming out of Jerome's mouth since the bullet had passed through his left rear cheek.

Jake took his arm from Nora and gave her a gentle push toward the tent and away from the cursing, bleeding man on the ground, then stepped closer to Jerome.

Nora kept her eyes on Jerome as she passed, walked to the tent, then stopped to watch what Jake was going to do with him.

Jake reached Jerome, pointed his Colt at him, and said, "Now, mister, I don't know your name and I don't particularly want to know what it is because it doesn't matter. You were hurting Nora and you should be damned grateful I didn't shoot something more necessary than your fat ass.

"Now, I'm going to give you exactly one minute to get on your feet and hit the road. Or if you'd rather, go and sit in that nice cold water for a spell, but do it a long distance away from this camp. But either way, I will make you a promise. If you so much as look at my woman again without my permission, I will put the next .44 right where your legs join together. Do you understand?"

Jerome had no choice but to grumble, "Yeah."

Jake stepped back a few feet and waved the barrel of his revolver a couple of times to let him know it was time to move.

Jerome made it to his feet surprisingly well, but when he began to walk, he threw a few blue curses into the atmosphere as he began to hobble away toward the stream.

130

Jake watched him go to make sure that he walked far enough away.

Nora had listened to Jake's threat and felt a flush when Jake had called her his woman but thought it was just a cover for being alone with her. Whatever the reason, hearing him say the words still thrilled her.

Once Jerome was more than a hundred yards away, Jake holstered his pistol, pulled the hammer loop in place, and turned back to see Nora smiling at him as she stood by the tent.

"We'll just glance his way from time to time to make sure he behaves. I don't think he'll be moving that quickly."

Nora shook her head and said, "No, I don't think so, either."

Jake stepped close to her, smiled, then took a knee and began to pull pegs out of the ground as Nora stepped back toward the dead campfire and finally began to fix her wardrobe disaster.

Jake had surprisingly paid scant attention to Nora's state of undress because he'd been so afraid for her initially, then so impressed with her ability to recover afterward. It wasn't until he began to dismantle the tent that he noticed and quickly looked away to avoid making her even more uncomfortable than she must have felt.

He had the tent disassembled in five minutes and everything packed in another fifteen.

Nora had saddled Satin and Coffee, and they were ready to go twenty minutes later. They rode out of camp, leaving Jerome Blankenship to ponder his wayward path as he sat in the creek watching them ride away.

―――――

Once on the road, Jake and Nora lapsed into a normal, un-Jerome-related conversation, enjoying a pleasant morning talk about anything that didn't involve scams or shooting.

They reached Sterling by eight-thirty, had breakfast, and Jake stopped by the sheriff's office to tell him of the encounter. The sheriff was still laughing when Jake left his office.

As he mounted, Nora looked his way and asked, "I take it you're not in trouble for shooting that bastard?"

"Hardly. The sheriff complimented me on my accuracy."

Nora laughed, and the Jerome incident faded into story-telling memory.

They entered Hutchinson just before noon, and Nora was still wearing her trousers as opposed to her riding skirt, but it didn't seem to cause much notice. Neither did her wearing a Colt, which surprised Jake, so he figured she may as well keep it on.

"Where to first?" she asked as they walked their horses down the main street.

"Let's get a couple of rooms and we'll go from there."

"Alright."

They stopped in front of the Blue Hen Hotel as Jake wondered who came up with the name. They stepped down and Jake registered as did Nora. Jake paid for both rooms which raised the eyebrows of the clerk, but neither Jake nor Nora cared. They walked to the second floor and each entered a room and dropped off their saddlebags and Winchesters before returning to go downstairs. All of Nora's clothes and other things were in one pannier, which Jake carried to her room.

With all of their unloading done, Jake said, "I'll go and drop off the horses at the nearest livery. Do you want to have some lunch before we started looking around?"

"Is it alright if I take a bath first?"

"Yes, ma'am. Just knock on my door when you're ready. I should be back by then."

"Thank you, Jake. I'll see you in a little while," she said as she smiled, then turned, headed back into her room, and closed the door.

Jake waited until the door closed, then left the hotel, took the horses to the livery, and paid for one day, paying a little more for some extra oats for the three animals.

When he returned to his room, he stretched out on his bed and had almost drifted off when there was a knock on the door, which startled him.

He hopped up from the bed, opened the door, and found a smiling Nora standing in front of him. For the first time since Chet had deserted her, she had taken extra time getting ready. She knew she could never be pretty, but she could at least try to look nice.

Jake thought she was still cute, and he suddenly liked cute very much.

"May I escort you to lunch, Miss Graham?" he asked with a slight bow.

"Why thank you, Mister Fletcher. You are most kind," she answered as she took his offered arm.

He escorted Nora across the hotel lobby, out the door, and soon entered a nice restaurant two blocks south of the hotel.

After they had placed their order, Jake said, "After lunch, we'll start by going to the sheriff and asking if he knows anyone named Haskins."

As Nora nodded, he added, "You know, Nora, having you along will be another advantage besides you being such good company."

"And that is?" she asked with a slight smile at the compliment.

"If I go around asking for someone, they might not give me an answer. But having a woman along tends to make people a little more talkative."

"Glad to be of service, then."

"Did you want to walk around town after that or ride?"

"I'd prefer to walk if that's alright."

"We won't cover as much ground, but we'll see more people because we can go into stores."

———

After a very satisfying lunch, they began the search for Charlie, Ralph, or Lucy Haskins. The first stop was at the sheriff's office.

Jake had been right about having Nora with him when they entered the jail and there was no suspicion when he asked his questions with a woman standing beside him.

Even with Nora nearby, though, they only received negative responses at the sheriff's office and then the post office. After that, they just walked arm-in-arm, a typical young couple window shopping and going into some of the stores. At one store, Jake noticed Nora looking at a pair of kid gloves, so he insisted that she get them. She protested, but not too loudly, and she did smile a lot when they were leaving the store.

Jake had sent a telegram to Deputy Marshal Jenkins in Denver advising him that he and Nora Graham, a victim of Charlie Haskins, were in Hutchinson, had found nothing but were going to Wichita soon.

Then, with the day done, they returned to the same restaurant, went in, and took seats at the same table.

While waiting for their dinner to arrive, Nora asked, "What do we do tomorrow?"

"We head to Wichita. Did you want to make it in one day or two? It's fifty miles or so. It would be pushing it a little, but it can be done."

"I'd just as soon break it into two days. Is that alright?"

"Of course, it is. We can take our time. I'd just as soon not arrive in Wichita too tired, because I think it's better than a fifty percent chance that they're there."

———

In Wichita, Lucy and Charlie were having dinner as well. They were eating at the fanciest restaurant in the city. Having over fifty thousand dollars in the bank allows for such extravagance.

"Ralph has found us a new one in Eureka. It's only about fifty miles east of here. He's a widower named George Smith, not quite forty, and the good news is that he's hunting for a wife. He owns a pair of flour mills, one there and one in Hamilton, about ten miles north. Ralph says he's good for at least five thousand if not more."

"When do I go?" she asked.

"I'll give you the details tomorrow and you'll leave in two days. You need to get in there fast before he finds himself another bride."

"Did he figure out a way to get him out of town once we're married?"

"This one is going to be a bit more difficult. He doesn't have any parents or kin, so I think it might be time to up the game."

"What do you mean by 'up the game'?" she asked with raised eyebrows.

"A lot of his money is in those mills. I'd guess between the cash and the mills, we'd be looking at over fifteen thousand dollars."

"What do you mean by 'up the game', Charlie?" she asked more pointedly.

"I think we arrange an accident for George after you're married."

Lucy was stunned and shook her head as she replied, "No. Absolutely not. I'm not going to stand for that, Charlie. We settle for what we usually do."

Charlie stared at her and said in a low voice, "No, Lucy, we aren't going to settle for anything. This is our chance to make a big grab because it's so perfect. Besides, it seems we're going to be losing your services in a few months, doesn't it?"

Lucy felt her pulse quicken as she asked, "What does that mean?"

"You're pregnant, Lucy."

"What gave you that idea?" she asked defiantly.

"I have my sources. I kind of suspected a problem when you spent three weeks in Colorado. Ralph wasn't too happy about it, either. Imagine how unhappy he'll be if he finds out you're carrying that cowboy's baby. You'd better play along, Lucy. Ralph will take care of the accident. You just do your job and remember to play the grieving widow at the funeral."

Lucy had no escape. She knew what Ralph would do. She would also have to depend on Charlie to not tell Ralph of her condition. *Could she trust him to do that? And how did he know she was pregnant when she wasn't even sure?*

As Charlie watched his wife wonder about what he would do, he already had every intention of telling Ralph about Lucy's condition. As soon as this pigeon was plucked, and the money deposited into his account, he'd tell Ralph about her pregnancy. Ralph would go insane with jealous rage and probably kill Lucy, or at least ruin her beyond any use. *Even if he ran off with her, so what?* Whatever the results, he'd take care of Ralph and he'd be one of the richest men in the state and beholden to no one.

After that homely little woman rancher, he'd found out how easy it was to woo unattached women with money, so he could continue his own line of work without two hangers-on. Having a large bank account would make it easier for him to work in the wealthier circles, too. Oh, yes, Charlie would definitely tell Ralph.

———

Jake and Nora had a leisurely start in the morning after a nice breakfast. There was no rush as they were only going to ride about thirty miles that day.

It was a chilly morning, and Nora was using that as an excuse for wearing her new gloves. They weren't the fancy gloves that women wore to cotillions, but more practical, yet every bit as elegant, and she loved the gloves.

They were even more special because she hadn't asked for them, but Jake had noticed that she liked them and bought them for her which meant a lot to her. The last time someone had bought something for her without being asked was when her father had bought her a horse when she had turned sixteen more than eleven years ago. The circumstances for this gift were a lot different, though, and she wondered if Jake knew how significant the gloves were to her.

Jake had no idea how special the gloves were to Nora. He just knew that she had admired them, and he wanted her to have them. He was glad to see that she was wearing them and seemed to like them so much. Everything about her was different.

Nora was probably the least attractive woman he had ever spent any time with, yet he had wanted to please her more than any of the others, and he'd only known her for two days. But it had been two days in which they had been together constantly and had shared more in those two days than most young couples would share in six months.

Nora hadn't worried about fashion statements when they left and continued to wear her britches. They had left the hotel with the saddlebags and pannier then loaded up the horses before heading to breakfast. Even Jake didn't worry about any disparaging looks from other women any longer but wasn't pleased with some of the looks that Nora elicited from some of the men, though. Those britches most certainly did show her smooth behind to good effect.

But now they were on the road and not being watched by anyone. They had passed a freighter hauling unknown crates into Hutchinson and exchanged good mornings as they passed going in their opposite directions, but that was the only traffic they had seen.

After the freighter had passed, Nora asked, "Jake, what happens if we find one and not the others?"

"I think if we find Lucy or Charlie, we grab them and haul them down to the sheriff."

"Won't the others get away?"

"If they have a good prosecutor, he'll be able to get the information he needs from the one we catch and should be able to round up the others."

"Do you think they've split up all the money?"

"Now, that's a good question. What do you think?"

"I don't think so. I just have a feeling that Charlie is in control of this whole thing."

"I agree with you. My impression about Lucy was that she was a follower, not a leader. If Charlie is in charge, then he could maintain control a lot better if he was the keeper of the bank. I should have asked about Ralph while I was in Chaffee."

Nora suddenly closed her eyes as Satin kept trotting eastward.

Jake noticed she had gone quiet and looked at her. She seemed to be deep in thought, so he just waited for her to tell him what she was thinking.

When she finally spoke, it was slow as if she was dragging a memory from deep in her mind, which she was.

Nora still had her eyes closed as she said, "Chet, or rather Charlie, said he had a mean brother that was good for doing the dirty jobs."

"Did he say the brother's name?" Jake asked quickly.

"Let me think for a few more minutes."

Suddenly, her eyes popped open and she smiled when her brain gave her the answer.

"He said his brother's name was Rafe."

Jake nodded and said, "You know, some men named Ralph pronounce it as Rafe. So, it sounds like his cousin is the muscle and the behind-the-scenes worker, the one who sends the telegrams and finds the suckers like us. Do you remember anyone asking about you before you met Charlie?"

"I don't think so."

"Do you remember seeing any strangers in Albert? It's not that big."

Nora thought about it for a few seconds before answering, "There was one man I recall because he gave me the creeps. He was a little taller than you and heavier. He was about five years older than you and just looked like he didn't belong there. He was only there for a few days. I saw him once at the church and once at the dry goods store."

"That was him!" Jake exclaimed, "I was getting a haircut and this black-haired guy was waiting for his turn. I remember thinking that it was funny because he didn't seem to need a haircut. We got to talking and he asked what I did and when I told him I was a rancher, he said he might have some cattle to sell because he was getting out of the ranching business.

"He said he'd let me have them at a good price, $17.50 a head, but I'd have to buy the whole herd of over two hundred critters, and I said I was interested. Who wouldn't be? I could just keep driving them to the stockyards and make a thousand dollars quickly. After I said I was interested, he asked if I could afford to pay cash. I said I could, and then he asked me where my ranch was. I told him I owned the C-F connected south of town then he said he'd talk to his partner and let me know. I never heard from him again. I left the barber shop and kind of expected he wouldn't sell at that price anyway, so I forgot about it. I met Lucy four days later, so it really dropped out of my mind because she had that effect on me, obviously."

"Describe him to me."

"Black hair and brown eyes. I couldn't tell his height because he was sitting, but it was possible he was my height or taller. He wasn't short, I know that. There was something else about him that I do recall. He carried his pistol on his left side and had one of the biggest blades I've ever seen on a gun belt. That thing had to be ten inches long."

"I remember that knife! It was one of the things that made him so spooky to me."

"He didn't spook me at all. I just thought he looked like a jerk. I was surprised when he said he was a rancher."

"Well, you're not a woman. Trust me, the way he looked at me sent chills down my spine, and not in a good way."

"So, that was Ralph. He finds them and tells Charlie who sends Lucy, or, in your case, Charlie. So, now we know what all three of them look like and all we have to do is to find them. I find it odd that both Ralph and Charlie are left-handed."

Nora smiled and replied, "I never noticed that Ralph was, but I do hope that we find them. You make it sound so simple, sir."

Jake grinned back as he was already trying to get a clearer mental image of Ralph Haskins.

_____

They were making better time than they had expected as they talked excitedly about what they had learned. The horses all seemed to have adjusted to the road and they found themselves twenty miles out of Hutchinson by their lunch break.

The horses were munching grass as Jake and Nora ate a cold lunch of some sausages and bread that they bought before they left Hutchinson. They still talked about Ralph and how he fit into the scam while they ate, but added more diverse topics, mostly involving Jake's time with his Uncle Ernest.

_____

As Jake and Nora were heading to Wichita, Charlie was contemplating his next move. He had briefed Lucy on the specifics of her target, now he had to bring Ralph in from Kansas City. He'd wait until she left in three days, then he'd wire Ralph as soon as she was married to the mill owner and have him come to Wichita. He'd arrive the following day, and then he'd explain his deadly assignment.

The assassination would need to appear accidental, something that would be believable, and Lucy would have to have an alibi for the time it happened, too. That would require some degree of coordination because he'd want her to be someplace public.

He had a hard time coming up with the accidental death, though. Mills have accidents all the time, but George Smith didn't do manual labor anymore. A horse accident wasn't believable either, as the terrain around the town didn't lend itself to accidents.

Charlie leaned back in his chair and recalled Ralph's background on Smith. *What were his faults?* He went to church every Sunday, which was how Lucy would meet him. She would be the demure young woman, recently widowed, looking for her cousin who said she lived in Eureka, only to discover she had meant Eureka, Colorado, not Kansas.

It was such a good story this time, he smiled. But this target seemed to have no vices that he could use, so he revisited the horse accident. *What if the horse had been spooked?* He leaned forward again and thought of what would most likely spook a horse, then decided he'd have to have Ralph get a timber rattler and keep it alive until he gets the victim out on the road and off his horse.

Once he had the man on the ground, he smacks the man on the head with his pistol, runs the horse around as if he panicked then leaves the mashed snake on the road as if the horse had trampled it in its excited state.

Nobody would doubt for a minute what had happened. The horse gets spooked by the snake and rears, throwing Smith from the saddle, then when he hits the ground, he breaks his neck. The horse then crushes the snake in its panic, then runs away. It would be a perfectly believable accident, leaving Lucy his rich widow. A pregnant widow, he thought as he laughed.

Then once the money was safely stashed in his account, he'd let Ralph know about the baby. All in all, it was one of the best plans he'd ever come up with.

———

Even as Charlie was grinning in his room, events were taking place that would throw his plan into shambles. The approach of Jake and Nora was one unplanned event, and the second was a woman named Maude Brown.

Maude Brown had been George Smith's girlfriend in high school. After he had gone off to fight in the War Between the States, she had waited for his return. When she had been told that he had died, she was disconsolate, couldn't bear to be in the same town anymore, and had gone east to Kansas City.

After settling there, she joined her brother in his flower shop and married a year later. She had been devastated to find that George Smith had returned looking for her and found her gone. His was such a common name that when the George Smith who had died was reported as killed, four different families were notified, all in Kansas. George had finally married himself after discovering that Maude had wed, and they had lost touch over the years.

After George's wife succumbed to tuberculosis, he often thought of contacting Maude, but knew she was married, so he refrained. Ironically, she wasn't married at the time. Her husband, after five years of marriage, had been arrested for robbery and assault, had been sentenced to twenty years in the state prison, and had been killed in a prison fight four years before George's wife died.

She only heard that George had been a widower for almost two years when her brother had been told by a friend who had just passed through town. As soon as she heard the incredible news, Maude posted a letter to George letting him know that she wasn't married and that if he wanted to renew their romance, she was willing.

George was more than willing. He had received the letter from Maude as Jake and Nora were enjoying lunch on the plains. He quickly sent a one-word telegram to Maude. It simply said, 'YES'. He would have added a series of exclamation points if the telegrapher hadn't complained about the number of strokes it took for one and that the receiver might misinterpret as it wasn't used very often.

————

Jake and Nora stopped about fourteen miles outside of Wichita. Road traffic had increased the closer that they were to the city, and they could have made it by late evening, but Nora wanted to stop and camp to spend another night alone with Jake. She still harbored the same concerns about what would happen if they found the three connivers and their adventure together would come to a screeching halt.

Jake wanted to spend the night with Nora as well, just because he enjoyed being with her. He'd found a good campsite and they left the highway riding a quarter of a mile south of the roadway. There were only two trees, but plenty of water and grass for the horses.

Jake and Nora unsaddled the horses and Jake unloaded Coffee, then set up the tent before making a fire pit. He broke up some downed branches and wound up with plenty of firewood and kindling.

After he had the fire going, Nora set about cooking as Jake sat and watched her and wondered if she knew that bending over as she cooked was, to put it gently, inspirational.

Nora may not have known it, but she hoped that she was being noticed. She remembered how Jake had looked at her when she was wearing the pants in the kitchen at the ranch house, and she wanted Jake to look at her that way. He had paid her genuine compliments about things that mattered, but he hadn't said anything to show he was interested in her as a woman and could understand why he wouldn't.

He might think of her as a sister or just a riding companion, but she just didn't know. And then, there were the kid gloves that was a sign that maybe Jake did really see her as she hoped he did. Nora wanted to know but didn't know how to ask.

She finished cooking, then set the plates of hot food on the ground to cool as she slid the frypan to the ground as well.

Jake poured the coffee, handed a cup to Nora then took a seat on the ground with his back against his saddle before Nora did the same. She was just three feet to his right as she blew on her coffee and took a sip.

After Jake picked up his plate of food and took a bite, he said, "Nora, you can make camp food taste better than we get in restaurants."

"I enjoy cooking. It's fun. The cleanup isn't, though. If you had a Dutch oven, I could bake some bread or biscuits."

"I'll remember that if we have to keep going," Jake replied with a smile before taking a big spoonful of her very tasty stew.

Nora was still thinking about how to bring up the subject of their relationship as she picked up the dirty plates to wash in the nearby creek.

Jake took the frypan and utensils and walked with her to the creek, then crouched next to her and began washing.

Nora exhaled slowly, then asked, "Jake, why did you buy the gloves for me? They really weren't necessary."

"I know. But I saw you admiring them and knew you wouldn't ask. I thought if I bought them, you'd be happy. It's that simple."

"But, why would you do that? I, well, I just don't understand."

Jake answered her question with one of his own, when he asked, "What don't you understand, Nora? It was just to make you happy. It was such a small thing. They did make you happy, didn't they?"

"You know they did, but it wasn't just because of the gloves, it was because you bought them for me even though I hadn't asked for them. Nobody has done that for me since my father bought me a horse when I was sixteen."

"That's sad, Nora. You're a generous and thoughtful person. You should be treated that way all the time."

Nora was getting nowhere, despite his thoughtful replies. She finally decided to take the plunge, hoping that she didn't get the same reaction as she had gotten from Johnny Doorman nineteen years ago.

"Jake, do you like me?" she asked bluntly.

Jake stopped scrubbing, looked at her, and replied, "You know I like you, Nora. I'm surprised you felt you needed to ask that question."

"No, I know you like me. But what I'm asking, what I'm wondering is if you like me like a man likes a woman or as a brother likes a sister."

Jake smiled and replied, "I surely don't see you as a sister, Nora. I definitely like you as a man likes a woman."

Nora released her breath that she had been holding since she had spoken, then said softly, "But you haven't acted like it."

"No, I haven't, but it was for a good reason, Nora. I was worried about hurting you. You just went through that horrible experience with Charlie, and then, you told me about how you grew up, so I didn't know how you'd feel if I said something wrong. I thought I'd just wait until I knew you better and I was sure I could say something without risking hurting you. I never want to hurt you, Nora."

Nora felt a flood of warmth flow through her. *This wasn't like Johnny Doorman at all!*

Nora kept her eyes on the plates as she carefully said, "I'm not going to be hurt, Jake and I want to be close to you. Will that be alright?"

Jake had his eyes focused on Nora, choosing his own words just as carefully, as he replied, "It's more than alright, Nora. It's as if we were meant to find each other."

Nora turned her big brown eyes back to look at Jake, smiled, and said quietly, "It seems that way, doesn't it?"

Jake smiled as he nodded, then asked, "Then you wouldn't mind if I kissed you, Nora?"

Nora whispered, "I'd like that very much, Jake."

They each dropped what they were washing, then stood by the stream in the waning light and faced each other.

Jake put his hands on the sides of Nora's face, then leaned forward and kissed her softly.

Nora was overwhelmed that such a simple kiss could give her such a feeling of being loved and wanted and felt her knees weaken. But it wasn't for additional support that made her put her hands behind Jake's neck to pull him in closer as she pressed the kiss harder and more passionately. She didn't understand why she had done it; it was just that she wanted more. She was already growing so excited even as she experienced her first kiss.

Jake dropped his hands and wrapped her closer to him.

She could feel him pressed against her as the kiss continued and felt urges that she didn't even know existed within her as she began to slowly slide her hips across him.

Finally, their lips separated and they each took a deep breath as they looked into each other's eyes.

"That was a very special first kiss, Nora," Jake said quietly.

Nora didn't answer verbally, she just smiled and kissed him again.

Jake felt her body moving against his and felt his own needs explode. She may not be as well-endowed as Lucy, but she was definitely a woman and he had no doubt that Nora knew how much she was affecting him.

He then slid his lips to her neck, sending shivers down her back. She pulled his head against her neck as she tilted her head to give Jake easier access. Her toes were curling, and her knees were threatening to give out by the time he stopped, then he leaned back slightly and looked into her big brown eyes.

"You are a very special woman, Nora," he said softly.

She whispered, "Jake, you're probably the only person who thinks that way."

"Then the rest of the world is filled with blind idiots."

"It doesn't matter what anyone else thinks, Jake. As long as you think that, then I'll be happy."

As difficult as it was, Jake still had enough concerns about Nora that he finally released her and stepped back slightly.

Nora sighed, then they turned, picked up the fallen dinnerware, and rinsed it before returning to the fire.

After setting the plates and utensils by the fire, Nora surprised Jake when she asked softly, "Will you stay with me in the tent tonight, Jake?"

Jake was torn with the question. He knew if he stayed with Nora, he might not be able to control himself because he wanted Nora badly, but he cared for her even more. When she had told him she was a virgin, it had shocked him, and now it worried him. She may not know what to expect and may find it disgusting and not at all what she obviously expected it to be.

He just simply didn't know and was worried that she might wind up having her dreams shattered. If he stayed with her in the tent, he'd have to avoid getting carried away.

"Yes, Nora. I'll stay with you."

Nora smiled and then said, "I'll feel better."

Jake smiled back, before they prepared to turn in for the night, each anticipating different results after they entered the small tent.

Once they were inside the tent, their different expectations were obvious.

Jake pulled off his boots and slid into his bedroll then smiled at Nora, who, after taking off her boots, began unbuttoning her shirt as he watched, unsure of what she was doing.

It was a heavy flannel man's shirt, but as she reached the fifth button, Nora pulled the shirt apart, and he knew that there was nothing manly beneath the cloth.

She looked at Jake, smiled, then leaned over and kissed him, her long brown locks falling about his face.

Jake felt her wet lips slide across his, then quickly pulled both arms out from his bedroll and sat up, rolling Nora onto his lap. There was barely any light in the tent as he looked at her face and knew that he was fighting a losing battle. Wanting Nora was winning, and it wasn't even close.

For Nora, there was no battle or even a mild skirmish. She wanted Jake. She wanted him to end her twenty-seven years as a virgin and wanted to know what it was like to be truly loved. She recalled that long-ago talk she'd had with her mother about what to expect, including the pain of losing her virginity, but she didn't care. She was being driven by something much more powerful than distant memories or warnings that were probably meant to keep her from dallying with men as if that was ever possible. But now, she wanted to do much more than just dally. She wanted Jake to make love to her with as much passion as possible.

She looked into his eyes and saw him staring down at her, then took his left hand in her right, pulled it inside her open flannel shirt onto her left breast, and for the first time in her life, felt the pleasure of being fondled by a man, a real man.

Jake leaned forward and began to kiss Nora. Now that his hand was where she wanted it, she put her right hand behind his neck and pulled him close.

Jake began undoing the remaining buttons on her shirt, opening the shirt, and had to extricate himself from his bedroll to begin seriously addressing Nora.

They were both on their knees facing each other as Nora unbuttoned his shirt, then began to slide her fingers over his heavily muscled chest before she surprised him and slid her lips to kiss him where her fingers still played.

Jake slipped Nora's shirt from her shoulders and began kissing her in places she had never even been touched before by a man, much less felt his lips, and the sensation made her shudder in unmatched pleasure.

Jake began working on her pants at the same time Nora removed his shirt. She continued to kiss his chest as he unbuttoned her trousers before she had to lay on her back to allow Jake to pull her pants free.

Jake was stunned to see that she was naked already. All she had been wearing all day was the shirt and the pants and the very idea aroused him even more. If he had known that she had been hoping for this moment, it might have happened at their noon break.

She smiled at his stunned expression and asked with a light laugh, "Surprised?"

"Surprised and pleased. Nora, you are truly an inspiration."

"Show me how inspired you are, Jake," she said in a throaty voice she didn't know she had.

Jake removed his loosened trousers and tossed them aside. It may have been getting cooler outside, but the temperature in the tent was rising rapidly.

Jake did have a lot to show Nora as this was her first time and she needed guidance, so he talked to her and explained things as he did them.

Nora found his voice almost as stimulating as his touches and kisses. She did as he suggested and began exploring his body at the same time. She thoroughly enjoyed running her hands and lips over Jake as he did the same to her. When she added her own voice to the increasing tempo of their lovemaking, Jake was even more surprised. *How could the virgin Nora be so uninhibited?*

Nora thought she couldn't wait any longer when Jake suddenly rolled her onto her stomach and began kissing her back and then the glorious backside that had first inspired him.

She began to feel her desires rise even more as his lips and fingertips slid across her skin, so she spread her legs apart to let him know she was ready, but all he did was discover the inside of her thighs which drove her close to madness as she began to squirm on the bedroll.

She began asking using language she had heard but never used before, language that seemed appropriate here and now. She was already sweating as Jake slid his palms and fingers over her. The sensations were irresistible, and Nora wanted them to keep going but she knew she wanted Jake to end them even more.

When he finally rolled her onto her back again, she thought it was time and grabbed Jake, demanding that he finish this. *Now!*

Jake wanted her just as much as she wanted him, but he wanted Nora to experience even more pleasure. He laid on his back beside her, then slid her onto his own wet torso and slipped his hands across her perfect behind as he pulled her against him.

Nora was surprised to find herself atop Jake and disappointed and not disappointed at the same time. She wanted him to go on but was almost losing her mind wanting him to end it. His hands were all over her, making her even more frantic. She was pleading with him to take her as she writhed and slipped across him.

Finally, she could stand it no more. She grabbed Jake's hair and looked him in the eyes and shouted at him to do it now, sounding like a dockworker as she did.

Jake had already reached that point himself, knowing that he wasn't going to hold out much longer either.

He rolled her onto her back and as she screamed for him even louder and more insistently, at last, Nora felt Jake take her. She gave no thought to her losing her virginity or her age as she exploded with lust and a savage desire to savor every moment of pleasure. She hadn't even noticed the pain her mother had described vividly to her as he finally joined with her.

She felt like an animal as she emitted sounds that she had never thought she was capable of making and didn't care. She was a real woman now and had her man.

Jake was awed by Nora. This sweet, quiet woman with a gentle face was letting it all go. He never would have guessed she would react this way, and he had been worried about her hating it.

After almost five minutes of thrashing and shouting, they finally collapsed in a sweaty, fleshy heap together on Jake's bedroll and were breathing heavily as Jake pulled Nora against him, stroked her head, and then kissed her softly.

It took two more minutes before they had reached normal breathing and heart rates, and it was Nora who spoke first.

"Jake, should I apologize for all those things I said? I never use words like that. I sounded like a prostitute."

Jake kissed her again before saying, "Nora, when we're in private like this, you say whatever you feel. I'll tell you something honestly, Nora. I've been with other women before, but none have come close to your passion. You were nothing short of astounding."

Nora was privately thrilled to be told that she was better than all those other women but had to ask, "Even Lucy?"

"Yes, Nora. Even Lucy."

"I made you happy, then?"

"You exhausted me, Nora. You are more woman than I could ever have imagined, and do you know what the best part is?"

"No. Tell me," she replied in perfect contentment as she lay on Jake with her head on his chest.

"That you're still the same compassionate, warm, and wonderful woman I've come to know since we started. This part of you was just unexpected, and I'll be honest with you when I tell you that I was expecting you to be disillusioned. I loved you before this happened, Nora. I just couldn't tell you because I didn't want to risk hurting you."

Nora was in an incredible state of total euphoria that she thought was impossible as she whispered, "You've made me so very happy, Jake. I've loved you since we were together for just a few hours and it's just been growing since. My only fear was that you didn't care for me like a man loves a woman. I could have lived with you just liking me as a sister, but it would have broken my heart to see you with another woman."

"There is no other woman, Nora, and there never will be one."

Nora smiled to herself and snuggled in closer. She was so totally happy and content that she never wanted to leave the tent, but she did wonder if she'd go just as crazy the next time and hadn't a clue how long that would be or how often. *Once a week? Twice?*

She was about to ask, as Jake began tracing his finger up her thigh and across her breast and began to kiss her again. She felt herself getting aroused again and was surprised. With her knee across his stomach, she was aware that he wanted her again and felt a deep, warm fire growing within her and began to kiss him harder, more hungrily.

"Again?" she asked in her hurried, husky voice.

"Again," he replied as he rolled her onto her back.

She discovered fifty-five minutes later that she would go just as crazy the second time as she had the first and if there was supposed to be any discomfort at all, she never noticed. She wasn't worried about her language any longer, either.

Jake had used the same language and it made her more excited. If anything, the second time was more thrilling than the first because she knew what to expect now and had actually been a more active participant, something that Jake couldn't imagine.

Nora and Jake stayed close and finally slid into a single bedroll to get some much-needed sleep with the added advantage of providing each other with body heat.

CHAPTER 5

Nora slowly opened her eyes to find Jake's green eyes looking into her browns as he said softly, "Good morning, Nora."

She smiled, sighed, then replied, "Good morning, Jake. This is a perfect way to welcome a new day."

"I couldn't agree more, Nora," he said as he kissed her gently.

"I suppose we need to get going. Wichita awaits."

"Not to mention my bladder. It won't wait much longer. Okay, let's try and wiggle out of here. You're thinner, so you could get out easier."

"I don't suppose you're going to close your eyes."

"Not in a million years, Nora," he said as he grinned at her.

His answer gave Nora a thrill knowing that Jake wanted to see her naked when just a few weeks ago, that bastard hadn't even thought she was worthy of sharing her bed. Now, she was extremely pleased that he hadn't. Jake would be the only man she would let touch her.

"Then you get out right after me, and I'll watch, too."

"What have I done to you, woman?" he asked as she started to slide out of the bedroll.

"Made me the happiest woman on earth," she answered as she popped free.

Jake looked at Nora in the early morning light filtering through the tent. She was as he had felt her last night, not overly curvy, but more than enough to keep his attention.

Nora did as she said she would and sat back on her legs and waited for Jake to leave the bedroll. He was not in the least embarrassed as she watched him, either. Nora marveled at his masculinity. He was all man and he was her man.

She pulled on her shirt and then her pants while Jake dressed as well before they scampered from the tent and ran to opposite ends of the two trees to answer nature's call.

Jake then washed quickly and started a fire for breakfast as Nora tiptoed over and set the coffee pot on the grate as well as the frypan. As soon as she laid the bacon on the hot pan, she stood and was immediately snatched by Jake.

"I haven't told you that I love you this morning, Nora. and I'm embarrassed for failing you. Please accept my apologies."

She laughed and hugged him before saying, "I accept your apology. Will you accept mine as well?"

"You'll never have to apologize to me, Nora."

He kissed her and then was interrupted by crackling bacon that had tossed droplets of burning fat onto his hand.

He shook his complaining hand, then said, "Your bacon is calling, ma'am. I'll start saddling the horses."

She turned to flip the bacon, and Jake gave her cute behind a soft tap before walking away to prepare the horses for the day's short ride into Wichita. He packed the panniers and loaded them all except the one for the cooking gear, then collapsed the tent and put it in a pannier.

After a very congenial breakfast with a multitude of ill-disguised innuendo and lewd suggestions, they mounted their horses to complete the journey.

As far as they were concerned, they were a married couple now, with or without the ceremony, rings, or paperwork from the state of Kansas.

———

In Wichita, Lucy was packing her bags. The train for Eureka would depart at 9:50, leaving her enough time to get some breakfast at the café before she left. Charlie had bought the ticket and given her thirty dollars for expenses, which should last her a week. She didn't tell him she had another hundred and fifty from her personal kitty. She also had one more secret she hadn't mentioned to Charlie. She wasn't pregnant after all. Her monthly had arrived two days earlier, but she didn't know what advantage it gave her, just that it had given her a tremendous amount of relief.

What she didn't know was that it made no difference to Charlie at all, even if he had known. His plans were set. He hadn't given Ralph the details of his plan for the elimination of George Smith yet, though. He'd arrive in Wichita in three days and Lucy would be in Eureka later today. When she married Smith, she'd send a telegram to Charlie that would start the fatal part of the operation.

———

In Eureka, George Smith was anxiously awaiting Maude's arrival. Her train was due in from Kansas City at 2:20 this afternoon, and he'd already prepared the house for her arrival. There would be no courtship. He was planning on asking her to marry him an hour after she stepped off the platform, if he waited that long, and knew that she would accept. He kept checking his pocket watch every minute or two, wishing that damned hour hand to reach the Roman numeral two.

———

Jake and Nora were taking their time to ride the fifteen miles, and by nine o'clock, they were only just a few minutes out of Wichita and could see the skyline.

Nora was still wearing her britches, but she was looking forward to spending some time in a hotel because she needed a bath.

"Jake, will we sleep in separate hotel rooms?" she asked.

"We'll get two hotel rooms. Where we sleep is up to us."

"I can't wait to have you in a real bed," she said as she grinned at him.

He grinned back, anticipating that very thing, but as circumstances unfolded, that expected event would be delayed by more demanding and more tragic happenings.

———

Lucy was on the platform waiting on the train, her trunk waiting in the baggage loading area. She held a travel bag on her lap and was deep in her thoughts as the train's warning whistle sounded down the line.

———

Jake and Nora heard the whistle, and as they approached the crossing to the city, the train was pulling into the station to their right. They waited until the train completely stopped before they walked their three horses across the tracks because they had been known to overshoot slightly which would have been a nasty introduction to Wichita.

As Jake and Nora crossed over the track. Nora was on his left as they made the crossing, and Jake was looking at her, telling her a story. She was laughing, and Jake was smiling as he glanced at the large platform and the boarding passengers when his smile dropped. He stared at the blonde woman standing near the passenger car, waiting to board, and recognized her instantly. There was no mistaking Lucy with her blonde hair and sensational figure.

Jake said quickly, "Nora! Don't turn around. Keep looking at me. Lucy is getting on that train."

"Are you sure?" she asked as she continued to look at him.

"Positive," he replied as she climbed onto the car's platform and disappeared, then said, "She's gone now. Keep riding forward. We can't catch her now, but we can find out where she's going."

"How?" Nora asked.

"You will, my love. You'll go to the ticket master and tell him you just arrived and you're looking for your cousin. You were told she was taking the train but didn't know where she was going."

"Can I change the story a bit?"

"You can make up anything you believe sounds right. I trust you, Nora."

Nora nodded and felt a rush knowing that he had confidence in her, a confidence that no one had placed in her before and wasn't sure that it was earned.

They rode further past the depot, then pulled up before the Railway Hotel before Nora dismounted, handed Satin's reins to Jake, then stepped onto the boardwalk as the train pulled out of the station.

Nora turned and smiled at Jake before she turned and stepped toward the station. she reached the ticket window and stepped in front of the cage.

"Excuse me, sir. Has my cousin purchased a ticket? I'm very worried about her. She and her husband had a very big argument and she said she wanted to go home to her parents."

"That's terrible. What does she look like?"

"About my height, blonde hair, and a very nice figure. She always got all the boys in school, and none of them paid me any attention at all."

"I'm sure you did fine too, miss. She didn't buy a ticket, but she did check her luggage to Eureka."

"That's odd. Her parents live in Topeka."

"Maybe she's going to stay in Eureka for a few days and let things cool off."

"That's probably it. Thank you so much, sir. We'll wait and see if she's going to return."

He smiled at Nora as she turned and stepped along the platform. He watched her walk away appreciating Nora. She may be wearing pants, he thought, but that was a real lady.

Nora took the reins from Jake and climbed back on Satin, saying, "She's going to Eureka."

"Eureka? Why would she go there? Do you think she's going to go back to find me?"

"No, he meant Eureka, Kansas. It's about fifty miles due east. Do you think she saw you?"

"No. I don't think so. I didn't know Kansas had a Eureka, too."

"That's okay, I didn't know Colorado had one until I met you."

Jake grinned at Nora as she smiled back at him.

———

Lucy had seen them as they rode past but hadn't identified them. She just had fixated on the oddity of seeing a woman riding a horse that looked like her Sugar wearing britches, a Stetson, and a Colt. She never looked past the woman to her companion. She only gave him a glance as the train was leaving and his hat's brim blocked his face. She gave them no more thought as the train accelerated toward Eureka.

Now that they knew where Lucy was going, Jake asked, "How do you want to handle this, Nora? We can wait and take the train tomorrow and take a break today, or we can continue on and get there early tomorrow morning."

Without a moment's hesitation, Nora said, "Let's ride to Eureka."

Jake smiled at her and replied, "I'll follow you anywhere, ma'am."

They turned and continued north through Wichita, stopped at the greengrocer, and bought some more eggs and a loaf of bread, then Jake had to send another telegram to Deputy Marshal Jenkins telling him of their discovery.

With their needs in Wichita satisfied, they pressed along the eastbound road after it left on the north end of the city. They were moving at a medium trot to cover the fifty miles in decent time, even though they were planning on arriving the next morning.

"It appears that Lucy is going to marry the next pigeon," said Jake loudly over the noise of the combined twelve hooves.

"Isn't this kind of close to their home for that?"

"I don't think Wichita is their real home. I think it's just a place where they start scams. I still think they live in Kansas City. If they're going to try to do one so close to Wichita, they may be pulling out after this one and maybe start working in Missouri."

"What do we do when we get to Eureka?"

"I'm not sure yet. Do you have any ideas?"

"Not a one, but we need to notify the sheriff, don't we?"

"Yes, ma'am, and we'll do that as soon as we arrive. Then we get a room at the hotel and may even run into Lucy then. If we do, we grab her and walk her to the sheriff's office. We'll explain what she did and then we see how she reacts. If she agrees to cooperate to avoid a long prison sentence, then it might work out better because we need to know where the money is. We agree that Charlie probably has it, so the only question will be how much loyalty she has for Charlie."

Then he paused before continuing, "Nora, when Lucy and I were together for those three weeks, I didn't get a feeling that she was distracted at all. You know, she didn't seem to have anything else on her mind other than what we were doing. I've been going through that time in my head ever since I found out what she had done. I mean, looking back, I wonder why she stuck around so long. The banker in Beaver Creek was cleaned out after four days. You were locked up after five days. Why wait three weeks to take my money and cattle?"

"Maybe she liked you, and after last night, Mister Fletcher, I can understand why."

Jake felt a bit guilty talking to Nora about Lucy but still said, "She liked me enough to send me to the poor house, but it's hard to describe what I recall. Maybe it's just because I can't imagine loving someone and doing what she did with me and other men. That's what makes me believe that she'll turn on Charlie faster than we expect. What if we grab her and before we take her to the sheriff, she tells us she'll tell us everything if we don't have her arrested?"

"That's your call, Jake. She's the one who fleeced you. Now, what happens to Charlie is my decision and I won't have any problems at all in sending him to prison for thirty years."

"I agree with you on that. I'd like to get him alone for a little while for what he did to you, and it wasn't just about the money. I can't imagine what it must have been like being locked in that closet for two days."

"Do you know what the worst thing was? Even worse than having no food or drink or having to use the closet as a privy?"

"I can't imagine what would be worse than that."

"I couldn't lay down. I had to stand or sit. I tried so hard to break the door, but I was too small and couldn't get any leverage. Between the incredible discomfort, the smell, and the hunger and thirst, I almost broke down a few times. At the time, I had no idea why he was doing this to me and thought that maybe I had offended him somehow. The first few hours, I was more sad than angry or disgusted. I wanted to ask him what I had done.

"But after the sun went down, and the little bit of light from under the door disappeared, I began to get very angry. Nothing I could have done deserved this and I vowed to slap him silly when I got out. But a day later, I was a blubbering mess and only thought of getting out of that prison. I was so ashamed of myself for what I had to do to stay alive.

"When the door finally opened, I was sitting in my own mess and in a daze. I had given up, Jake. I thought I would die. He pulled me up, made a face at the stink, told me how badly I smelled, and said he wasn't going to be charged with murder. I was so glad to be free and able to lie down, I did just that. I fell to the floor and stretched out. I heard the front door slam and departing hoofbeats.

"After a few minutes, I crawled to the kitchen and pulled myself up to the pump and gave it a few strokes, and put my head under the water. I let it run across my head and sucked it in as it went past. Once I had done that, I stripped off all my stinking clothes and threw them outside. I was so hungry that I began eating anything I could find. I was still naked, but I was alive and in my house. I filled a bucket full of cold water and carried it outside, then went back in and got a bar of soap and washed myself. Only then did I start feeling human again. I had to wait a couple of days until I got my strength back and found he had taken my horse. It gave me time to clean out the closet and air the house out, too. Then I walked to town, figuring I'd buy a new horse. That's when I found he had almost cleaned me out. I knew my cattle were gone, but when I found my bank account emptied, I was so crushed, I just walked back to the house. I was lost, Jake."

"He's a heartless bastard for doing that to you, Nora."

Then she turned and smiled as she said, "But then you arrived, Jake. You saved me. You cared for me and I'm not lost anymore."

Jake leaned across between the two horses and kissed Nora, his heart going out to this woman who had endured so much yet now meant so much to him.

————

In Eureka, the eastbound train was departing the station, and Lucy was walking toward the hotel with her monogrammed traveling bag. Her trunk would be delivered later.

She was thinking about that horse and woman rider she had seen in Wichita. The horse she was riding looked like the horse that Jake had bought for her that she had never ridden, except when she left. She had been touched by his thoughtfulness for buying the horse but felt guilty about it, so she didn't ride it until she had to. She had almost left a note of apology on the horse when she left but thought it would be the height of hypocrisy.

But today, the more she thought about it, she swore that the animal that the oddly dressed woman was riding looked like the same horse. *And what about the other two horses?* She hadn't looked at them very long, but the pack horse looked like one of Jake's other two that he kept in the barn and the other one being ridden looked like his as well. *Could it have been Jake Fletcher? Why would he have gone to Wichita? And who was the woman with him if he had?*

No, it wasn't possible, she finally concluded. If it had been just the man with the three horses, she'd suspect that she was being tracked down by Jake, but the woman's presence negated that concern.

Lucy would just do this job and then be done with it. She was still angry about the 'accident' that Charlie was planning, but there was nothing she could do to prevent it.

As she walked down the boardwalk to the hotel, George Smith was almost waltzing to the depot. It was early, but he was so anxious to see Maude again, he'd happily wait for two more hours. He passed the pretty blonde woman going the other way and tipped his hat. She sure was a looker. He'd be interested if it wasn't for Maude. He and Maude had been so close before he went off to that damned war and fate seemed insistent in keeping them apart until it changed its mind. They were a perfect match back then and he knew they still would be when she arrived.

Lucy had acknowledged the man tipping his hat by nodding her head but didn't give him a second thought.

———

Jake and Nora were still trotting and had gone twenty-two miles since leaving Wichita when they decided to stop for a break. It was just past noon when they pulled over to the side of the road.

There was a pond nearby, so the horses were allowed to drink their fill and eat from the abundant grass while Jake cut some slices from the fresh loaf of bread and then some slices of the ham that Nora had pulled from the pannier.

It was almost like a pleasant spring picnic as they sat and ate their sandwiches and drank from canteens.

Nora then asked, "Jake, what will it be like for you when you get to talk to Lucy again?"

"Odd. I don't know how she'll react, though. She could turn into a raging witch or break down into a mass of sobbing female. I simply have no idea what to expect. But whatever it is, I won't believe it. She's very good at saying or doing anything that she wants and making it sound believable."

Nora asked in a subdued tone, "Will she try to get you to want her again?"

"She might, and I'll be honest with you and let you know that despite all that has happened, I might have been an even bigger fool and let her back into my life before I met you, but not now. You are my great big wall to protect me from her and you are my anchor. She could strip naked in front of me and it wouldn't change my mind."

"Would you watch?" she asked with a smile.

"I'd watch, but then I'd drag you off to some private place and have my way with you because I love you, Mrs. Fletcher, and as I said before, you're much more impressive."

Nora smiled with relief and satisfaction hearing his words and the form of address he used as she said, "Then I hope she does."

Nora was feeling a bit randy at the thought of being dragged off by Jake, so without warning, she launched herself at him.

He caught her, despite the surprise, and landed on his back on the dirt, surrounded by prairie grass.

She was frenetically kissing and groping him as he returned the favor as he began sliding his hands under whatever cloth protection she was wearing.

Jake was simply amazed at how Nora had changed in this one aspect of her personality. Maybe being released from the doom of permanent spinsterhood and virginity had released her inhibitions as well. He didn't care about the reasons as much as the result as they rolled in the Kansas dirt.

But mad groping was as far as they could do at the lunch break before Nora slid to Jake's side and assumed the position that she normally had found herself when they were naked the night before.

"I'm sorry, Jake. I just couldn't help myself. I began imagining you taking me away and making love to me again. I needed that."

"Don't worry, Nora. It was a pleasant way to end our lunch break. Luckily, it wasn't providing any entertainment for anyone on the road."

She turned her head and looked at the road a scant fifty feet away, then laughed before she said, "I hadn't thought about that, but it may not have stopped me anyway."

Jake pulled her close and kissed her again before giving her cute behind a mild slap.

"Let's get going to Eureka," he said as he rose and helped her to her feet.

After they brushed off the grass and dirt, they mounted and started the three horses east at a medium trot.

In Eureka, Lucy was in her room preparing for tomorrow and was reading her victim's description that had been provided by Charlie and noticed that it was a lot like that man who had passed her on the boardwalk. She'd find George Smith at the church tomorrow morning and after a few innocent smiles, she'd talk to him afterward and knew that he would be panting like a coon dog after a few minutes.

———

Just down the road, the westbound train was pulling into the station and her target, George Smith was almost bouncing like a teenager. He wondered how much Maude had changed in seventeen years. She never mentioned any children and he hadn't had any, but never could figure out why it had been that way. Maude would be thirty-five now and he wondered if they would still have time. In the end, it didn't matter if they had children or not, he would have his Maude.

Maude was just as eager as she looked out onto the platform and picked out George easily. He had put on a little weight and his hairline was receding a bit, but he was still her George. The train was almost at a stop when she stood, picked up her travel bag, and walked quickly down the aisle.

She stepped down onto the platform and walked slowly toward George who was approaching her. They met in the center of the platform, where she dropped her travel bag before he took her hands.

"Welcome home, Maude," George said as he looked into her eyes and smiled.

"It's good to be home, George," she replied softly as she gazed back at him.

He took her arm and her travel bag, then walked back to the boardwalk then headed to his house. Just minutes later, in the privacy of the parlor, they were locked in an embrace and kissing as if they had never missed those seventeen years apart. She readily agreed to be married after church tomorrow and wasn't in the least surprised to learn that George had already notified the Reverend Wilcox of his plans to marry Maude after tomorrow's service. Just by his walking into church with a smiling Maude on his arm would be the signal to the reverend that the ceremony was on.

———

Lucy was tired and was napping as her mark was going over the wedding plans with his intended.

———

Jake and Nora were just ten miles out of Eureka when they found an excellent location for the night. Jake had used his field glasses to find a spot almost a mile north of the road. He had spotted the trees in the distance and knew water had to be nearby. It was worth the cross-country trip when ten minutes later, they pulled up to the trees and found a wide stream that made a horseshoe bend to the trees before breaking back to the northwest. The horses were soon unsaddled, and Jake hitched them in the bend where the grass was the thickest.

"This is beautiful, Jake," Nora said when he returned to their new campsite.

"It is. It may be our last night on the road, Nora. If we get Lucy tomorrow, then we can have the sheriff in Wichita arrest Charlie and maybe Ralph if we know where he is."

"I hadn't thought of that. You're right. We could be finished after we get Lucy," she said, then paused, and continued, asking, "Jake, what happens after that? To us, I mean."

Jake stepped up to Nora and put his hands on her shoulders.

"What would you like to happen, Nora?" he asked quietly.

She looked down and asked even more quietly, "Could we get married, Jake?"

Jake tilted her face back toward him and kissed her gently.

"I had already assumed we'd be getting married, my love. I would have asked more formally later tonight. I thought you were wondering about that."

Nora's attitude shifted remarkably as she broke into a big smile, hugged Jake, then began to cry softly.

Jake just held her close and put his hand on the back of her head. He really had planned to ask Nora later, but this would do. He thought she knew that when he'd addressed her as Mrs. Fletcher.

Nora was beyond happy. She wasn't sure that Jake was going to ask her to marry him, especially with the prospect of seeing Lucy again and despite addressing her as his wife. There was still that doubt about competing with a beautiful woman, despite Jake's assurances. She held him possessively hoping that Jake really was her man.

Nora eventually released Jake and they set to making their campsite. It was only five o'clock when it was done, and Nora had suggested that they don't set up the tent. It was such a beautiful day. Early May was an almost perfect time for weather, so he laid out the bedrolls and dug a fire pit near the stream.

There was plenty of firewood in this location, so he didn't need to wander very far at all. There would be no repeat of the Jerome incident.

Nora had pulled the cooking grate and frypan from the pannier and was carrying them back to the fire pit when Jake took them from her hands and put them aside. He had been thinking about her question earlier and had figured out why she had asked it. Tomorrow was Lucy Day and Nora must still feel as if she couldn't compete.

He scooped Nora into his arms and carried her to the bedrolls.

She knew what was on his mind and began to kiss him as he carried her before he gently lowered her to the bedrolls and just seconds later, were rapidly removing any covering cloth.

An hour later, with the sun fading in the west, they lay entwined on the bedroll. With no restrictions on standing or movement as there had been in the tent, they had been free to do new things to enhance the experience. Again, Nora had surprised herself with her slut-like behavior but had reveled in it as well and knew that Jake had enjoyed her. She would do anything to please Jake and knew for a fact that he did anything that she asked of him. It was an incredible time for them both, and Nora had the added incentive of trying to ensure that Lucy would be just a distraction.

Jake continued to be astonished at Nora. The bedroom Nora was so different than the normal Nora, and he loved them both.

As they lay tucked in close to each other, he had his hand on the back of her head as he said, "Nora, no more doubts from you. No more worries. I want to marry you and spend the rest of my life with you. Period. Tomorrow, you can look Lucy in the eye and know that you are the better woman. You are better in everything that matters. You don't have to back down. You own me body, heart, and soul."

"You knew, didn't you? I was worried, Jake. I'm sorry. It's just hard to think that someone as plain as I am could ever compete with someone like Lucy."

"Get that out of your mind, Nora. First of all, you aren't plain. You may not be beautiful in the face like Lucy. Few women are. But you are not plain. You are cute, and I prefer cute. When you smile, you make me smile from the inside out. But you are much more beautiful than Lucy or any other woman I've known on the inside, where it counts. If that wasn't enough, you are a wonder in bed. I'm still in awe of that."

"But I don't have Lucy's curves, either."

"No, you're not as generously endowed there, but what you have is so wonderfully shaped and the only one who will ever really know how perfect you are underneath those clothes is me. You have more than enough bumps and curves to keep me entertained, Nora. And, in a few years, when Lucy needs stronger corsets to keep everything together, you won't."

Nora laughed lightly and replied, "I've never worn a corset. I wondered what they're like sometimes."

"As long as we're married, Nora, I hope you never find out."

"Then I never will. Besides, I don't want to slow down our adventures."

He rolled Nora onto her back and began to kiss her again. Nora was hoping that it wouldn't end with just kisses, and Jake fulfilled her hopes. She just couldn't get enough of Jake. *What a difference two weeks could make!*

———

Twelve miles away, in Eureka, George and Maude were making up for lost time. Wedding night be damned. This was their wedding night.

Lucy slept alone.

———

CHAPTER 6

Jake was the first to awaken on Lucy Day and slipped out of the bedroll as Nora watched appreciatively thinking that her man was all man and she didn't need to feel possessive any longer. She was confident in Jake's love but was still surprised in her lovemaking. *Where had that come from?* They had enjoyed each other three times last night. Yet, here she was watching Jake and already wanted him back in the bedroll with her. Then he did something that surprised her.

He looked down at her, smiled, and without a word, ran a short distance, dove headfirst into the cold water of the nearby pool formed by the stream.

When he surfaced, he shook his head, grinned at her, and shouted, "Come on in, Nora. The water's only almost icy cold."

"Not on your life, Mister," she yelled back.

She had no intention of freezing in that water, but she needed a hot bath. What she did do was slip out of the bedroll, exposing herself to the cool morning and to Jake's smiling eyes. She smiled and did a pirouette, giving him the full view, not feeling the least bit of shame or embarrassment. This was for Jake, her Jake.

After breakfast, interrupted by kissing and other touches of affection, they finally were able to get mounted, and on the road just two hours after sunrise. Nora had dressed in her riding skirt and blouse, and Jake told her that she was just as cute as she was when she wore the britches.

As they were so close to Eureka, Jake asked, "It's Sunday, Nora. Do you want to go to church first? We'll be there by eight-thirty and most services don't start until nine o'clock."

"What if we get there and Lucy is in there? I met Charlie at church. Where did you meet Lucy?"

"At a church social. I wonder if they think by being in church, it gives them more credibility."

"Then should we go? And what if the town has more than one?"

"Good point. If we get there in time, we can watch the folks going in. We'll have to hide the horses, though."

"Of course! She'd spot Satin and probably Sandy and Coffee, too."

"When we get to Eureka, we board the horses at the livery. Then we walk to the church. If there's more than one, we may need to split up and look at the people separately, but Lucy should be easy to spot."

———

In Eureka, Lucy was getting ready for church. It was step one to meeting George Smith, but she wasn't going all out. She was still bothered by those horses. But not going all out didn't mean she wasn't going to be forgettable. It was impossible to make herself unforgettable to any man.

———

George and Maude were also getting ready for church and their wedding day. Her trunk had been delivered to George's house and she had dressed in her Sunday best. George was wearing the nicer of his two suits, a herringbone tweed and Maude thought he looked dashing.

———

Jake and Nora arrived at the edge of Eureka at 8:20 and quickly boarded the horses, and Nora thought it wise to leave her Stetson and pistol with the horses, so she didn't attract attention. Jake agreed with her decision. A man with a Stetson and a Colt was not only expected, it was almost mandatory. A woman with either was noticeable.

He had Nora on his arm as he headed for the Lutheran church, which was the closest. The Catholic or Episcopalian churches were already having their services, so if Lucy's victim was in either one, then she'd already be inside.

They decided to stop at the café across the street from the church and have some coffee first. It had an unrestricted view of the church, so they'd be able to watch as the congregation entered. So, after they selected the perfect viewing table, they took a seat and were soon just watching as they sipped their coffee.

———

George and Maude were anxious about their wedding, so they were among the first to arrive. Besides, George wanted the reverend to see them together, so he'd know that he had a marriage to perform.

Lucy waited in her hotel room just two buildings down from the Lutheran church and Jake was paying close attention to the hotel door, certain that Lucy was in the hotel if she wasn't already in one of the other churches. Whether she was going to church or not was the question, and it wasn't long before they had the answer.

Lucy left her room, walked across the lobby, then stepped out into the bright Sunday morning sun, stopped at the entrance, and then turned and slowly walked down the boardwalk.

"There she is, Nora!" Jake said excitedly but in a subdued voice.

Nora looked at Lucy for the first time and felt a pang of jealousy and a twinge of her recently forgotten inferiority. *How could she compete with that woman?*

She kept her eyes on Lucy as she said, "I can see how you were smitten, Jake. She really is outrageously beautiful."

Jake stopped watching Lucy walk toward the church and looked at Nora.

"She'll never come close to you, Nora. Let's go and follow in another minute."

Nora smiled, but having seen Lucy, she was uncertain again.

After Lucy had reached the church and gone inside, Jake stood and tossed a quarter on the table before he and Nora, stood, then left the diner. As Nora walked beside Jake, her hand was firmly gripping his forearm, almost cutting off the blood supply to his hand. Jake noticed the difference and wondered how he could possibly convince Nora that she was the better woman.

They were almost the last ones in line as they entered and took a back pew before they soon spotted Lucy, who was sitting on the opposite side, three rows in front and on the end. Jake could see her scanning the congregation, probably looking for her target, and hoped she didn't turn around, and as it worked out, she didn't get the chance.

Reverend Phillip Wilcox had entered the church and stood before the assemblage.

"Good morning to everyone. I see some new faces among our worshippers this morning. Know that you are all welcome in this house, which is also a special day for two of our congregation. After our normal services, you are all invited to remain for a celebration of love and patience."

Jake continued watching Lucy to make sure her head didn't turn his way. If it did, he'd turn quickly away.

"As many of you know, our good friend George Smith lost his wife, Evelyn, two years ago and has been grieving her loss since then."

Jake noticed a jerk in Lucy's attention when the preacher mentioned George Smith. *Was he the one?*

"Well, the Lord has smiled on George. As many of you who have lived here a long time could recall, George and Maude Simmons were sweethearts when they were young. A mistake during the war resulted in Maude leaving our town in grief over the mistaken belief that her George had died. When he returned a year later, she had already married and was living in Kansas City. George married, but when Evelyn died, George was alone. No man should be alone.

"Yet, Providence shone the light upon them, and Maude learned of George's loss and wrote him a letter. She asked if she should return to him. He wired her telling her yes, and she returned yesterday. So, after our ceremony this morning, everyone is invited to attend the marriage of George and Maude, reunited at long last through the good Lord's graces."

Jake was certain that her mark had been taken and could see her jaws tighten and her face cloud, but then he saw something that caused him a bit of confusion. After her initial surprise, a wry smile played across her lips. *Why is she smiling if she just lost her mark?*

Nora noticed the smile as well and was just as confused as Jake, then tugged on his shirt and he looked at her.

He leaned over and whispered, "I'm sure that her mark was George Smith."

Nora nodded and they both looked forward again.

The service began and everything seemed normal, but Jake wondered if Lucy was going to stay for the wedding ceremony.

———

In Wichita, Ralph Haskins was getting off the train much earlier than he'd been expected. He wasn't supposed to show up for a day, but he had been bored and wanted to find out what the whole story was. He suspected that Charlie had decided to modify their methods after his little adventure in Albert. He had said that if he had left her in the closet a little longer, they could have had the ranch too, but the ranch wasn't worth the money and he'd be a prime suspect in any murder investigation for the plain woman's death. He then said that if they chose their next victim more wisely, then they could get a big payday, and Ralph easily understood what it meant.

He carried his travel bag down the street, crossed over to the other side, turned at the first right, and went down three buildings to a large house. He stalked up the walkway, onto the porch and didn't knock as it was a rooming house.

He climbed two flights to the top floor and passed what was Lucy's room. He knew she wasn't supposed to be there, but he stopped and tried the door anyway. It was locked, so he just

183

shrugged and stepped to the next door, knocked, and waited until Charlie opened the door.

"What are you doing here so soon?" Charlie asked as he swung the door open.

"I got bored. I thought I'd come here and find out what was going on. You sounded like you were going to go about this differently."

"We are. Come on in and I'll give you the details."

———

The church service was nearing the end and Jake was still curious about what Lucy would do. She would most likely leave the church and get ready to leave Eureka, but without a train leaving for Wichita for more than six hours, that might be a problem for her.

The reverend concluded the service. Surprisingly, no one moved to leave, not even Lucy. Jake glanced down at Nora and raised his eyebrows. She shrugged her shoulders in response, having expected Lucy to leave as well. Maybe Lucy didn't want to draw attention to herself by being the only one to depart.

It wasn't the reason for Lucy remaining in her pew. She was staying just to see George Smith and Maude get married. She had been to six weddings, and all of them were hers. The first was to Charlie, then there was the jeweler in Hutchinson, a banker in Garfield, a rancher outside of Garden City, then the banker in Beaver Creek, and finally Jake Fletcher near Eureka.

Each of them, except Charlie, had looked at her with wondrous expressions on their wedding days, but that last one had nearly ruined her. Not with the suspected pregnancy, but with the way he treated her. He wasn't nearly as handsome as

Charlie, but while her other victims had worshipped her, Jake had treated her as an equal. He would ask her opinion, and then when she had allowed him to consummate the marriage, he did things for her that no man had done before. She had enjoyed herself so much in those twenty-three days, and not just the passionate times, and felt a rush just remembering them.

And now, she wanted to see if George had that same look on his face that she had seen so many times before, except at her own real wedding.

George and Maude stepped forward to the front of the church. George gazed at Maude's smiling face as he held her hands in his. The minister smiled at them both and began the marriage ceremony.

Jake sought out Nora's hand and clasped it tightly in his to keep reminding her that she was now his wife and soon, they'd make it legal in the eyes of the state.

She looked up at him and smiled. "Soon," she thought.

The minister read the words. Vows were exchanged, followed by rings. George kissed his long-awaited bride and the couple turned to face the congregation to a round of applause.

Lucy then examined the look on George's face. It was the same face she had witnessed five times before from a close distance and was saddened to know she would never see it again. She had a sickening feeling that Charlie and Ralph would be angry at her for failing in this job, even though it wasn't her fault.

George and Maude walked down the aisle, left the church and the congregation began filing out.

Lucy stood there, wondering what she could do. *How could she get out of this? Go to the sheriff?* She shook her blonde head knowing that wasn't possible. She was the last person in the pew, so she stood, then turned to leave and was met by a familiar face standing two feet in front of her.

"Good morning, Laura. Or should I call you Lucy?" Jake asked.

Jake expected her to run, or maybe slap him and accuse him of grabbing her while Nora just wanted to rip her hair out.

Instead, Lucy said quickly, "Come with me."

She pulled his arm and was surprised that he stayed put and then noticed the woman next to him. She was a bit taller than she was and rather plain-looking and was uncertain why she was even there.

Jake answered her unasked question when he said, "Lucy, this is Nora Graham. Charlie did to her what you did to me and we're here to set things right. Did you want to talk to us or to the sheriff?"

Lucy made a quick decision and replied, "Alright, both of you follow me."

Jake and Nora stepped away from the pew, and Lucy stepped into the aisle. Jake followed with a strangle-hold-gripping Nora on his right arm. She was not about to lose Jake to this woman and still failed to realize that she had the upper hand, not Lucy.

The trio left the church and walked toward the hotel, then stepped into the lobby before Lucy walked quickly down the hallway to her room as Jake quietly undid the hammer loop to his Colt. Nora noticed because she still had her death grip on his arm.

Lucy went inside and after they entered behind her, closed the door, then plopped onto the edge of the bed and took a deep breath.

She focused on Jake as she said, "I know you must hate me for what I did to you and I can understand that, but things have changed. You've got to help me stop Charlie and Ralph."

Jake had expected something like this and wasn't buying it, at least not yet.

"Lucy, you have never told me the truth before, so why should I trust you now?"

"I know that. You could turn me over right now and I don't care anymore. I have to get away from those two."

Jake looked over at Nora who gave him the 'I have no idea' look.

Jake looked back at Lucy and said, "Go ahead and tell me what's going on, Lucy."

"It's this job. The one where I was supposed to marry George Smith wasn't like the others. Charlie was inspired by his one job with Nora. After he let her out of the closet, he thought how much easier it would have been to leave her in there, then let her die, so he could sell the ranch later."

Nora felt her legs weaken at the thought of how close she had been to death and Jake could feel her shudder.

"He thought he'd be too easily fingered for her murder, so he let her out. Now, he's planning on killing George Smith to make it look like an accident, but there's more. I think Charlie is going to try to kill me. I thought you had gotten me pregnant and somehow, he found out."

Nora had to sit in a chair after hearing her casual reminder that Jake had bedded Lucy more than he'd been with her.

Jake was a bit sick in the stomach himself at the thought of Lucy carrying his child but remained standing as she continued.

"But I discovered that I wasn't pregnant after all. I didn't tell him that I wasn't, but the way Charlie looked at me when he told me that he wouldn't tell Ralph made me very afraid. I don't think that my being pregnant would make any difference anymore. I could see in his eyes that he no longer needs me.

"I think he lied and will tell Ralph that I'm pregnant, or just tell Ralph that he can have me. Ralph has always been obsessed with me. He's a cruel and vicious man and has no redeeming qualities at all. Charlie could tell him to kill me and it wouldn't bother him at all. He'd tell Ralph to enjoy himself as much as he wanted first. This is all the truth, Jake and I'm terrified."

Jake looked over at Nora and saw her downcast eyes. He didn't know if it was because of what Lucy had said or her mere presence, but he had to do something.

"Lucy, where is all the money that you and Charlie stole?" Jake asked.

"He's the only one who has access to the money. It's in the First National Bank in Kansas City. I assume it's under his legal name, Charles Haskins. He gives me a little money before each job, and I know he gives Ralph a lot more for his work."

"How much is it?"

188

"If I'd have to guess, I'd say over fifty thousand dollars."

If she had given him a smaller amount, then he would have guessed she was lying about everything else and ended the conversation.

But she was close to his estimate, so he continued his questioning by asking, "Where do Charlie and Ralph live?"

"Right now, Charlie is at our rooming house in Wichita on 5th Street. I'm not sure of the number because we just go there. We have three rooms on the third floor. We have a house in Kansas City on Walnut Street, too. It's number 123. Ralph has a room in Kansas City on 16th Street, but I don't know the number there either."

Jake looked again at the downcast Nora and asked, "Nora, what do you think?"

Nora didn't lift her head, but simply replied, "As hard as it is to fathom, I believe her."

Jake nodded, then looked back at Lucy and said, "Alright, Lucy. Here's the way we're going to approach this. First, I need to know how long it will be before you have to notify Charlie that you've married George Smith."

"As soon as I'm married to him. That's usually a week or so."

"Obviously, that's not going to happen, but it gives us some time to come up with a good plan. What I'm going to do is to send a telegram to a United States Deputy Marshal in Denver that I've been working with. I'll see if he can freeze or seize the account in Kansas City. Without money, they can't do much. Then, we'll get them rounded up."

"What about me?" she asked.

"I have no idea yet. You'll have to hope that none of your victims press charges. After their money is returned, most probably won't. I know that I won't, but Charlie won't be that lucky. He's facing a lot of charges and I doubt if my fiancée is going to let him get off the hook. Isn't that right, Nora?"

Nora heard him tell Lucy that she was his fiancée and she felt a flood of relief wash through her before she looked up and smiled.

"No, I won't. He's going to go to jail for a long time."

Lucy then asked, "What if everyone gets their money back and nobody presses charges other than Nora, and there's still money left?"

Jake wasn't sure but wanted her cooperation, so he replied, "That would be yours, I'm guessing. You're still married to Charlie, aren't you?"

"Yes. I can live with that if that's what you believe will happen."

"Alright. You two stay here and I'll go down to the Western Union office and send the telegram. I'll be right back."

Nora knew that she had been asked to stay to make sure Lucy didn't go anywhere but was already uncomfortable with the notion.

Jake didn't have any choice but to smile at Nora before he left the room and closed the door behind him.

Lucy looked over at Nora and asked, "That was you on my horse in Wichita, wasn't it?"

Nora bristled and replied, "No, that was me on my horse in Wichita."

"I'm sorry, I didn't mean it that way. But you and Jake saw me there, didn't you?"

"I didn't. Jake did. I didn't see you until this morning."

"Jake said you were his fiancée. When did that happen?"

"A few days ago. We've only been together for a short time."

"I guessed that. Charlie only returned from your place a few weeks ago. I was appalled when he told me what he had done. It bothered me, believe it or not. Taking money is one thing. Hurting people is another."

"But you always hurt people. You crushed Jake and probably those other men. Then you could have ruined his life by taking everything from him."

"I left him his ranch, almost four hundred dollars, and the horse. I could have done worse."

Nora felt her anger rise as she snapped, "Don't use that as a justification for what you did. Jake is the best man I've ever met. Why he should love me, I'll never know. When you hurt him, you may as well have shot him, but I never would have met him if you hadn't."

Lucy's reply did anything but calm Nora's anger when she smiled gently and then said softly, "Jake is special, isn't he? He got me in trouble with both Charlie and Ralph when they wondered why it was taking me so long to take his money. Ralph knows how much he had, so I had to return with close to that amount."

"Why did you stay so long?" Nora asked, almost punishing herself when she did.

"I enjoyed almost every minute of my time with Jake. I had never been with a man like him before or since."

Nora quickly said, "I like him, too."

"Have you bedded him yet?" Lucy asked with a devilish smile.

Nora wanted to appear worldly, so she answered the question with a firm, "Yes. Yes, I have."

"He is a real man, isn't he?"

"Yes."

Lucy could see her redden and asked, "Are you embarrassed by this kind of talk?"

"A little," Nora confessed.

"I'm sorry. It was just conversation between women who appreciate what Jake provided when compared to other men."

Nora suddenly blurted, "He's the only man I've ever been with."

"You were a virgin?" Lucy asked with arched eyebrows.

Nora was a deeper shade of red as she simply nodded, wondering why she had said such a stupid thing. She felt she was losing the edge.

When Nora nodded, Lucy giggled and then exclaimed, "Wow! You were heading into spinsterhood! That must have been a real shock for you then, spending a night with Jake. I know how spectacular he is in bed, but it must have almost killed you."

"No, it wasn't a shock," Nora answered quietly, hoping the conversation would end.

Lucy tilted her head and examined the plain woman a bit closer wondering what in tarnation a man like Jake saw in her.

But after that brief inspection, said, "Well, at least your first time was your best."

Nora didn't reply, but let her eyes drop to the floor again and wished Jake would return quickly.

———

As the women talked, Jake handed the message to the operator:

US DEPUTY MARSHAL HANK JENKINS DENVER COLO

LUCY HASKINS HERE IN EUREKA UNDER GUARD
SAID HASKINS PLANNED ON KILLING NEXT TARGET
CHARLIE IN WICHITA ROOMING HOUSE ON FIFTH STREET
SAID CHARLIE HAS ALL THE STOLEN MONEY
PERSONAL ACCOUNT IN FIRST NATIONAL BANK IN KC
UNDER CHARLES HASKINS
NEED TO FREEZE OR SEIZE ACCOUNT
OVER FIFTY THOUSAND DOLLARS
WILL WAIT FOR YOUR REPLY

JAKE FLETCHER EUREKA HOTEL EUREKA KANSAS

After paying the eighty cents to the intrigued operator, he returned to the hotel and rented two more rooms before he walked to Lucy's room and knocked.

Lucy opened the door and as he entered Nora looked up at him as she sat on the bed and felt an enormous amount of relief, but was still very disconcerted from her conversation with Lucy.

"The telegram is on its way to Denver and hopefully we'll get a reply soon. I rented two other rooms, one on each side of Lucy's."

"Which one is mine?" asked Nora.

Jake wasn't about to give her an answer before he said, "I'm not sure. I'll figure it out later. How about lunch, ladies? I'm getting hungry."

As Nora stood, Jake took her arm and then followed Lucy out the door. There was a reason he didn't want to assign Nora a room and figured that she'd understand why he hadn't soon enough. His Nora was a smart lady.

They hadn't taken ten steps down the hallway when his smart lady realized why he'd answered that way and smiled at his reasoning. He didn't want Lucy to be able to sneak into his room later that night. If she didn't know who was in which room, there was an equal chance she'd slip into a room and possibly find Nora. If she didn't know which one Jake was in, she'd have to stay put. Now, Nora, on the other hand…

Nora was on Jake's right arm and Lucy had his left as they crossed over to the café where Jake and Nora had seen Lucy. They took a table and ordered their lunch, making small talk rather than letting the waitress and other diners know the situation.

———

In Denver, Hank Jenkins read the telegram he had just been handed and walked back to his boss. He had desk duty that day, but the marshal was in his office on that Sunday, just hiding from his wife who was in a bad mood. His boss, United States Marshal Cecil Cooper whistled when he read the telegram.

"That is a lot of money to steal from potential husbands. Go ahead and notify John Breedlove in Kansas City. Use my signature. See if he can get a judge to freeze that account pending investigation. Good job, Hank."

"Boss, I didn't do anything much on this one, to be honest," he said as he wagged the telegram, "This feller did all the work."

"Well, pass along the good work comment, then. Tell him it may take a day because it's Sunday, but we'll let him know what we'll do about it. Tell John that it's his area, so he may want to go and pick this guy up, too. It's a Federal issue because they're crossing state lines."

"I'll do it and let you know what I send."

"Good man."

Hank left the office, then headed for the well-used route to the nearby telegraph office and sent:

US MARSHAL JOHN BREEDLOVE KANSAS CITY MISS

**SUSPECT CHARLES HASKINS OF KANSAS CITY
BELIEVED TO HAVE SCAMMED 50 THOUSAND DOLLARS
REQUEST FREEZING HIS 1ST NATIONAL BANK ACCOUNT
PENDING YOUR INVESTIGATION
SUSPECT IN WICHITA 5TH ST ROOMING HOUSE
TWO VICTIMS TRACKING SUSPECT AND ACCOMPLICE
CURRENTLY AT EUREKA KANSAS HOTEL
SEE JAKE FLETCHER AND ADVISE THIS OFFICE**

US MARSHAL CECIL COOPER DENVER COLO

The operator tapped out the message and Hank took his copy back to the marshal.

———

An hour later, United States Deputy Marshal Harry Little in the Kansas City office read the telegram and had the same reaction as Marshal Cooper had when he'd read Jake's and whistled. That was a lot of money to scam from folks. It was big enough that he decided to run it over to the marshal's house even though it was Sunday.

The marshal read the telegram and told him to track down Deputy Marshal Carroll and have him take the next train to Eureka and to notify Denver and this Jake Fletcher character in Eureka right away.

The wheels were in motion.

———

For three hours, Lucy talked to Jake and Nora in her hotel room. She listed all her victims and their locations. As Nora was the only woman who Charlie had scammed, it accounted for all their victims of the marriage scam.

Jake had been writing down the information as she gave it to him, including the amounts. When he totaled the numbers gained from the six phony marriages, the grand total was just over forty-two thousand dollars.

"Where did the rest of the money come from?"

"Different kinds of scams, mostly from people whose names we didn't even know."

"Now I know why you asked about the extra money."

She smiled and replied, "Now you know."

"Well, that's not my problem. I'm going to go downstairs and see if there has been a reply to my telegram."

"It is Sunday, Jake. Don't get your hopes up," advised Nora.

"This coming from the most optimistic person I know," he said as he smiled at her before giving her a nice kiss.

Nora was more than pleased. The kiss was more than just a peck and was a way to let Lucy know that he preferred Nora.

Lucy noticed and was not only confused by Jake's apparent attraction to the woman but also saw a challenge. She never had lost to another woman, never.

Jake stepped down the hall and approached the front desk. He didn't have to say anything when as soon as he was close enough, the desk clerk took out the message from his room box and handed it to him.

"Thank you," Jake said as he took the yellow sheet.

"You're welcome."

Jake quickly unfolded the yellow sheet and read:

JAKE FLETCHER EUREKA HOTEL EUREKA KANSAS

US DEP MARSHAL CARROLL ARRIVING NEXT TRAIN FROM KANSAS CITY PLEASE MEET AND BRIEF

US DEPUTY MARSHAL HARRY LITTLE KANSAS CITY MISS

"Do you know when the next train is due in from Kansas City?" he asked the clerk.

"That would be at 8:45."

"I'd like to get a room for a visitor. Can I do that?"

"If you have his name."

"I do," Jake replied as he copied the deputy's name onto the register and paid the two dollars.

He took the proffered key, slipped it into his pocket, and said, "Thank you," before turning back to the hallway.

"Well, that was fast," he thought.

He soon reached the door, knocked, and was rewarded when Nora opened the door this time. She wanted to kiss him but felt that would be Jake's decision under the circumstances.

Jake closed the door behind him and said, "Ladies, we're going to have a visitor in four hours. United States Deputy Marshal Carroll is arriving from Kansas City on the next train to talk to us."

"That was fast," Nora commented.

"They must think it's important."

"Will he arrest me?" asked Lucy.

"I don't think so. It'll be his call, but right now, it's just an investigation. I'm sure that once he's talked to all of us, he'll want to go to Wichita and find Charlie."

NORA

"Ralph may be there, too, but it's just a feeling, nothing more. If Charlie wanted something done, he'd contact Ralph. He probably already had Ralph coming before I was supposed to marry George Smith, so once he got that telegram, he'd send Ralph down to kill him."

Jake replied, "We'll let the deputy marshal know that."

"Jake, I'm going to take a bath. I know you took one earlier, but that water looked just too cold to me," Nora said.

"It was very cold, but it was okay after a while."

"I'll be back in a little while," she said as she pulled off her boots, picked up her travel bag, and left the room, closing the door behind her.

"She must trust you," said a smiling Lucy as she rocked on the edge of her bed.

"I want her to trust me. She had such a miserable childhood and then, just when she thought she was going to be married, Charlie pulled his little game. Did you know she thought she was going to die in that closet?"

"I know. Charlie thought it was funny. He said how bad she smelled when he let her out."

"I owe him for that, Lucy. I owe him big time."

"You really do love that Nora, don't you?"

"Every bit of her, and she's not 'that' Nora, she's my Nora. She's more of a woman than any other female I've ever met."

"*Including me?*" she asked with her eyebrows raised, knowing that he must be joking.

"Including you. She doesn't wear that Colt for decoration, Lucy. She's very proficient with it, and a Winchester, too, I might add."

"But you can't tell me that she's my equal in bed, Jake. Be serious."

"No, she's not your equal, Lucy," Jake replied.

"Well, at least you're honest."

"She's way better than you are in bed, too. She's nothing less than spectacular."

"Her?" she asked with a sneer, *"You prefer that to me?"*

"Yes, Lucy, her and not 'that'. I prefer Nora Graham to you and every other woman, and soon she'll be Nora Fletcher. But it's not just because she's so amazing in our lovemaking, Lucy. You have to understand that I loved her before I even kissed her. She is so deep and so complete. We talk, we laugh, and I don't have to explain anything to her. It seems like I've known Nora my entire life. I'd do anything for her and protect her."

Lucy didn't answer, but inside she was seething. *How could Jake like that plain, under-endowed woman to her?* She remembered those three glorious weeks and knew that he must have forgotten how special they were. This wasn't right.

What neither one knew was that Nora was outside the door listening to each and every syllable that had been spoken. After closing the door, she wasn't quite as confident as she wished she could be and had stayed there to hear what would happen, almost expecting to hear sounds of passion erupt from beyond the door. But after hearing Jake's defense of their love, she wanted to rip open the door and jump on him. Instead, she turned and quietly walked to the bathroom, smiling for all it was worth.

———

Twenty minutes later, a wet-haired Nora returned to the room wearing a clean set of clothes. When Jake saw her, he smiled broadly, knowing what wasn't under those clothes. Nora smiled every bit as wide as she stepped inside and sat down.

As she pulled on her boots, she asked, "Did I miss anything?"

"Not much. Lucy just wanted to know how long we've been together."

"Not long enough to suit me, I'm afraid," Nora replied. "I wish I had met you when I was twelve."

Jake laughed and then said, "You'd probably have made fun of me. I was this gangly kid with big knees. I hated it when it got warm and the kids started wearing shorts. You know, the kind that were pants a couple of years earlier and had either gotten too short or been ripped by horsing around? I had two pairs of shorts for every pair of pants that I owned. When I put on shorts, it was like I had these two sticks with hornet nests in the middle."

"How did you do in school, Jake?" asked Nora.

"Okay. I had to. The rule was I couldn't go to Uncle Ernie's ranch unless I had at least a B in every subject. I worked hard, but the toughest thing to get a B in was deportment."

"You were a bad little boy?" asked Lucy.

"Not so much bad as I was a bit of a smart aleck. Sometimes, the schoolmarm would say something in a lesson that would get me started. She didn't like it, either."

"Like what?" from Nora.

"Oh, for example. We were talking about the War Between the States. Now that's so fresh in a lot of folks' minds that it's a bit touchy, but the schoolmarm didn't care. Miss Faircloth was talking about the battle of Richmond and said how heroically General Ulysses S. Grant won the battle, so I raised my hand. She hated to call on me, but with all the other students looking at her, she kind of had to.

"She pointed at me and said, 'What is your question, Mister Fletcher?', and I said, 'It's not a question, ma'am. It's just that Ulysses S. Grant didn't win that battle'. Well, she went nuts and began giving dates and casualties and everything else about the battle. Then she asked, 'What do you say now, Mister Fletcher?'. And I repeated myself, saying, 'Sorry, ma'am, but Ulysses S. Grant wasn't even at Richmond.'.

"She stomped over to a thick book she had on her desk and began thumbing through the pages, and found a lithograph of General Grant standing over the earthworks at Richmond."

"So, she was right after all," said Lucy.

"Not for a smarty-pants eleven-year-old. She called me up front, rammed her finger into the book, and almost screamed, *'Then who is that, Mister Fletcher, standing in the earthworks over Richmond?'* I looked at the picture one way and then another. Finally, I looked up at Miss Faircloth and I said, 'Yup, that's General Grant, there. But it's not Ulysses S. Grant.'. She threw up her hands and shouted, *'Then who the hell is he?'* The whole class was shocked that she almost blasphemed right there in the schoolroom and were still staring with wide eyes and open mouths when I finally finished.

"I just looked at her and said, 'Why, ma'am, that's United States General Hiram Ulysses Grant. When he got to West Point, they screwed up his name, but I never cottoned to calling a man something other than his real name. Don't you agree?' That little episode alone almost cost me my time at the ranch. She gave me a C, but when I explained the reason for it to my father, he thought it was outrageously funny. My mother was just shocked that the schoolmarm had used that kind of language in school."

Both women were laughing at the story before Nora said, "I'm sure you have others."

"Oh, sure. Some really did get me in trouble, too. No practical jokes or anything, just a kid who was too full of himself. After your hair is dry, Nora, how about we all go and get a nice dinner?"

"It's almost dry, so let's do that and then we can go meet the deputy marshal."

———

Three hours later, they were all on the train platform awaiting the deputy marshal from Kansas City and Jake noticed how nervous Lucy was. He would be if he was in her position as well. He just hoped the deputy was happily married and didn't put it past Lucy to convince the lawman to let her go. Honestly, he wouldn't even mind if he did, but then again, she had made those snotty comments about Nora. Whatever the deputy marshal decided was his call, he just wanted Charlie even worse than Nora did.

The train was a little early and as it slowed to walking speed, Jake saw a man a little older than he was, maybe thirty or so, hanging over the end of the moving car's boarding steps. He hopped off as soon as the platform was available. He had saddlebags with him, and as he spotted Jake he stepped in his direction.

When he was close enough, Jake shook his hand and said, "Deputy Carroll, I'm Jake Fletcher and this is Nora Graham and Lucy Haskins."

"Ladies," he said, tipping his hat, then turned to Jake and said, "Mister Fletcher, I know we all need to talk, but I really need to get something to eat. I've got to pick up my horse, though."

"I'll take care of the horse if you'll give me the tag. Nora, can you show Deputy Marshal Carroll to the diner and I'll join you in a few minutes."

"I appreciate it," Deputy Marshal Carrol said.

Nora and Lucy escorted the deputy marshal to the diner as Jake walked to the railroad stock corral and handed the stockman the deputy's ticket. He led a tall dark gray gelding over to the rail, and after taking the reins, Jake led him to the livery, paid for the night, and let the liveryman take him.

Jake walked into the café and found Lucy laughing, making Jake worry already. Then he caught Nora's eye who gave him an 'it's okay' look. Jake appreciated Nora more each day and wondered how long it would be before they didn't have to talk at all.

He sat down at the table and said, "Your horse is at the livery, Deputy. He'll be taken care of and I already have your room key."

He handed Carroll the key, and as the deputy marshal accepted it, he said, "Thanks. I do get reimbursed for expenses, you know."

"I figured as much, but this is quicker."

"Thanks. Call me Jim, by the way."

"I'm Jake."

The waitress brought Jim his food and the others had coffee and a piece of apple pie while he ate his meal. When he had finished, the waitress removed the plates and the deputy marshal pulled out a pad and pencil.

"Well, Jake, you've woken a few folks up over this one, but we really do appreciate the help. We don't have nearly the number of men we need and folks like you and Nora make our lives a lot easier. So, fill me in on exactly what we're looking at here."

"I'll give you the basics of what happened to me. Nora can tell her story, but the one with all the information is Lucy. I knew her as Laura a couple of months ago."

Jake gave an abbreviated story of what had happened while Nora stared at Lucy as he told the story, wondering if she felt any remorse. Then, she told her story in more detail than Jake had. There was a reason for the added information as Jake's story would be filled in by Lucy, but no one could fill in Nora's gaps.

Finally, the deputy turned to Lucy as she started at the beginning, with her marriage to Charlie. She began listing the scams they would run over the years, and Jake was impressed with her memory skills. By the time she reached Jake's story, the deputy was on his fourth page of notes. She listed what had happened and how much they had taken from him as she had with each of the last six jobs, including Nora's. They matched what she had told Jake earlier. Nora knew, as well as Jake, that the amounts were accurate because each of them knew how much they had lost.

When she finished, Jim Carroll looked at Jake and asked, "Are you going to press charges against Mrs. Haskins?"

"Not if my money is recovered. I think she'd be a prime candidate for becoming a state's witness, pending recovery of the victims' losses."

"I'll run that idea past my boss. I'd tend to agree with you. Juries are notorious for failing to convict women, especially if no one died. I'm glad you stopped this one, though. I'm going to go and send a telegram to my boss in a few minutes. Now, we can take the train tomorrow morning and get to Wichita around 10:15. It's only an hour and ten minutes. When we get to Wichita, I'll contact the sheriff and ask for support in catching Charlie Haskins. If the cousin is there, we'll grab him, too. So, how about if we meet here in the diner tomorrow morning at 7:30?"

"We'll do that," Jake replied.

The two men and two women returned to the hotel, Lucy went into her room first then Jake handed Nora her key and winked at her when the deputy wasn't looking. She smiled demurely and as she accepted her key, her pulse quickened when she saw Jake's wink. It would be a doubly new experience for them, enjoying their newfound pleasures in a bed but with noise restrictions.

Jim Carroll waved at Jake as each went into their rooms.

An hour later, Jake stepped out into the hallway in his bare feet, checked both ways, tiptoed to Nora's room, eased the door open without even a tap on the door to let her know that he was entering before he stepped inside and closed it just as quietly behind him.

There was a three-quarter moon outside, so it was fairly bright in her room which allowed him to see her smiling face as he disrobed. She held up the blanket for Jake and he slipped in against her.

He kissed her softly and let his fingertips slide across her skin growing goosebumps as they passed.

"Jake, I have a confession to make," she whispered, causing him to pause in his ministrations.

"What could you ever have to confess, Nora?"

"I feel so bad because there was no excuse for what I did. You've told me over and over how much you love me, and I believe you, but I'm so unsure of myself and was still worried that Lucy would try to take you away from me."

"I'm not in Lucy's bed, am I, Nora?" he whispered into her ear.

"No. But when I left to go to the bathroom for my bath, I waited for a few minutes and listened at the door like an old biddy. I'm ashamed of myself, Jake. I really am. Why can't I just accept that you love me, and no woman can take you away from me?"

"Because you felt that you were less than the other girls in school for a long time and no one ever told you how wonderful you are. Those girls you went to school with did this to you, Nora. Then, when you went to live on the ranch, no one was

207

there to tell you otherwise. But I'm telling you otherwise now, Nora. I'm going to marry you and tell you every day just how wonderful you are. Maybe it'll take twenty years for you to believe me, but I'll still tell you."

Nora felt her big brown eyes mist over as she whispered, "How did I ever deserve you, Jake?"

"Nora, I'm the lucky one here. Now, look at me and tell me you want me to make love to you."

Nora wiped her eyes as she smiled and replied, "We have to be quiet, though, don't we?"

"It'll be something new."

Nora put her hands around his neck and pulled him in tight for a hard kiss. It may have been quiet, but it wasn't lacking in passion. It was difficult to avoid making their usual cacophony of loud sounds, but by trying to remain silent, they found a completely new and exciting experience.

When they finished, Jake just held Nora close and just slid his fingers softly over her hair. His heart was aching for her and all he could think of was how he could possibly convince her once and for all just how important she was to him.

Two hours later, he snuck back into his own room, leaving a happy and contented Nora curled up under her quilts. Neither had talked of what she had overheard Jake say to Lucy. Jake knew what he had said, and Nora knew she didn't have to remind him. He had reminded her more than once in the past few hours without saying a word.

But even as quiet as they had managed, a very jealous and disbelieving Lucy lay in her bed listening to their hushed lovemaking and was confident that it was just because Jake had forgotten how good she'd been, or maybe he was doing this to punish her. There was simply no way that the plain Nora could match her.

CHAPTER 7

At 7:30 the next morning, the four met at the crowded diner. Jake had already saddled the three horses and brought them to the railroad corral and bought three tickets with horse transport tags to Wichita. When they reached the train depot, Lucy's trunk had been brought from the hotel to the baggage area and tagged as well.

"I'll be back in a few minutes," Deputy Marshall Carroll said as he headed for the Western Union office.

"This should be interesting," Jake said to Nora as he walked off.

He returned in a few minutes and handed the message to Jake, who read it quickly and looked at Deputy Carroll.

"Wow! That's fast work."

"When your boss is on a first name basis with a Federal judge, it helps."

Jake handed the telegram to Nora.

She read it, smiled, and said, "They froze the account already."

Deputy Carroll replied, "Yes, ma'am. The bank confirmed the amount of over fifty thousand dollars. No drafts or withdrawal requests will be allowed unless authorized by Judge Cornelius L. Swafford. Haskins won't know about it, though. He can write drafts and probably get some cash, but not much. If he wires for money, it will be denied. That's when he'll know."

––––––

Three hours later, they arrived at the station in Wichita, collected the horses, and promptly left them at the nearby livery. They told the liveryman to just water and feed the horses but leave them saddled as they might be back shortly.

Jake and Nora left the four Winchesters in the scabbards. Walking around town with a Colt was one thing, but with a Winchester or a shotgun was something else.

They walked to the sheriff's office, so Jim Carroll could get some added manpower which happened very quickly. Just ten minutes later, U.S. Deputy Marshal James Carroll was flanked by two county sheriff deputies as he was heading toward 5th Street. Jake, Nora, and Lucy walked five feet behind.

––––––

At the rooming house, Charlie and Ralph were discussing how to eliminate George Smith. Ralph liked the accident idea until he was told about the snake. Ralph hated snakes.

"No. No damned snake, I'm tellin' ya!" he shouted as he paced the room.

"Alright, you come up with something better, then."

"I don't know yet. Give me a few minutes."

Ralph stopped his pacing and looked out the window to think of some other way than to handle a damned rattlesnake. He was just staring into the sky and then shook his head, still unable to come up with an alternative. He was starting to turn around when he glanced down and was startled by what he saw.

He continued to look out the window as he exclaimed, "Jesus! Charlie! It's Lucy, and she's bringing the law!"

Charlie bounced from his bed, raced to where Ralph was standing, and looked out the window.

"Damn that woman! Let's get out of here. We'll use the back stairs. Grab what you need. Fast!"

Charlie grabbed his wallet, which contained $262 dollars and three bank drafts before he bolted from the room. Ralph just grabbed his gun belt and his hat. His money was in his pocket. He had $21.55 but had no bank drafts. He kept his money in a box under his bed in his apartment in Kansas City and had over $1240 in the tin safe.

Both men reached the back stairs, then before they ran down the sixteen steps, Charlie scanned for any lawmen, saw no one in the alley, then raced down the stairs with Ralph close behind him.

When the lawmen entered the rooming house, Jake and the ladies stayed downstairs in the common room. As he watched the lawmen climb the stairs, he heard other sounds of boots on steps, but from further away from the back of the building.

"They must have seen us coming!" exclaimed Jake as he quickly stood.

Jake pulled his Colt, ran out the front door, and turned to the space between the buildings. He raced the length of the rooming house and popped out the other side just in time to see two men disappear at the end of the alley and head south toward the railroad station.

Jake turned back and when he emerged into the street again, he looked west and saw the two men running south. He turned and saw Nora and Lucy as they left the rooming house.

"Tell the deputy that I've given chase. They're running south toward the railroad station!"

He didn't wait for a reply but took off at a dead run, knowing that he wasn't a runner. He spent his time running on the back of a horse, but he had to at least see where they were going.

He rounded into the street where they had run and didn't see anyone moving quickly. There were a lot of people about though, so he spotted a pedestrian and asked, "Did you see two men go running past?"

"Sure did. They took off toward the depot and then turned into the livery," he replied as he pointed in that direction.

Jake thanked him as he sped off. Their planned route of escape made sense. They'd need to get out of town fast and couldn't afford to wait for a train. By the time he neared the station, he was out of breath and had to slow to a walk as he gulped for air. He needed to get in better shape.

When he was within a hundred feet of the livery, he saw the two men gallop their mounts out of the livery, then turn their horses and race away. He felt his stomach twist when he realized that they were riding two of his horses. He watched them bolt across the tracks and head out across the prairie at speed heading west.

Jake managed some speed of his own and trotted toward the livery, stepped inside, and found the liveryman stretched out on the ground. His head had been smacked with a pistol by the looks of it. Once he was sure that he was still breathing, he looked for a horse. Deputy Carroll's horse was still saddled, so he mounted and trotted him back toward the rooming house where he met the three lawmen jogging towards him. They were winded as well and stopped when Jake approached.

"Jim! They stole two of my horses and crossed the tracks running west! I'm heading back to check up on the liveryman. It looks like they pistol-whipped him."

Jim acknowledged his statement, and Jake turned the horse around to ride back to the livery. He got there quickly, jumped off the horse, and walked over to the prostrate liveryman. He was beginning to stir, so Jake looked for something to clean off his head, but there was nothing even close to dirt-free.

He took a knee next to the liveryman and said, "Mister, are you all right? You've been smashed in the head, probably with a Colt barrel."

He groaned and went to feel his head, but Jake stopped him by grabbing his wrist.

"It's messy up there, but I think you'll be okay."

"Those bastards! They took your horses!"

"I know. We'll get them back."

The three law officers finally entered the livery and Jake looked up as Jim Carroll said, "We need to get after those two. You said they headed west?"

"Yeah, you can pick up their trail easily right over to the south of the livery."

"Let's go, boys," Jim said to the two deputies.

The two deputy sheriffs left to get their horses which were in their own corral behind the sheriff's office as Jim mounted his horse and asked, "Are you coming?"

"I'll follow as soon as I get a saddle for Coffee."

"What?"

"Oh. That's my pack horse's name."

He nodded then said, "Well, follow along after us."

"Jim! Before you go, be aware that they have two Winchesters and a shotgun now. They were in the scabbards, but most of the ammunition is in the panniers, so they won't have anything more than what they have in the guns."

"Thanks for the update. Gotta go."

Jim turned his horse and after he met the two deputies out front, the three lawmen trotted away, and Jake watched as they picked up the trail and broke west after crossing the tracks.

———

Three and a half miles ahead of the deputies, Charlie and Ralph had reduced their speed to a medium trot to save the horses. They had crossed over to the road, hoping that the often-used surface would hide their path, and also rode in line, so they didn't leave a trail of two horses traveling together.

"What do we do now?" Ralph shouted over his shoulder.

"We set a trap for the trailers. We can't outrun 'em, so we need to pick 'em off. That'll give us time. We need to find a spot, so keep an eye open."

———

Back in Wichita, the liveryman was on his feet but was still a bit woozy.

"Do you have any saddles for sale?" Jake asked.

"Yeah. Sure. I've got four. Go and pick one out. They're on the last two stall rails."

Jake walked to the back of the big barn and found two that he liked. He pulled them both out along with the rest of the tack.

"How about these two?"

"Why two?"

"Because I need to buy a horse, too."

"Got six you can look at, they're in the corral in back. Just bring one around. I'm not too good at walking right now."

"I'll be back."

Jake trotted around the back of the corral and found six horses. One was a mare that looked a lot like Nora's Satin. She was a little darker but seemed like a good horse, so Jake took her by the bridle and led her to the front.

"How much for the horse and both saddles?"

"How does a hundred dollars sound? I owe you some."

"You don't owe me. Here," Jake said as he handed him the money before he quickly saddled both the new mare and Coffee and slid the remaining two Winchesters into their scabbards. He also moved two boxes of .44s into each set of saddlebags and one of the spare gunbelts for Nora.

As he walked them past the liveryman, he asked, "Are you gonna be okay?"

"Yeah. I'll head over to the doc in a bit. You go and find those bastards."

"I'll be back for the pack saddle and panniers later."

"I'll hold 'em for ya."

Jake led the two horses out the door, mounted Coffee, then led the new horse down the cobblestones toward the rooming house where he saw Nora and Lucy out front and headed over quickly.

"What happened, Jake?" Nora shouted as he was close enough to hear.

"They stole Sandy and Satin. Jim and the two deputies went after them, so we're going to trail behind to see if they need any help."

"What can I do?" asked Lucy.

"For right now, just head up to the rooms and see if they left anything. We'll be back in a few hours."

"Alright."

Nora climbed up in the saddle quickly, then she and Jake wheeled the horses and headed south, then soon left Wichita when they rode across the tracks. With the lawmen's tracks added to the Haskins', it was even easier to follow.

"This new mare is very pretty, too, Jake. Do we have to give her back?"

"No, Nora. She's yours, too."

"Jake, why did you take me with you? Isn't this a man's job?"

"I didn't want to leave you with Lucy. I didn't trust her that much. Besides, where I go, you go. You're my woman, Nora."

She smiled as she looked over at Jake. Words like that would go a long way to help dispel any lingering feelings of doubt.

———

Five miles ahead, the Haskins boys had found their ambush site. It wasn't great, but it was the best they could find. It was a small broken hill that had its western third cut away, probably by the railroad looking for some dirt to fill a shallow area. The rails ran just a hundred yards to the north of the hill, but the road was only thirty yards south of the hill. They rode their two new horses behind the missing chunk of dirt and hitched them to a small bush. Ralph made sure that the horses couldn't be seen by anyone coming from the east before he looked west to make sure there wasn't any traffic and found an empty roadway.

They quickly climbed the hill, Charlie with a Winchester and Ralph with both the shotgun and the Winchester. They stopped near the summit and sat down.

Ralph said, "I'll let loose with the scattergun first, then we can let them have it with the Winchesters."

"You know about this better than I do," answered Charlie.

"At fifty yards, the shotgun will do a lot of damage. Trust me."

Charlie just nodded as they waited on the hill for the law that was sure to arrive. They'd hear the horses and then set up for the ambush.

The three badged riders were a mile out when the Haskins settled into position and Nora and Jake were three miles behind them.

Jake had been handing cartridges to Nora, who had been feeding them into her Winchester just to make sure it was full. When she waved that she didn't need anymore, he filled his, then reached behind him, pulled out the spare gunbelt, and held it out to her.

Nora just nodded, accepted the Colt, and wrapped it around her waist. She didn't even think how odd it must have looked to any observer as she snugly tugged the pistol onto her hips.

———

U.S. Deputy Marshal Carrol was slowing down as he rode beside the two deputy sheriffs.

"I don't like this," he said loudly as he peered down the road, "We should be seeing them up ahead. They can't be more than three or four miles ahead of us, and we can see that far down that road easy."

"Maybe they cut cross-country," offered one of the deputies.

"Maybe. Let's spread and check both sides of the road and see if they broke north or south."

They were still riding west as the two deputies took the left side and Jim was trotting slowly on the right edge.

Their voices had carried even more than their horses' hoofbeats, alerting the ambushers on the hill.

"They're almost here!" loud-whispered Ralph after he had popped up and taken a peek.

219

They were about four hundred yards away when Ralph spotted them.

Jim was uneasy as he looked up and saw the hill, but it was empty. He kept an eye on it as they closed within a couple of hundred yards when everything changed.

One of the deputies thought he saw a hoofprint off the side of the road ahead and said, "I think I got 'em."

Jim looked over at him and nudged his horse to the south side of the road to check for the new trail.

Ralph and Charlie could hear the closing hoofbeats and when Ralph thought they were as close as they could get, he popped over the crest of the hill with the shotgun and saw the two deputies on one side and the other lawman almost in the middle of the road. He aimed at the two deputies and fired both barrels.

The sudden explosion of the shotgun took everyone, including Charlie, by surprise. The two deputies and their horses took the massive load of buckshot, throwing both deputies from their horses. The horses took multiple hits, reared, and screamed as they raced away, but Jim didn't have time to chase their horses as he grabbed his Winchester and leapt from the saddle.

He raced to the deputies to check on their condition as Ralph and Charlie began firing the Winchesters.

Jim sprinted across the road to the deputies and hit the dirt as the .44 caliber rounds began exploding in the dirt around him. He wheeled his repeater at the top of the hill and fired several rounds at the Haskins to keep their heads down then quickly checked on the two deputies. Both were alive but helpless. *Damn!* He was so angry with himself for falling into their ambush. He should have worked wide around that damned hill, but it was too late to do anything now. He was in trouble.

A mile and a half away, Jake and Nora heard the gunfire and they quickly set their horses to a fast trot. Jake pulled his Winchester and levered a round into the chamber as Nora did the same.

———

Jim was getting low on ammunition and had already reloaded with his spares on his gun belt. If he needed more, all he had was the five in his Colt. He needed to make his shots count now, no more shooting just to keep their heads down. He looked at his horse almost sixty yards away, eating grass. He had two more boxes of cartridges in his saddlebags but knew it would be suicide to try and get them.

———

Ralph and Charlie were even lower on ammunition. Ralph had his gun belt with three more rounds left and his Colt with five. Charlie estimated that he had only three in his Winchester but wasn't sure of that number.

"I'm going to swing around to my right a bit. I'll take a shot from the side. If I hit him, we make a break," said Ralph.

"Go!" yelled Charlie.

Ralph slid down the hill a bit and then crab-walked to the east where he managed a better shooting angle.

Jim was still looking at the summit with the large cloud of gunsmoke when the burn of a round hit him high on the right shoulder at the same moment the crack of the Winchester reached his ears. He twisted onto his back from the shot, his

Winchester laying uselessly by his side. He couldn't shoot it if he had to and couldn't shoot his Colt, either, unless he used his left hand, and he was a lousy shot with his left hand. He felt the blood soaking his shattered shirt. If they came down from that hill now, he'd be a sitting duck. *He should have checked that damned hill!*

––––––

Ralph stood and looked at the damage he had just caused and was torn before making a killing shot, but his depleted ammunition supply made the decision for him.

"Let's get out of here!" he shouted to Charlie.

Charlie didn't need to be told as he slid down the hill and was unhitching Satin and Sandy when Ralph reached him, then they mounted and rode away quickly, regained the road, and headed west at a fast trot.

––––––

Nora and Jake had cleared a slight rise and saw them riding off about a mile away.

"There they go!" shouted Jake.

They both set their horses to a canter, expecting to be able to catch them. Instead, as they got closer to the location of the shootout, they found the three lawmen down on the road.

When they reached the scene, Jake and Nora pulled up, then quickly dismounted. They found the two deputies groaning, but alive. Jake was more concerned about Jim's wound. It was a nasty shoulder wound that seemed to have done a lot of damage.

"Nora, check on the two deputies. I've got to get something to stop Jim's bleeding."

"Okay," she answered as she stepped over to the first deputy. He had taken four buckshot hits, but none were fatal. The worst was in his right side, just below the ribs. He also had hits in his right arm, his right thigh, and his right calf. He was bleeding, but not badly. The second deputy had been peppered with three hits. One was on his right jaw, which was ugly, but not too bad. The second was in his right pectoral area. He was fairly stocky, so it hadn't penetrated into his chest. The third was on the back of his right hip. Both would heal well as long as they avoided infection.

Jake had taken his last clean shirt from his saddlebag and trotted back to Jim.

"Jim, I'm going to try to stop the bleeding. Can you hear me?"

Jim opened his eyelids a crack, saw Jake, and said in a weak voice, "I screwed up, Jake. I should have checked that damned hill."

"Don't worry about it now. Let's get you fixed up."

Nora had gone to collect the deputies' wandering, injured horses as Jake began to wrap the shirt around Jim's wound. He folded over the back of the shirt and put it on top, then he had to lift Jim's lifeless arm a bit to slide the sleeves over his armpit before he then tied off the sleeves tightly on top to keep the shirt bandage in place.

"That's the best I can do, Jim. Hang on for a second," he said as he stood, then trotted over to Jim's horse and led him and Coffee and Nora's new mare over to where Jim lay on his back in the middle of the road.

Nora had brought the two wounded horses back to the deputies, then helped each of them struggle to his feet before she helped them step awkwardly into their saddles.

Jake was kneeling next to Deputy Carroll and said, "Jim, I'm going to get you to stand up. Can you do that?"

"I'll try. My legs still work okay."

Jake pulled him up by his left arm then helped him to his horse and managed to get him into the saddle. He had to lash Jim's feet to the stirrups to make sure he didn't fall. Once everyone was back in the saddles, he fashioned a quick trail rope, then they turned back east. Jake rode slightly ahead of Jim while Nora rode between the two deputies.

———

Four miles to the west, Charlie and Ralph trotted along the road looking every bit the part of two men out for a leisurely ride. They were only two miles out of the town of Goddard.

By the time Jake and Nora reached the sheriff's office in Wichita, Ralph and Charlie had stopped in Goddard, eaten, and stopped at the dry goods store. They had restocked on ammunition, bought some food, then rode out again an hour after stopping, continuing west.

———

The distressed sheriff told Jake and Nora he'd get the three wounded men to the doctor's office and send telegrams to the U.S. Marshal's office in Kansas City advising him of what had happened and include the information to the surrounding law officers with the two men's descriptions, names, and their horses' coloring. He told them he only had two more deputies now, and with the two Haskins probably out of his jurisdiction by now, either the neighboring county or United States Marshals would have to deal with them.

Jake listened to the sheriff's woes, then said "No, sir. The marshal will do what he can, but we'll go follow them now. They're not getting away."

"Who is going to follow them?"

"Nora and me. We'll keep the marshal informed."

"You can't take a woman with you!" the sheriff shouted.

"If it were a regular woman, I'd agree with you. But my woman isn't a regular woman. She's the best damned lady there is."

He turned to Nora, and asked, "You ready to go, Nora?"

"Let's go get those bastards," she replied loudly.

They left the sheriff's office, mounted and wheeled their horses away, leaving a confused sheriff in their wake.

———

They were twenty-two miles behind Charlie and Ralph when they left and were fast trotting west along the road and passed the scene of the shooting an hour later.

"Nora, we don't have any food. We're coming up on Goddard in a few miles, so we can buy what we need, but I don't want another pack horse. We'll travel light. Just think of what we'll need. You'll need another bedroll and slicker. We'll be roughing it and all we'll have is cold camps. I don't want them to spot our fire."

"Jake, every camp we have together is a hot camp, whether there's a cooking fire or not."

Jake laughed and said, "You are a special woman, Nora. I'm proud of you."

"I have to admit. I'm kind of proud of myself for a change."

"You remember that feeling. You have every right to feel that way all of the time."

"Thank you for putting so much trust in me, Jake."

"How can I not, Nora? You're going to be my wife if we can ever stop running around Kansas long enough to find a preacher."

———

They arrived in Goddard twenty-five minutes later, stopped at the dry goods store, and bought what they needed. They asked the proprietor if the two men had stopped by and he told them that they had picked up some ammunition and food and left about four hours earlier.

Jake paid for the order and they had to spend a few minutes setting up Nora's new ride. She now had stuffed saddlebags and a bedroll. Jake had bought a replacement shirt as well before they set off again, now seventeen miles behind their quarry.

———

As they were exiting Goddard, Charlie and Ralph were entering the town of Kingman. They were operating under the assumption that the three wounded or dead lawmen wouldn't be discovered right away, and it would take them a few hours to be returned to Wichita before any messages went out. They hadn't counted on Jake and Nora which was understandable.

As they rode into Kingman, town marshal Will O'Rourke was making rounds, saw the two men, and quickly identified them as the two in the telegram. He was in a difficult situation. His shotgun and rifles were in the office three hundred yards away, so he couldn't take on the two outlaws by himself with only a pistol. That would be sure death, so he began walking rapidly toward his office.

It was Ralph who spotted the marshal. He might not have noticed except that the marshal kept taking furtive glances at the pair as he walked. Ralph angled Sandy toward the peace officer.

Will O'Rourke noticed the change and picked up the pace as there was no reason to be stealthy any longer.

Ralph added some speed as well as he pulled out his now full Winchester and the marshal broke into a dead run. It became just that when, just as he began to run, Ralph fired from fifty feet.

Marshal O'Rourke was spun counterclockwise as the round entered the left side of his chest and exited into the boardwalk. He hit the boardwalk, dying just thirty feet from his office.

"Let's beat it!" Ralph shouted to Charlie.

Charlie had seen it coming and was ready to bolt. The two men raced their horses through and out of Kingman in less than a minute as a crowd formed in their wake to see what had happened. They only noticed the dead marshal after they had already gone.

———

In Kansas City, United States Marshal John Breedlove stared at the telegram he had just been handed. Jim Carroll had been seriously wounded and two Wichita deputies were shot as well. He needed to get this under control. He had the desk deputy get a hold of Deputies Trace Wilkens and Harvey Bradshaw. He'd send the two deputies to Wichita and stop those two bastards. The Haskins had just moved up the chain to the top of the Kansas City U.S. Marshal's list.

———

Two hours after Ralph and Charlie had left Kingman, Jake and Nora rode into town. They figured on having a quick lunch at the café before heading out, so they stopped at the livery and asked that their horses be unsaddled, brushed down, fed some oats, and watered, saying they'd be back in an hour.

It was the liveryman who told them about the shooting, so the first thing Jake did was to head over to the Western Union office and sent the following.

US MARSHAL JOHN BREEDLOVE KANSAS CITY MISS

**CITY MARSHAL KILLED IN KINGMAN BY HASKINS
LEFT HEADING WEST TWO HOURS AGO
WILL CONTINUE TO TRAIL**

JAKE AND NORA FLETCHER KINGMAN KANSAS

He paid the forty-five cents and handed the message to Nora to read as they left the office.

"When did we get married?" she asked with a big smile.

"Days ago. It's just not official. I thought you should at least get used to the idea."

"It's a wonderful idea to get used to," she answered as she folded the sheet and put it into her riding skirt pocket as a valued memento of the extraordinary honeymoon she and Jake were experiencing.

———

In Kansas City, Marshal Breedlove had briefed his two deputy marshals and sent them to the depot to catch the next train that was leaving in forty minutes. They had just enough time to get their horses ready, so they left the office.

Five minutes later, when a messenger arrived with Jake's telegram, the marshal bolted from the office and jogged down the street to the train depot.

Deputy Marshals Wilkens and Bradshaw saw him coming and headed his way.

He handed the telegram to Deputy Wilkins and said, "Change those tickets to Kingman. If you catch up to the Fletchers, find out what they know. If they want to assist, take all the help you need, but don't put the woman at risk."

"Got it, boss," said the senior man, Trace Wilkens.

———

Ralph and Charlie left the road and headed northwest a mile outside of Kingman. Now they understood that things had happened a lot faster than they expected. They were now known to all the local towns. How far out was the question. What they didn't know was that one of the men they had shot was a United States Deputy Marshal, so they were never going to be out of their jurisdiction, and they were not going to give up the search.

"What do we do now, Charlie?" asked Ralph.

"We find a nice quiet ranch or farm and settle down for a few hours. We're gonna need some sleep and the horses will need some rest."

"Sounds like a good idea."

They continued riding northwest heading cross-country.

———

Jake and Nora left Kingman heading west, having just given their horses a rest and some oats and water. There were only two clear tracks to follow now, making their job easier. Then they disappeared from the road a mile out of town, so Jake stopped, then he and Nora dismounted. It only took a minute to pick up the trail again heading northwest. Before they got back in the saddle, Jake began kicking the dirt with his boot, making a heavy line in the road pointing northwest. Then he found some rocks and began building a marker on the ground with an arrow pointing in that direction.

They mounted again and continued heading northwest as the sun grew low on the horizon. They began searching for a campsite of any sort four miles northwest of the road, and finally found something decent near a tiny creek, but there weren't any trees.

They dismounted and quickly set up their barebones campsite, unsaddled the horses, and stretched out their bedrolls as the horses grazed. They had a cold dinner of beans, ham, and some slices of bread and it wasn't bad at all.

Once they had settled down and were just sitting together in front of their saddles, Jake smiled at Nora who was snuggled in close.

"You know, Nora. This is kind of romantic out here. We're all alone on the prairie, a full moon is coming up and there's a small creek bubbling off to the side. It would be a shame to let it all go to waste."

"My thoughts exactly," she smiled as she reached over and started popping his buttons while Jake matched her button for button.

It wasn't exactly warm out, but it was warm enough for Jake and Nora to spend a busy hour plus on and off the bedrolls. Nora felt liberated after the silent episodes the night before and Jake wasn't exactly quiet, either.

After their sweat-coated bodies began to feel the breeze, they slid into one of the bedrolls and just carried out a normal, naked conversation. They talked, but Jake couldn't resist kissing his woman. Nora simply was overwhelming him and the longer he knew her, the more he was fascinated with what he found. She seemed to have no end to the depth of her abilities.

"Tomorrow, we get up early, and as soon as we can pick up the tracks, we go."

"I know. At least it won't take us long to have breakfast."

Jake laughed and said, "You know what, Nora? We have one huge advantage over those two."

"What? They don't know we're here?"

"Well, that too, but they can't do this," he answered before kissing her and sliding his hands along her now dry body.

"I hope not," she answered in her husky voice then pulled him closer, if that was possible inside their one-person bedroll.

Just before dusk was gone, Charlie and Ralph found some plowed earth, which told them that there was a farm nearby. They followed the furrows due north until they could see the lights of the farmhouse.

Inside the farmhouse, Madeline Curry was making dinner for her family. Her husband, John, was out in the barn, cleaning up the plow after a day of planting. She knew he'd be tired and was making a nourishing supper. Their two children, Joseph and Amanda were upstairs. Joseph was eight and Amanda was six. They both helped around the farm already, as most farm children did. Joseph helped his father as much as a little boy could and Amanda collected eggs and tried to help her mama with housework. They were good children.

Ralph and Charlie walked their horses to the side of the house, not noticing John Curry in the barn. They dismounted and Ralph pulled his Colt as they walked toward the house silently. Charlie only had the Winchester, so he had it in his hands as well. Ralph had his hammer back, expecting trouble, still twitchy after the Kingman incident. They walked around the front of the house and had almost reached the porch steps when John Curry walked out of the barn, unarmed and carrying his work gloves when he saw the two men.

"Hey! What are you two doing?" he shouted.

Ralph didn't even care who was shouting, as he turned his pistol and fired. From twenty feet, it was difficult to miss, but he did. Charlie was on edge as well, and after Ralph fired, he let loose with the Winchester. He didn't miss, his .44 drilling right through the left side of the farmer's chest as if it wasn't even there.

John Curry flopped onto his back in shock, took two shuddering breaths, then stopped breathing altogether.

Inside the house, Madeline heard her husband's shout and the immediate response of the two gunshots from two different weapons. She was accustomed to violence and knew what had just happened. She didn't panic but quickly pulled down the family shotgun from its rack above the kitchen door. It was only loaded with birdshot, but it would have to do. Her first thought was to protect her children, understanding that her husband was probably already dead.

She trotted to the stairs as the children were hurriedly trotting down with terrified expressions on their small faces.

Madeline said firmly, "Go back upstairs, both of you. I want you both to hide together. Do not come out unless I find you. Go!"

They had many questions, but their mama had told them what to do, so they quickly turned and ran back up the stairs.

Joseph took Amanda's hand as they jogged down the hallway and entered his room where he pulled her under his bed. He hugged his sister close once they were in the darkness. They were scared out of their wits, but their mama told them to hide.

———

"He's dead," declared Ralph after looking at John Curry's body.

"He shouldn't have come out like that," Charlie rationalized.

"His bad luck. Let's get into the house."

233

Ralph turned, and he and Charlie headed toward the house. Ralph had put his pistol in his holster, the danger eliminated, or so he believed.

They had almost reached the house when the screen door flew open and a small woman with a shotgun was glaring at them, the two big barrels looking like tunnels.

"You two bastards just killed my husband. Drop those guns right now!"

Charlie complied with her threat and dropped the Winchester in a loud clatter then put his hands in the air.

Ralph would have none of it. This was just some damned farmer's wife and he was sure that she wouldn't pull that trigger.

He stared at her and calmly pulled his Colt. As he did, she pulled the trigger and both barrels exploded. She was aiming a bit high and she hadn't known it. The range was so short that the pellets never spread much, so the shot blasted past Ralph's head, taking off his hat as two birdshot pellets caught the top of the taller Charlie's head.

He screamed, and Ralph ducked after the pellets had already gone past. He was stunned that he hadn't been hit. He had his Colt in his hand as he rushed the woman.

She threw her used shotgun at him, striking his right knee with the barrel, then turned and ran into the house with a cursing Ralph hobbling behind.

She ran as fast as her skirts would allow her and reached the kitchen where she headed for her knives and almost reached them when she felt Ralph's hand grab her by the hair.

He yanked her backward and slammed her down, the back of Madeline's head hit the wooden floor and she blacked out.

The children heard the commotion and remained quiet because their mama had told them to.

Charlie had regained his wits and walked into the house. He was still shaken by his brush with death and his head hurt. The pellets hadn't even stayed in his scalp. They had ricocheted off his skull but had left two wounds that were bleeding. He wasn't happy about it, either.

Ralph was standing over the unconscious Madeline as he entered the kitchen.

"That bitch almost killed us!" Charlie said as he passed Ralph, walked to the pump, and began dousing his head.

"Can't trust no woman. Damned Lucy got us into this mess."

"Well, this one ain't gonna give us any more trouble. I'll give her some trouble first, though," grinned Ralph.

He scooped up Madeline and carried her into the main room. There was a rug on the floor, which was good enough for what Ralph had in mind. He didn't lay Madeline down but simply dropped her.

After she thumped loudly to the floor, Ralph bent over her, ripped open her dress, and raped her as she lay on the floor. It didn't matter one bit to Ralph whether she was awake or not.

"Say, Charlie, you want a turn?" he shouted when he was finished.

Charlie thought about it and said, "Nah. I'm hungry."

Ralph took his Colt from the chair where he had left it when he pulled down his pants, cocked the hammer, and shot Madeline through her naked chest.

"You ain't gonna get another chance to shoot nobody," he snarled as he returned his pistol to its holster.

Charlie heard the gunshot and knew what Ralph had done. He was beginning to fear his cousin and wondered if it was even safe to be around him any longer. He had found Madeline's dinner and began to take it out of the pan and put it on the plates when he noticed there were four plates on the table.

"Hey, Ralph. Come here," he said loudly.

Ralph walked in, looked at the food, and said, "What? Oh, real food. That smells pretty good."

"No, look. There are four plates. They must have kids or farmhands or something."

"Nobody came with all the gunshots. Maybe they were expecting visitors."

"Nah. Not likely. I'll bet they got kids. Did she look like she had kids?"

"How the hell should I know?"

"Never mind. Let's eat and then we'll go search this place."

They both took seats and began shoveling in the food.

Joseph and Amanda had heard the voices and knew their mother was now dead, too. They'd heard what the bad men had said and knew that they couldn't stay in the house anymore.

"Amanda, we've got to get out of the house, or those bad men will kill us," he whispered.

"Alright," she answered quietly as she tried to keep from crying.

"Take off your shoes."

She slid off her shoes and Joseph did as well, then he whispered, "Take them with you and follow me."

She did as Joseph told her. She loved her big brother. He always watched out for her and now she needed to do whatever he told her. He took her hand as they left the cover of the bed and silently walked down the hallway.

They reached the stairs and were worried about the creaky steps, so they stayed on the side and took them slowly, one careful step at a time. They'd done it before when they wanted to sneak into the kitchen for some cookies.

In the kitchen, Charlie and Ralph were helping themselves to seconds as they talked about where they would go after they left the farmhouse.

"We need to get out of the area. We're only about fifty miles from the Nations. We can cut through there and head to Colorado."

"Sounds like a plan."

As they talked, Joseph led Amanda down the last steps, and they saw their naked mother lying dead on the floor. Amanda began to cry but didn't make any noise. She just tried not to look. Joseph wanted to cry as well, but he knew he had to protect Amanda. He was the man of the house now.

He led her through the still-open front door and down the porch steps. They saw their father in the moonlight and walked past him to the barn. Once there, they put their shoes back on and climbed the steps to the loft. They had spent many hours in the loft before, so they were very familiar with what was there. They took a horse blanket with them and went to a corner of the loft where there was some hay. Joseph spread it on the floor and laid the horse blanket down, then let Amanda lay down and he curled up next to her. He pulled the blanket over them and they stayed silent. Joseph knew their lives depended on it.

In the house, Ralph and Charlie had finished their food and left the dirty dishes in the sink.

"Let's go find us some kids," smiled Ralph as he pulled his Colt.

"They're kids, Ralph, you don't need that."

"Kids talk, Charlie. Right now, nobody can pin this on us."

Charlie left his Winchester out in the main room as they began the search. They went to every room and looked in every nook and niche finding nothing. They could tell that there were two children, though, a boy and a girl.

"So, where'd they go?" asked Charlie.

"How the hell do I know? Maybe they're staying at somebody's house. We haven't heard a peep from them."

"Then why the four plates?"

"Habit maybe. Or maybe they're on their way home now."

"That could be. If they're coming home this late, that means somebody's got to bring them. Let's get that body out of the front yard," said Charlie.

"You do it. I'm gonna stretch out."

Charlie was going to argue but decided against it. He went downstairs and looked at the dead woman, shook his head then reached down and threw the rug over her body. He didn't want to be reminded just how much trouble they were in now. *Damned Lucy!*

He went outside, grabbed the farmer's body by the top of his coveralls, and slid it over to the side of the barn. Then he remembered that the horses were still tied off on the side of the house, so he walked to the horses, then led them to the barn, where he stripped off the saddles and put them in stalls.

Joseph and Amanda had heard him enter and then leave. Joseph thought about taking the two horses, but Amanda had never ridden a horse and he thought it was too dangerous. He'd wait until they left, assuming that they weren't going to stay in the house after what they'd done.

———

Deputy Marshals Wilkens and Harvey Bradshaw arrived in Kingman at 8:50, left their horses in the livery, and got a hotel room. They'd set out at first light.

CHAPTER 8

First light found Jake and Nora already in the saddle, following the still fresh tracks northwest. They were nine miles from the farmhouse.

Twenty minutes later, Ralph and Charlie were out in the barn saddling Sandy and Satin.

Joseph and Amanda heard them and had already taken care of nature's call in the far corner of the barn earlier. They knew the heavy barn smells would hide their presence and were now huddled under the blanket as they listened to the two men who were just six feet below them.

"Those kids still bother me, Ralph."

"Don't worry about it. That's why we're gettin' outta here. We got plenty of food and fresh horses. I even got the sixteen dollars from their little stash in the kitchen," he said as he laughed.

Charlie just shook his head and they rode out of the barn and headed southwest for the Nations.

―――――

Joseph waited for another half an hour before he thought it was safe to exit the loft.

They were coming down the steps when they heard hooves and quickly reversed themselves and climbed back into the loft.

Joseph told Amanda to stay put as he cautiously approached the open loft doors.

Jake and Nora trotted to the front of the house. The tracks had led to the house, and they didn't know what to expect.

Jake leaned over to Nora and said, "Just call out 'Hello, the house'. A female voice would be less threatening."

She nodded as Jake held his shotgun toward the door with the hammers back.

"Hello, the house!" Nora shouted.

Joseph heard the shout and felt a sudden sense of relief. *It was a lady!* It wasn't the bad men at all. *It was a lady!* Joseph trotted to the open loft doors and saw the woman and a man, both had guns and the man had a shotgun pointed at the door. He knew they must be looking for the bad men and took a chance.

"Hello!" he shouted.

Jake and Nora both turned and saw the small boy perched above them in the loft.

Jake said loudly, "Good morning. What are you doing up there, son? We're looking for two very bad men."

"Are you deputies or something?"

"No, they shot three deputies and we're following them until the U.S. Deputy Marshals come behind us. Have you seen anybody?"

"They came last night and killed my mama and papa. One of them dragged my papa behind the barn. My mama is in the front room. She didn't have any clothes on."

Jake felt sick and Nora was shaken by the news before Jake asked, "Son, are you alone?"

"No, my little sister Amanda is with me."

"Why don't you both come down. My wife will take care of you while I clean things up."

"Okay."

Nora was so upset that she didn't even comment on Jake's *my wife* comment.

Jake released the hammers and slid the shotgun home. He had work to do.

"Nora, I'll take care of their mother. You hold them here until I can cover her up and bring her out."

"Alright."

Jake jogged inside and found the lumpy rug, then pulled it back and saw the naked woman with the bullet hole in her chest. She had obviously been violated and he was sure that it had been done by Ralph because Charlie didn't like to get his hands dirty. He wrapped her in the rug and lifted her from the floor then carried her through the front door where he saw Nora standing holding the hands of the two children.

He walked past them and stepped behind the barn where he found her husband. He laid her down next to him and returned to the children and Nora.

They took the children inside and listened to their story as Nora cooked breakfast for everyone.

———

Deputy Marshals Wilkens and Bradshaw were out of Kingman and had just found Jake's marker.

"That's handy," remarked Trace Wilkens.

"Let's go," replied Harvey as they left the roadway and followed the four sets of tracks.

———

Jake found a paper and pencil and wrote a note to whoever was following them with a brief synopsis of what had happened, where the bodies were, and that they would drop the children off in Cunningham, the nearest town. He also said that the children had reported that the two were headed for the Indian Nations.

He hung the note on the door and let Nora climb into her saddle. He handed her Amanda before he mounted Coffee, then reached down and picked up Joseph and rode out of the farm, then found the trail easily from Joseph's directions.

As they followed the Haskins' trail, Jake was astounded by Joseph's steady demeanor and his handling of the situation and wondered when he would have to let all his emotions go.

Meanwhile, Nora was chatting with Amanda, finding her to be a delightful little girl. The ride to Cunningham was relatively short and just a short way off the trail they were following.

So less than an hour later, they rode into town and stopped at the sheriff's office.

After letting Joseph down, Jake helped Amanda down, then he and Nora walked with the children into the sheriff's office and told him what had happened at the O'Rourke farm and that the two children were now orphans. Then Jake made a snap decision without asking Nora.

"Sheriff, we'll stop by on the way back. If Joseph and Amanda don't have any relatives who want to care for them, Nora and I will."

The sheriff nodded and said, "I appreciate that. I'll make inquiries. Mrs. Jordan, the reverend's wife, will take care of them in the meantime. She has a real soft heart."

"Thanks, Sheriff. We need to run," Jake replied before he looked over at Joseph and said, "You take care of Amanda just like you already have, Joseph. You're a hell of a man already."

Joseph smiled and offered his hand to Jake. Jake shook his hand as Nora picked up Amanda and gave her a kiss. Amanda hugged Nora and kissed her on the cheek.

Jake and Nora waved at the children before they left the jail, then crossed the boardwalk to their horses and mounted quickly. They had to go west to pick up the trail again and were just five miles behind Ralph and Charlie when they left Cunningham.

"Jake, did you just offer to adopt Joseph and Amanda?" Nora asked as they trotted along.

"I did. I know that I should have asked you first and we're not even officially married yet. But they're such amazing children, Nora. Was I out of line?"

"No. You were the same wonderful man I've loved from almost the minute I met you. Amanda was so loveable. I wanted to hug her all the time."

"Well, we'll see how that works out, but now let's go and find those two and end this."

They picked up the pace and followed the easy trail.

———

Deputy Marshals Wilkens and Bradshaw reached the farm and found the note before they walked behind the barn and saw the two bodies. They knew that Jake and Nora had stopped in Cunningham and told the sheriff there of the deaths, so they correctly assumed that they would be taken care of by the local undertaker.

They found the trail and started following at a fast trot, already wondering just about this remarkable pair who were making their job easier.

———

Ralph and Charlie were operating on a flawed principle that they couldn't be followed into the Nations. They didn't understand that it only applied to law officers and while they were being followed by law officers, but between them and those law officers was a determined couple. They had wanted to get Charlie first, but after what Ralph had done to the children's mother, Ralph had been moved closer on that short list.

They were still four miles ahead of their unlikely pursuers, but they were still almost thirty miles from the Nations. They could make it if they hurried, but they weren't hurrying because they felt safe. They only had thirty more miles to go and no one was behind them, or so they thought.

———

Jake could tell by their trail that they weren't far behind and said loudly, "We're getting close, Nora. They can't be more than five miles ahead of us, maybe less. Let's pick it up a bit and close the gap."

She nodded, and they nudged the horses up to a fast trot.

Not five minutes later, Jake picked up some dots on the horizon. He still had those old field glasses he picked up in Albert, so he pulled them out of his saddlebag, happy that he hadn't stored them in Sandy's saddlebags.

Then he said, "Hold up, Nora. I see something."

She pulled her new mare to a stop as Jake looked through his field glasses and saw the two riders, then handed the field glasses to Nora.

"Straight ahead on the horizon."

She had them in view as she said excitedly, "There they are! What do we do now?"

"Let's push them. As long as we stay close, they can't set up an ambush like they did to the deputies. Let's make them nervous."

"Let's do this, Jake," Nora said.

They set the horses to a canter as they began eating up the distance.

Ralph and Charlie hadn't looked back when they were at the peak of the rise that provided a good view of Jake and Nora, but after they dropped below the rise, they couldn't see them if they tried.

If Jake and Nora had known that they were gaining at such a rate, maybe they would have slowed down, but probably not. But when they crossed the same rise that Ralph and Charlie had crossed earlier, they were shocked to find themselves less than a mile behind.

"Let's slow it to a trot, Nora. We may need some reserve from our horses if they bolt. Let's get as close as we can. I can't believe they haven't picked us up yet."

They hadn't picked them up yet because they were discussing their most important topic of the day…money.

"When we get to Denver, I'll have the bank there transfer my account from Kansas City, so money won't be an issue."

"What if Lucy told them about the money?"

"She doesn't know where it is because I never told her."

Ralph didn't tell Charlie that he had told Lucy. He had been trying to ingratiate himself with her by telling her all the bad things that Charlie was doing behind her back, and now it was going to come back and bite him in his hairy behind.

While they were talking, Jake and Nora had closed the gap to less than half a mile. They were just eight hundred yards away when they were finally spotted.

It was then that Charlie, out of boredom more than planning, turned to look behind them and shouted, "Jesus Christ! There's somebody right on our ass! Where did they come from?"

Ralph swiveled in his saddle, saw them, and added his own curse as he yelled, "Damn! They're gaining, too!"

"Let's run and find someplace to hold up and take a few shots to send 'em packin'."

They set their horses to a gallop as they raced southward, taking the occasional glance behind.

———

"They finally spotted us," Jake said unnecessarily as they kept their horses' pace to a fast trot.

Ralph and Charlie weren't panicking, but it was close. They just couldn't figure out how anyone could get so close without them knowing about it. The fact that they hadn't checked their backtrail since leaving the farm didn't occur to them.

They were losing their pursuers and had reopened the gap to almost a mile when Ralph spotted a low gully to the right and pointed it out to Charlie. They angled toward the gully and rode straight into the bed where they leapt from their horses, ripped their Winchesters out, and waited. They didn't worry about securing their horses because there wasn't enough time.

———

Jake and Nora had seen them drop down into the gully, and when they got within two hundred yards they stopped.

"It's that woman I married!" Charlie said with a half laugh when he recognized Nora.

"And she's with the last guy that Lucy married. I think they're pissed at us," Ralph laughed, relieved that they were dealing with amateurs.

But they were also dealing with something else and would soon discover the difference.

———

Nora asked, "What are we going to do now, Jake. They're in there pretty good."

"I'm going to try something to make their life difficult and you get ready to do the same."

Jake cupped his open hands around his mouth and shouted, "Sandy! Sandy!"

Nora smiled and started shouting, "Satin! Satin!"

The Haskin boys started laughing as Charlie snorted, "Those two must be nuts!"

Their two horses' ears perked up at the sound, then they both nickered, and when Jake and Nora shouted again, they bolted.

"What the hell!" Ralph shouted as he tried in vain to grab Sandy's reins as he flashed past.

Both horses scrambled out of the gully and ran to the shouts of the humans they knew and who had treated them well.

Ralph and Charlie knew they were utterly and completely screwed when the horses were gone carrying their supply of ammunition, food, and water.

Jake and Nora welcomed their equine friends and Coffee seemed pleased at the reunion as well as Satin went over to inspect the new mare.

Nora was rubbing Satin's neck as she said, "Jake, that was brilliant. Now what?"

"I want you to put lead ropes on Coffee and your new horse. We're going to back off another two hundred yards, but keep them in sight."

"Okay."

Jake knew that Nora could handle it. She was a ranch woman after all.

Nora had them all tied and ready to move in ten minutes.

"I'm ready, Jake," she said.

"Those two can only go east or west in that gully and not very far on foot. They'll need to come after the horses. Hopefully, our friends with the badges will be here soon."

————

Their badged friends were five miles north of where they stood and making fast progress. The trail was very easy to follow. It was like a straight line pointing toward the Indian Nations. They only hoped they could get there before the Haskins reached their sanctuary.

————

Ralph and Charlie were desperately trying to come up with something.

"Why don't we split up and come at them from different directions?" Ralph asked.

"Look where they are. They can see everything for four hundred yards around. We'd be picked off before we could get a shot off."

"But they've got Winchesters and so do we, and one of 'em is a girl!"

"Yeah, but the rancher will have plenty of time to kill us both. They can be lying prone on the ground making a tiny target and with a great shooting platform while we'd be moving."

"Well, what can you come up with then, smart man?"

"I'm thinking."

While Charlie was thinking, Jake was looking behind him for the lawmen and soon spotted them about two miles back.

"Here come our friends, I think. I'm a bit surprised they're here already," he told Nora, handing her the field glasses.

She turned and looked through the lenses and said, "Two riders. I can't make out badges, though."

"They don't usually wear them when they're trailing. It reflects the sun something fierce."

"Oh. I'm always learning something when I'm around you, Jake."

"Have I told you I love you today, Nora?"

"I'm not sure. It's always welcome to hear, though."

"I love you, Nora. You're the most incredible woman I've ever met. One of these days, I'll have to get you to marry me."

"You'd better after all the exercising we've been doing together."

"You know, if we didn't have two murderers on one side and two United States Deputy Marshals on the other side, I'd ravish you right now."

Nora smiled, then walked over and put her arms around him, and kissed him.

Both the marshals and the murderers noticed.

"I'll be damned. Look at that," said Charlie, "That yokel actually likes that plain woman, and after he had Lucy, too."

"Don't bring up that bitch," growled Ralph.

The marshals had a different reaction.

Trace Wilkens just said, "Now, I don't care how successful this mission is, don't be expecting any thanks along those lines from me."

They were within half a mile when Jake waved. They waved back, wondering why they were stopped. They didn't notice at first that they had all four horses.

Harvey finally commented, "Say, Trace, they've got all four horses, but I don't see any bodies."

"They've probably got 'em holed up. They're waiting for us to help them out."

Charlie and Ralph noticed the approach of the two lawmen and knew they had to do something and do it now.

Charlie said, "Alright. Here's what we're gonna do. We're going to take off west at a crouch. We look for someplace where we can have better protection and visibility. If we can hold them off, we can get the horses back."

"Charlie, we don't have any food, water, or ammunition anymore."

"Do you want to just give up and get hanged for sure?"

"No. Let's go."

They crouched at the waist and ran just as the two deputy marshals arrived and dismounted.

Deputy Wilkens shook Jake's hand and said, "United States Deputy Marshals Trace Wilkens and Harvey Bradshaw. You must be Mister and Mrs. Fletcher."

"That's right. The Haskins are in that gully ahead, but I doubt if they're still there. They had to go either east or west. They each have Winchesters, but now they have no food or water and limited ammunition."

"We were wondering about that. How'd you get their horses?"

"They're our horses. They stole them when they escaped from Wichita. When they ran into the gully, I just hoped they hadn't hitched them. So, when we called out to them, they ran over. Must have made their day."

The two lawmen laughed, and Trace said, "That's rich. Now, here's what we're gonna do. You're not supposed to be here in any official capacity, and your wife sure isn't. What I think would be best is if me and Harvey split, and each take a swing around the gully. One of us may come under fire, and the other will double back in the gully and get them in a crossfire."

"I'm pretty sure they're going west," said Jake.

"Why do you think that?" he asked.

"I saw a small dust cloud trailing that way about five minutes ago. How about if you both cut them off and my wife and I will back you up in the gully? You'll have equal firepower and if they come back, they'll run into more rifles."

"You can help, but I can't allow a woman to be involved."

"Nora is a good shot and I'd rather stand with her than any man I've ever worked with. I know they're going west. If you continue your pursuit, you won't have to worry about your left flank. Who will be there covering that flank is my decision. How's that work?"

Deputy Marshal Wilkens mulled it over before answering, "Okay. I can live with that if you can. Harvey, let's head west."

They mounted and started their horses west at a trot.

"Nora, we're going to take Satin and Sandy down into the gully. It's pretty shallow. Once we're down there, we'll begin a slow walk west. Have your Winchester ready."

"It's ready, and so am I."

He smiled at her as he said, "Let's go, Nora."

They hitched Coffee and the new horse to a young cottonwood, then mounted and rode Sandy and Satin down into the gully and turned them west. Both of them had their Winchesters cocked as they slowly walked their horses along the gully's bed.

———

Ralph and Charlie had been jogging hunched over for almost ten minutes and they were exhausted. They finally stopped, finding nowhere else to go to mount a defense.

"Let's stay here and fight it out, Charlie. This damned gully ain't never gonna get us anywhere."

"Alright. They were north of us, so they'll be coming from that direction. But they may try to flank us so keep an eye out to the east. I'll watch to the north."

"Okay. Let's wait on 'em."

United States Deputy Marshals Trace Wilkens and Harvey Bradshaw were walking their horses about one hundred and fifty yards from the gully. They were out of normal Winchester range, but a lucky shot could still get them. They were putting themselves at risk to find out where the Haskins were.

Ralph peeked over the edge, spotted them, and then dropped back down and said, "Here come two of them. It must be the lawmen. Do we fire?"

"Wait. They're looking for us. If we let them go past, they'll miss us."

The deputy marshals were almost to their position but didn't see them in the gully as they clung to the near wall.

A quarter mile to the east, Jake and Nora were in the gully still walking their horses. Jake could see the marshals from his saddle. The sun was lower in the sky now and he estimated they had another hour of light left.

He waved to Nora, and they stopped then dismounted.

He brought his head close to hers and said, "I think they're close. Let's walk."

Nora nodded. They wrapped their reins around some rocks on the gully wall before they stepped forward, their cocked

Winchesters pointed down the gully. The deputies were now directly opposite the hiding criminals walking their horses slowly as they searched for the two men.

Ralph wanted to fire at them badly and knew they were right there, but he held his fire. He rolled slightly to his right to keep his rifle aimed at them. When he did, his right foot hit a fist-sized rock that rolled down the gully and smacked into another rock, making a loud click. The sound was almost like a Winchester hammer being cocked and was enough to alert the two lawmen.

The two deputies turned and hit the dirt almost like a ballet. The two outlaws, realizing their position had been given away, popped up to the edge of the gully and began firing. They knew their ammunition situation was desperate, so they avoided blanket firing and were taking aimed shots at the two deputies.

As soon as the first shot was fired, Jake and Nora crouched, trotted down the gully, and soon arrived at a mild curve and stopped. The shooting was just on the other side of the curve.

"Are you ready, Nora?"

She nodded and hefted her Winchester.

Jake took two side steps into the center of the gully and Nora took one. With their Winchesters level, they stepped forward, made the turn, and saw the two men firing. Ralph caught the motion out of the periphery of his vision and rotated his Winchester toward the new threat, but it was too late.

Jake and Nora opened fire as soon as he began to turn.

Ralph took two .44 caliber rounds in the chest and slid down the gully, no longer bleeding as his heart had stopped pushing blood through his arteries.

That left Charlie, and Jake was going to fire but stopped his index finger short, and lowered his Winchester but Nora didn't lower hers as she kept him in her sights but didn't fire.

"Charlie Haskins! Drop the rifle. Now!" she shouted.

Charlie had heard the shots and watched Ralph slide down the gully. Until Nora shouted, he wasn't sure what had happened, then suddenly turned and saw the woman he had married holding a Winchester pointed in his direction.

He almost wanted to laugh. A woman with a Winchester was funny enough, but this woman he knew to be a mousy, frightened woman who he'd last seen covered in her own body waste was even less dangerous. She was a joke and the man had his Winchester down, so he wasn't worried at all as he quickly turned his repeater to take aim at the woman, but never got a chance to pull the trigger.

Nora fired when she saw him turn. Her bullet rammed into Charlie just above his right clavicle and went through his chest severing his brachial artery before it exited.

He dropped to his knees in shock, his Winchester falling to the ground as he stared at Nora in total disbelief for five full seconds as his life's blood pumped into the Kansas air. Charlie Haskins, the pretty man who said that Nora didn't meet his standards, then fell face first into the floor of the gully, shuddered, and then died.

Nora slowly lowered her smoking rifle and wondered why she didn't feel sick about it. She should have. *Shouldn't she?*

"Deputies! It's all over. They're both dead!" Jake shouted.

Trace Wilkens and Harvey Bradshaw scrambled up from the ground, mounted, and rode to the gully's edge. They looked

C.J. PETIT

down and found the two men who had been shooting at them at the bottom of the gully.

"We heard your wife shout. Who made the shots?" asked Trace.

"We both hit Ralph, I think. He turned when he saw us, and we didn't let him get a shot off. I let Nora take care of Charlie. He had locked her in a closet for two days, so I figured she had the right. She warned him to drop his rifle, and he saw me with mine pointed to the ground, so I guess he thought he could beat a woman in a shooting contest. And maybe he could with most women, but not against my woman. She's the best."

Nora smiled at him as he turned and smiled back.

Deputy Wilkens stared at Nora for a second, then said to Jake, "Give us a hand dragging these two out of that gully. Mrs. Fletcher, could you go and retrieve the two horses, please?"

"I'll do that. You can call me Nora."

"Thank you, Nora," replied Deputy Bradshaw.

Nora turned and walked back to Satin. She'd bring Sandy back to her husband and smiled to herself at the thought. It sounded so normal now.

The three men watched her leave and Trace said, "You have one hell of a wife there, Jake."

"She's more woman than any other that I've met. I wouldn't trade her for any of them."

Jake then helped the deputy marshals lift the two bodies from the gully. They went through their pockets and found a total of $65.45. The deputy marshals insisted that Jake take it because they didn't want to have to account for it, but the real reason was that they felt that he and Nora had earned it.

Nora arrived with their four horses, and Jake and the deputies put the bodies on Coffee and the new mare.

Deputy Wilkens said, "The closest town is Coats. That's about fifteen miles northwest. We're going to bring these bodies in and send a telegram to our boss and the sheriff in Wichita. We'll need statements from both of you."

"We'll just follow you in and stay there overnight. We'll need to ride to Cunningham in the morning. What will you do after Coats?"

"Depends on what the boss tells us to do."

After mounting and setting back north at a slow trot, Nora and Jake had Sandy and Satin just inches apart, their legs almost touching.

Jake looked over at Nora and mouthed, "I love you, Nora."

She knew a verbal reply was unnecessary as she spoke to him with her big brown eyes and a smile on her lips.

By the time they reached Coats, it was past nine o'clock. While the deputies went to see the sheriff, Jake and Nora went to the local eatery and enjoyed a filling supper with a decidedly rural ambiance.

They left the diner and headed for the sheriff's office when they were done, meeting the deputy marshals on the boardwalk just a hundred feet from the café.

Jake and Nora traded locations with the lawmen who headed to fill their stomachs while the self-married Fletchers spent a good hour in the sheriff's office writing their lengthy statements.

Jake finished his first, then looked at Nora who was still writing, but soon paused. They hadn't talked about the final confrontation with the Haskins yet and he felt it was time to broach the subject now that she'd written about it.

"Nora, how are you doing?" he asked.

Nora looked over from her sheet and replied, "I was wondering why I don't feel worse for shooting Charlie. I didn't feel any remorse and I didn't feel any sense of fulfillment, either. I'm beginning to think that there's something that's not right about me inside."

"There's nothing wrong with you at all, Nora. I wondered that myself after shooting those three men a few weeks ago and thought there was something wrong with me, too. But I had given them a chance to surrender, so what happened was because they chose not to drop their guns. Besides, they were there to do me harm. Now, you already had been hurt in many ways by Charlie Haskins, yet you still gave him a chance to drop his weapon, so when he didn't and thought he could shoot you, you had no choice. You shouldn't feel bad about it at all."

"I know, and maybe I'll feel better after a while. But I do have one question for you. Why did you lower your Winchester?"

"As I told the two marshals, I felt that you had the right. I'll admit that I was worried about the decision and was ready to pull my Winchester back on target if you'd lowered yours. I had one other reason that I'm almost ashamed to tell you."

"Will you tell me now?"

Jake nodded, then replied, "I thought if I had my sights on him, he'd throw down his weapon and give up. But from the way you described him, he didn't think much of you, and I was counting on that poor and very misplaced opinion to drive him to do what he did. If he surrendered, he'd be dragged back to Wichita and stand trial. You'd have to sit on the witness stand and tell what he'd done to you and his defense attorney would attack you any way that he could. I didn't want that to happen and I didn't want that bastard to live for another thirty years at the state's expense. That's why I almost goaded him into taking the shot."

"You thought all of that in just a few seconds?"

"No, ma'am. I thought of that before we even called our horses out of the gully. It was just a question of how the circumstances unfolded after that."

"Well, Nora, go ahead and finish up your statement. It's getting late and we still have to get the horses stabled and get a room at the hotel."

"One room, Jake?" she asked as she smiled.

"One room, Mrs. Fletcher."

———

Five minutes later, they left their statements on the desk with the sheriff who had to wait for the two U.S. deputy marshals to return from dinner, exited the jail, led their horses to the livery, and paid the liveryman to board and feed the horses. They had their saddlebags over their shoulders, then walked to the hotel where Jake signed the register as Jake and Nora Fletcher for their single room.

Once in the spartan room, while Jake was putting things away, Nora trotted down the hallway and took a quick bath, then, after she'd barely set foot past the threshold of their room, Jake made his exit to head down the hallway.

When he returned to the room, Nora, damp hair and all, was already under the blankets. She smiled at him and pulled the top of the blankets down revealing her lack of clothing.

Jake was soon fittingly dressed in his birthday suit and joined his wife under the covers.

———

Early the next morning, just as the morning sun began sending rays of bright light through the window, Jake's eyes slowly opened to find Nora sleeping peacefully inches away. He'd expected that she might have had nightmares over the gunfight or the discovery of what the Haskins had done at the Curry farm, but she hadn't awakened in terror or even a loud moan.

He stared at her almost angelic, cute oval face in awe. How could so many people have underestimated her for so long? No, she wasn't gorgeous. No, she wasn't voluptuous. But those were window dressings. The frightening thing, in a way, was that he still didn't think he had reached anywhere close to the limit of her abilities yet.

He continued to study her soft, gentle face, almost childlike in its innocence. After almost five minutes, Jake leaned over and kissed her forehead softly.

Nora opened her eyes slowly and smiled at him and Jake felt a warmth inside him whenever she did, especially like this.

"Good morning, sweetheart," he said softly.

"Hello, my husband," she answered just as quietly.

They just smiled at each other for a minute or so before Jake asked, "Shall we get some breakfast, our horses, and then make that ride to Cunningham to see about the children?"

"I suppose. But this is so nice."

Jake kissed her on the forehead again, then asked, "Nora, after we legally get married, where do you want to live? We have two ranches and our money will be returned, so we have many options."

"I'm not sure yet. What do you want to do?"

"Before I met you, if I had gotten my money back, I had planned on buying more cattle and just going back to doing what I was before, but you've changed all that. Now, as long as I'm with you, no matter where it is, I'll be happy."

"That's how I feel, too. Let's go have breakfast and we can talk as we ride."

"That sounds like a plan, Nora."

He slipped out of bed and waited for his nude wife to join him for a morning kiss and a small amount of fondling before they both dressed. They checked out and after breakfast, were riding northeast, leading their two extra horses.

Jake said loudly over the hoofbeats, "A lot of what we decide to do with our future depends on what we find out when we get to Cunningham, Nora."

"I know. You never did describe your ranch in Colorado. You've seen mine. Is yours better?"

"It's twice the size, and I have better water, but the terrain is about the same, as is the house. Your barn is better, but I have Eureka nearby and they have a lot more services than Albert."

"It sounds like we should sell mine and move into yours. We'd have enough money to stock it easily and do whatever else we need to do to improve things."

"I can see that. Let's see what we find in Cunningham."

Nora nodded with a smile of anticipation and Jake hoped it worked out for her. He really liked Joseph Curry, but he knew that soft-hearted Nora was already deeply attached to Amanda and hoped that she got her wish.

They reached Cunningham just after noon and rode first to the sheriff's office, both nervous to learn if their future would include the two Curry children.

Jake could see the anxiety in Nora's face as they dismounted and tied off the horses. After they crossed the boardwalk, Jake held the door open, and Nora glanced nervously at him as she entered.

As soon as they passed the threshold, the sheriff rose from behind the desk and said loudly, "Howdy, folks! Welcome back. Did you catch up with them fellers who killed John and Madeline Curry?"

Jake was taking off his hat as he replied, "Yes, sir. My wife and I took care of them both. Two United States Deputy Marshals returned their bodies to Coats last night."

"Well, praise the Lord for that. I just thought you might like to know that little Joseph and Amanda will be well cared for. Madeline's sister Irene and her husband Patrick are going to adopt them. They're good folks and didn't have any children of their own and I know Irene will treat them like royalty."

Jake knew that the news hurt Nora, but she just smiled and said, "I'm happy for them, then. Thank you, Sheriff."

"No, the thanks all belong to you and your husband, ma'am. You rescued them young'uns and brought justice to their parents' killers. Bless you both."

"Thank you, Sheriff," Jake said and shook his hand.

He then took Nora's elbow and led her from the office, and as soon as Jake had closed the door, she began to weep softly. Jake didn't care what people walking by thought as he pulled Nora close to the wall and held her tightly. His heart was breaking for her. She didn't sob or shudder, she just quietly cried. He didn't say anything because nothing he could say would ease her heartache. He surely wasn't going to say anything stupid like, "maybe it's better this way," or some other banality.

After a couple of minutes, she said softly, "I'm all right now, Jake. We need to get some lunch."

"Alright, Nora. It still won't be as good as your cooking. I can't wait to get some of the Mexican dish you make again."

As they walked with arms locked to the diner, Nora asked, "So, you really liked it, did you?"

"I loved it. You have more abilities and gifts than any other person I know, Nora."

"I have something even better. I have you, Jake," she replied, then asked, "Jake, when we dropped the children off, the sheriff made it sound as if there weren't any relatives, but just now, it seemed as if he knew her sister quite well. Why did he do that?"

"I was wondering about that myself and the only thing that made sense to me was that because I asked first, he didn't want to tell us until he was sure that they would accept the children. This way, we'd be able to adopt them when we returned if the aunt and uncle didn't take them in."

"I guess that makes sense, but I had my hopes up."

"I know."

After lunch, they walked the horses to the train depot where they found that the next train for Wichita left at 6:05, so Jake bought two tickets and four horse transports. After he was given the tags and brought the horses to the corral, he noticed that all four had Winchesters in their scabbards.

He turned to Nora and said, "You know, Nora. We could go into the gun shop business with all the guns we've been collecting. We have the two Winchesters and pistols at your house and the four Winchesters on the horses along with the two shotguns."

"That's something I hadn't thought of. So, what will we do for four hours?"

"I know what I'd like to do with you if we had someplace private."

"My! My! Are you always this way?" she asked as she grinned.

"Only with your inspiration, my love. I have an idea. Follow me."

He took her by the arm and walked west along the boardwalk, but Nora had no idea where he was leading her until he stopped before a whitewashed building with a cross atop its steeple.

She turned her startled face to look at him and exclaimed, "You're kidding! *Now? Dressed like I am?*"

Jake grinned at her and replied, "Do you want to wait until we get to Wichita? You can wear whatever you want if you do."

"Would you mind waiting? You know how much I want to marry you, but can I have just this one concession?"

"You can have as many concessions as you like, but don't keep turning me down, woman. I may have to tap your cute little noggin and carry you off in an elopement."

"I don't think it will come to that," she said as she smiled.

———

It was late evening, bordering on early nighttime when their train pulled into Wichita. There was no one in the livery next to the station where they'd left them before, so Jake unsaddled all four horses, brushed them down, and put them into stalls before stepping outside to retrieve Nora.

"Where to now?" she asked.

"We get something to eat and then get a room. Tomorrow, we go to see the sheriff and find out what has happened to Lucy in our absence."

Nora was surprised and said, "You know, I had totally forgotten about Lucy. What happened, do you think?"

267

"I have no idea. She should be in her room at the rooming house, but I don't know if they made any arrangements yet. With Deputy Marshal Carrol being shot, a lot of things may have changed."

They found an open restaurant and had a plain but satisfying dinner. By the time they reached the hotel and got a room, it was well into the night. Nora hadn't spoken much during the meal and Jake wondered if remembering Lucy had something to do with her unexpected silence.

When they were snug under the blankets, Jake held Nora close knowing that she wanted to talk, but he had to let her start the conversation, which took a while.

Almost twenty minutes of silence followed, twenty minutes of having a naked woman pressed close was strangely not erotic to Jake as he was concerned about Nora.

When she finally spoke, it wasn't about Lucy at all.

Nora said softly, "She was such a wonderful little girl, Jake."

Jake felt somewhat relieved when he realized the cause of her behavior. If she was still worried about Lucy, he didn't know what else he could do or say.

"I know, Nora. I saw how you two chatted for that entire ride. You had her giggling and smiling as if nothing bad had happened to her."

"You taught me that, Jake. When I was so upset about what Charlie did to me, you told me stories and got me laughing. I was able to do that for her and it made me feel so useful."

"You're always helpful, Nora, you just don't see it as easily as I do. You don't see most of the wonderful person that you are, but I do. I was thinking about you the other night, of course, because I think about you a lot, you know. But this time, I was thinking how it was almost frightening how deep a person you are. Just when I think I might have a handle on really understanding you, you show me something new. I can't wait for us to spend our life together, Nora. I want to go on exploring your depths and discovering everything I can about you."

"I love you, Jake. You're everything to me."

Jake leaned over and kissed her softly. She slid up a little and sighed. Five minutes later, she was sound asleep.

Jake stayed awake for a little while longer, understanding that Nora was content as she slept beside him, but knew that she needed to have that one last gap in her heart filled. He knew that his Nora was desperate to be a mother. After all those years when believing her life would be spent as an aging virgin spinster, she probably never recognized that need until she had little Amanda on her lap. All he could do was to keep doing what they both enjoyed so much and hoped that her other wish would be fulfilled soon.

He kissed her softly once more, then closed his eyes and let sleep overtake him.

CHAPTER 9

They both awakened in the same position they had been in when they drifted to sleep. Jake woke just a minute before Nora and just ran his fingers through her hair that was spread across his chest.

Nora seemed to be in a better mood than she had been immediately after the loss of Amanda, gave Jake a quick kiss, popped out of bed, and threw on some clothes. Then she quickly left the room and headed to the bathroom, returning twenty minutes later, clean and smiling.

Jake skipped the bath because he was anxious to find out what was going on with Lucy, so ten minutes later, he and Nora took their saddlebags downstairs and had breakfast in the hotel restaurant.

Once they finished eating, they left the hotel, and with arms locked, walked to the sheriff's office to get updated on Lucy and the condition of the injured lawmen. They arrived at the sheriff's office and Jake held the door as Nora entered.

The sheriff himself was at the desk, no doubt brought about by the temporary loss of two of his deputies.

"Morning, Sheriff," said Jake.

"Well, howdy do! Glad to see you two back. I hear you got those two bastards who shot up my deputies and the U.S. Deputy Marshal."

"Yes, sir. How are your deputies and the marshal?"

"The deputies will be back on the job in a couple more days. The deputy marshal is still here. They're moving him to Kansas City later today. If you want to see him, he's still over at Doc Bristow's house. It's on 3rd Street."

"We'll go and see him later. What happened to Lucy Haskins?"

"I have no idea. The U.S. Marshal's office is dealing with her. I'm just glad you two could make those two bastards pay."

"I guess they didn't want to come back and hang, as they knew they would be."

"That they would."

"We'll go over and see how Jim Carroll is doing."

"Before you go, I got a telegram from Marshal Breedlove in Kansas City. He asked that you both stop by when you can."

"Then, I guess we'll go to Kansas City tomorrow."

"Have a nice trip."

He shook Jake's hand and didn't know what to do with his pistol-packing woman until she offered her hand as well. He grinned and shook Nora's hand before they turned and left the office.

After leaving the jail, Jake and Nora walked north and logically passed 1st and 2nd Streets before turning on 3rd Street. The doctor's house was easily found with its very professional sign hanging out front. They turned and walked down the paved entrance and stepped up onto the porch. Jake knocked and thirty seconds later, the door was answered by a middle-aged woman whom they both assumed was Mrs. Bristow.

"Good morning, ma'am. We're friends of Jim Carroll, the U.S. Deputy Marshal that was shot. Could we see him?"

"Certainly. He's awake and wants out of here. Follow me."

Jake let Nora precede him and followed as he usually did, and for the same reason that he did when he first met her.

They were led to the doorway of a nice-sized bedroom where Mrs. Bristow stopped, then said, "Deputy Carroll, you have visitors."

She smiled and walked away before they entered the room.

Jim Carroll's face lit up when he saw Nora and Jake, and said, "Well, this is a pleasant surprise."

"How are you doing, Jim?" Jake asked.

"A lot better than I thought I'd be. If you hadn't wrapped me up so quick, the doc didn't think I'd be here at all. As it is, I'll be off work for about thirty days and then I'll be doing desk work for a while."

"Jim, what happened to Lucy?"

"That's the big question we're all asking. Nobody seems to know. After our little dustup out west, by the time we went looking, she had cleared out. There was nothing there at all."

"That's surprising. I thought she'd make a deal for the remaining money."

"We did, too. As it turns out, I hear you and Nora made it a moot point. The money will be unfrozen and those who already have claims against him, like you and Nora, should get your money back pretty soon. It would have taken a lot longer if it had gone to court. But Lucy being gone kind of bothers me. I don't think she was totally honest with us, either. It's just a gut feeling."

"That's very possible. She may have been working an angle, telling us what she wanted us to hear so she could make a break. But without the money, what could she do?"

"Maybe there was more money elsewhere that she knew about."

"That could be. Well, it won't bother me a bunch. We're going to head back to Eureka, Colorado in a couple of days. But first, your boss has requested we stop by your office in Kansas City. Do you know what that's about?"

"I'm not sure. It may just have to do with the money. Well, I wish you both the best of luck."

Jake shook his left hand and Nora kissed him on the cheek before they turned, left the room, and then went to the doctor's house.

As they were walking down the street, Nora asked, "What do you make of Lucy's disappearance?"

"I think Jim has the gist of it. She may have been afraid of both Charlie and Ralph, but once it looked like we had them, she began to work for herself. She may have had her own bank account, which I kind of doubt because the money wasn't there. I thought she was being honest when she said that Charlie kept all the money and doled out as little as possible. If she wants to get money, it's got to be what Ralph may have had socked away. How she could get it, I don't know. Unless he didn't keep it in the bank."

"But it doesn't matter to us, does it?"

273

"Not a bit. Let's get over to the store and you buy whatever clothes you think will work for our wedding."

She grinned at him and replied, "That sounds like a marvelous idea."

So, the clothing store became their first stop. After Nora had picked out all the things she wanted to wear and Jake had selected some new pants, a shirt, and a vest, they stopped at a jewelry shop and bought a wedding band set. They returned to the hotel and Jake took a bath while Nora changed. When he exited the bathroom, he found his bride wearing a very simple and elegant dress and couldn't recall the last time he had seen her in a dress.

He dressed quickly, and they stepped back into the May sunshine just forty minutes after entering the hotel. It was only a little after ten o'clock when they walked to the courthouse.

Once they found the right room, they were soon filling out the paperwork and as she wrote in the blocks, Nora suddenly laughed.

Jake looked over at her and she asked, "How did you answer the question, 'Are you presently married?', Mister Fletcher?"

He grinned at Nora realizing that there were potentially more than two ways to answer the question, but replied, "How about a simple 'no', Mrs. Fletcher?"

Nora nodded, wrote 'no', and continued to finish the other required empty rectangles as she lightly giggled.

But they were both more reserved as they gave the completed forms to the clerk who reviewed them and then ushered them into the judge's chambers. The clerk and a secretary served as witnesses as the judge performed the almost anti-climactic ceremony. The vows were exchanged, and the rings were placed on their fingers following the long-established ritual.

After the judge intoned, "I now pronounce you man and wife", Jake kissed Nora like it was the first time, and each of them experienced the same thrill as they had with that first kiss on the Kansas plains.

They were congratulated by the witnesses and the judge, who followed them into the outer offices to sign the marriage certificate. At 10:40 in the morning, they walked out of the courthouse recognized by the State of Kansas as Mr. and Mrs. Fletcher.

"So, do you feel any differently, Mrs. Fletcher?" Jake asked, smiling at his new bride as they walked arm-in-arm down the boardwalk.

"No, I really don't. I've been married to you for a while now, haven't I?"

"You have. And now, it's official. I can finally tell you the deep secret that I promised myself not to tell you until after we were married."

Nora stopped dead in her tracks and looked up at Jake, taken aback by his comment. *Jake was keeping secrets? How bad was it?*

"Jake, nothing can be that bad. I'll always love you."

"Then I'll tell you the secret," he said as he looked down at his wife.

Jake leaned over to her ear, and right there, in the front of the county courthouse in the middle of a June Friday, he whispered, "I love you, Nora Fletcher."

Nora didn't know whether to be upset or tickled. She thought that as it was their wedding day, she'd choose the latter, so she just laughed and kissed him.

"It's close enough to lunch, Nora. Let's go and get something to eat."

"Alright."

He hooked his arm through hers again before they resumed walking. She was so absolutely happy that she didn't know if this wasn't all some extended dream or a fantasy that she had put together while in that closet.

They arrived at a nice restaurant and were seated, the waitress arrived, and they placed their order. It wasn't anything special, just beef stew, but what was on the table wasn't important anyway.

After they'd eaten, Jake ordered some ice cream for dessert, and the waitress brought their two large bowls of the frozen vanilla treat a few minutes later.

"Jake, I've never had ice cream before," Nora admitted as she took a spoonful.

"I've only had it twice, once in Kansas City and once in Denver. Speaking about Kansas City, I don't think the visit with the marshal is about the money. Well, at least not all about the money. I think this Haskins business isn't resolved yet."

"You mean there may be another relative?"

"No, not a new one. It's about Lucy. I just don't trust her. She was desperate to get out of the situation, but once she was free of those two, she just vanished. I don't believe we're free of her yet."

"Why?"

"Just a gut feeling, really. She may be mad at both of us. I started the search for her, and you added Charlie to the mix. Together, we really threw a snake into their corral. And there's something else that may sound self-aggrandizing, but I think she's jealous of you."

"*Jealous? Of me?*" Nora asked as she looked back at him.

"Remember when you were listening outside the door?"

"Don't remind me."

"You may have heard the words, but you didn't see her face and get her full reaction. She was in utter disbelief that I would prefer you over her. When I told her that you were a lot better than her in bed, I think it really irritated her. She was good and probably couldn't imagine anyone better, but when I explained to her that the physical part of our relationship, as spectacular as it is, is just a small part of why I love you so dearly, she didn't understand. I could see it in her eyes. I think she believes I'm mistaken and she's going to try to prove me wrong. She can't lose to any woman."

Nora sat back, her frozen dessert melting and forgotten.

"Is she dangerous, Jake?"

"I'm not sure. She's hard for me to read. She has so many facades that I'm not sure if there is a real Lucy in there anywhere. She's been so many different things for so long, it's possible that she doesn't know either."

"We'll have to be careful, then."

"Always," he replied as they both returned to eating their ice cream.

––––––––

Lucy sat in her room in Kansas City. She had gone to Ralph's apartment, emptied the box under his bed, and had almost fifteen hundred dollars with her now. Ralph had always tried to impress Lucy, had told her about the money, and even where he kept his spare key. She had the means to do what she needed to do now but still had to think about what it was.

That first day, after Charlie and Ralph made their escape, she had planned on going to the U.S. Marshal's office with Jake and that Nora woman, but when she heard about the deaths of Charlie and Ralph, everything changed. She understood that there would be no incentive for them to give her a deal and might even be arrested. But that extra ten thousand dollars from Charlie's account was a hell of an incentive to take the risk anyway and talk to the law. As the lawman had said, it would be hard to get a conviction, but that was before that idiot husband and his cousin shot up a deputy marshal, too.

Lucy was torn about this one, as she looked again at the large wad of cash in her travel bag. Then, she recalled that Charlie was going to get rid of her because he had decided to go solo and thought that maybe she could go into business on her own. *Why did she need someone to find her a target?* She could just find a rich widower on her own and get all the money. She didn't need Charlie or Ralph at all.

NORA

One thing she knew for certain, she would not be humiliated again as that plain woman in Wichita had done. *How could Jake have said those things?* Look at her and then look at that woman. It wasn't even close. She was convinced that he had either forgotten the rapture he had felt when he was with her, or he had lied to get her to tell him about the money.

If it was because Nora had taken him much more recently, then maybe she should just show him one more time what he was missing. Then he'd have to admit that she was the best and that Nora woman was nothing in comparison. She'd throw it in that nothing of a woman's face and just walk away, knowing that she was still the best.

Now, she needed to plan. *Where would they be going after they got their money back?* Not to her place near Albert, that was a nothing town. His place was more likely. Eureka, Colorado was a bigger town and his ranch was bigger, too. Then there was the money aspect of the job. Between the two of them, they'd get back over thirteen thousand dollars.

As she sat on the bed, her mind was busy with thoughts of revenge and money, the perfect combination.

———

After they finished their ice cream, Jake and Nora strolled down to the livery where they met the liveryman who had been smacked in the head. He said he had found the note and had heard that he and his wife had shot the two that bushwhacked him. He offered to take care of the horses until they got back from Kansas City at no charge, so Jake shook his hand before they left to return to their hotel room. They were newlyweds, after all.

———

The following morning found Jake and Nora on the train out of Wichita to Kansas City. It wasn't a long ride, and after stopping for a quick lunch, they walked to the United States Marshal's office for their first meeting with U.S. Marshal John Breedlove. It was only three blocks from the diner, so it was early afternoon when they entered.

They stepped into the office and found Deputy Marshal Trace Wilkens at the desk. He rose and smiled as they approached.

Jake shook his hand and said, "Good afternoon, Trace. The sheriff in Wichita said the marshal wanted to meet with us."

"Welcome to Kansas City, Jake and Nora. That's what I've been told. You got here quickly enough."

"We're going to head back to Wichita, pick up our stuff, and then head back home as soon as we're finished here."

"Sounds like a plan. Come on, I'll take you to the boss."

They followed Trace past a few empty offices before he knocked on the final door on the left. He didn't wait for an answer but just opened the door and said, "Boss, Mr. and Mrs. Fletcher are here to see you."

"Send 'em on in."

Trace held the door open for the couple as they stepped into the marshal's office, then closed the door behind them.

United States Marshal John Breedlove looked exactly as Jake had expected. He was a big man, just over six feet and about two hundred pounds, and had a confident, commanding air about him.

He stood as they entered and offered his hand to Jake.

"John Breedlove. Call me John," he said as Jake shook his hand.

"Jake Fletcher, John. And this is my wife, Nora. Call me Jake, please."

The marshal was a little surprised when Nora offered him her hand, but he shook her hand as well.

"Call me Nora," she said as she smiled.

"Please, have a seat," the marshal said before they each sat down.

"First item on the agenda is the money. We would have had a delay until there was an investigation, then a trial, and a decision, but with the death of Charles Haskins, and the evidence provided by you and my deputies, Judge Swafford ordered the account to be turned over to a bank auditor for dispersal to the injured parties. Most will be notified by certified letter, but as you're both here, you'll be able to go over to the First National Bank and see Mister Freeman, who's the auditor. He will cut you each a draft for the amount you lost. You can do that immediately after leaving here.

"The second item isn't as pleasant. It involves Lucy Haskins. We had already received approval from the U.S. Attorney to make a plea deal with her to grant her amnesty for her testimony. Then the other two made that escape, and once they fired on Deputy Marshal Carroll and the two Wichita deputies, the deal was withdrawn as they were now facing hanging offenses in addition to the previous charges.

"We never had a chance to tell Mrs. Haskins about the withdrawal of the deal because she disappeared as soon as she must have heard about the shootings. She's a pretty shrewd woman and must have known what was going to happen.

"Anyway, we weren't going to hunt her down because no one had filed charges yet. But then, during the course of our investigation into Charlie Haskins, we found that his cousin, Ralph had maintained an apartment here. We got a search warrant and went over there.

"The room was empty and so was a metal box that was laying on the bed. Now, Ralph had no bank account that we could find, so we're pretty sure the metal box had all the money he'd made working for Charlie. I have no idea how much, but it must be substantial, and our only suspect is Lucy Haskins.

"Witnesses at the rooming house reported seeing a beautiful blonde woman in the building just two days after they ran. She may be in Kansas City right now, and she may not be a blonde anymore, either. There aren't many of them, so she'd stick out. She'd have to wear something to make her look frumpier, too. The reason I'm bringing this up to you both is that we're concerned she may try to seek some sort of revenge. It's not uncommon. She probably sees you two as the source of all her problems, so I just wanted to warn you."

Jake said, "We figured that one out already. Lucy is hard to figure out because she's been hiding behind so many masks all these years, so I don't know what to expect from her. All we can do is be aware of her and protect ourselves accordingly."

"Speaking of that, Deputies Wilkens and Bradshaw were mighty impressed with both of you for what you did in saving Jim Carroll and the Wichita deputies and then trailing the two almost to the Nations. They said you also saved a couple of young children while you were following the Haskins."

"That was Joseph and Amanda. They were beautiful kids."

"Well, you both did a spectacular job," he said, then turned to Mrs. Fletcher and said, "And, Nora? The boys said that if you were a man, they'd ask you to join the U.S. Marshal's Service in a heartbeat."

Nora smiled and said, "Tell them both that I appreciate the comment."

Jake then asked, "We'll go ahead and go over to the bank now. Do you need anything else, John?"

"No. That's it. Feel free to stop by anytime."

They all shook hands again, before Jake and Nora headed out the door, then waved at Deputy Marshal Wilkens as they left the offices.

The very impressive First National Bank building was two blocks south, so they walked with arms tightly locked to the bank, and once they arrived, asked to see Mister Freeman. He had his own office and secretary, so the receptionist dropped them off with the secretary before departing.

"Marshal Breedlove told us to stop by and see Mister Freeman. I'm Jake Fletcher and this is my wife, Nora Fletcher."

"Oh, yes. The Haskins case. Come with me, please," the secretary said as he pulled a thick folder from his in-basket and led them into Mister Freeman's office after knocking twice.

"Mister Freeman, Mr. and Mrs. Fletcher are here. Here's the Haskins file," he said as he handed the folder to Mister Freeman.

Horace Freeman looked very much as one would expect of a banking auditor, he was fairly short and slim with a receding hairline and wore bifocal glasses, but had sharp, piercing gray eyes.

"Please, have a seat. Marshal Breedlove said you'd be stopping by," he said as his secretary left and closed the door.

"Now, I've been told by the marshal that you, Mrs. Fletcher, are the Nora Graham listed on the sheet of victims of the Haskins's frauds?"

"I am."

"Then congratulations on your recent marriage. Do you have any form of identification?"

"I do have our marriage license," Jake replied, "Would that suffice?"

"It would."

Jake handed him the marriage license, and after a brief examination, Mister Freeman gave it back.

"Now, I'm showing a total of $13,300 owed to you both. $7800 to Mister Fletcher and $5500 to Mrs. Fletcher. Would you rather have it as one draft payable to both or as two separate drafts?"

Jake looked at Nora. This was her call.

"One draft is fine," she answered, smiling at her husband of a day.

Mister Freeman wrote out the draft and handed it to Jake. Jake and Nora both signed receipts and their business at the bank was done.

They left the bank just a few minutes after two o'clock and Jake waved down a carriage for hire, then gave the driver an address on Broadway.

Once they were seated and the carriage began to roll, Nora asked, "Where are we going? I thought we were heading for the hotel?"

"We'll be going there later, but first we need to make a stop."

Nora put her hand to her mouth and exclaimed in a startled hush, "Your parents!"

"It wouldn't be fair to come to Kansas City and not see them."

"I know, but I'm not dressed right, Jake. I should put on a nice dress."

"You're perfectly dressed, and trust me, they'll be more than happy to meet you."

The carriage arrived at the residence of the senior Mr. and Mrs. Fletcher minutes later and Jake paid the driver then told him not to wait.

As they walked up the long walkway to the imposing house, Nora was more nervous than when she was shooting Haskins.

They stepped up the four porch stairs before they crossed the polished hardwood surface then stopped at the heavy oak door before Jake used the brass knocker to announce their presence. He could have just opened the door without knocking but he wanted the effect.

Nora was expecting a maid to answer the door, or if it was his mother, she imagined the older Mrs. Fletcher to be a stern, gray-haired woman wearing a corseted dress with a bustle.

When the door did open, she was stunned to see a dark-haired woman, a little taller than herself wearing a man's shirt and britches.

His mother's face broke into a huge grin as she saw her son with a young woman.

"Jake! Welcome. Come in and who did you bring to visit?" she said as Jake gave Nora a gentle nudge to send her into the parlor.

After she closed the door, Jake gave his mother a hug and a kiss on the cheek, then took Nora's hand and said, "Mama, I would like to introduce you to another Mrs. Fletcher. This is Nora, my wife and your new daughter-in-law."

If Jake's mother was grinning before, she almost split her face in half with the introduction. Without hesitation, she took one long step forward and hugged her new daughter-in-law.

"Congratulations to you both. And, Nora? Thank you for rescuing me from a mother's perpetual worry about her son's bachelorhood."

She hooked her arm through Nora's and led her to the kitchen.

Once inside, she said, "Have a seat, both of you. I was just going to have some coffee. Your father is off at work but should be home in two more hours. We received your letter about the loss of your money and cattle. Do you need some cash?"

Jake smiled and said, "No, mama. We both got all our money back. Nora had been swindled as well by the husband of the woman that I kind of married. That's how I met her. We've been running around Kansas these past few weeks tracking down the scam artists, and now that it's all behind us, we'll be moving back to the ranch in Eureka."

"Do you want to tell me the story or wait until your father comes home?"

"We'll wait. It's a long story."

His mother looked over at Nora and said, "Nora, I must apologize for my appearance. It's a bad habit, I'm afraid. I find this manner of dress much more comfortable when I'm working around the house. I'm not a very gracious lady, I'm afraid."

Nora smiled at her mother-in-law and said, "To be honest, I was very relieved to see you dressed like that. I've been wearing pants almost since I met Jake."

"I'm a bit unconventional myself and enjoy tweaking the stuck-up noses of the upper-crust ladies that I meet. I've got to start dinner going, so we can talk as I work."

"I'd love to help. I enjoy cooking."

"That would be marvelous. I'll tell you some stories about Jake when he was a troublesome boy."

For over an hour, Jake sipped his coffee and watched the two most important women in his life. He was the focus of most of the stories his mother told and often had Nora laughing and shaking her head.

Jake tried to defend himself on occasion but to no avail. He was happy to see how well Nora and his mother got along, but he knew they would. Nora was her kind of person. They were almost finished when the front door opened, and Arnold Fletcher entered his house. He heard the sound of women's laughter, knew Rose had a visitor, and quickly crossed through the parlor, down the long hallway, and stepped into the kitchen. As soon as he entered, his face lit up when he saw Jake sitting at the kitchen table.

Jake hadn't heard him come in above the ladies' mirth, and quickly shot out of his seat and greeted his father with a bear hug. Arnold was almost as tall as Jake and a bit heavier around the middle. He was dark-haired with gray streaks, yet there was a marked resemblance between father and son.

"Papa, I'd like you to meet your new daughter-in-law, Nora."

Arnold smiled even more broadly, turned to the women, and promptly enveloped Nora in the same kind of hug that Jake had given him.

Then he stepped back and smiled at Nora, saying, "You are as cute as a button, Nora. I suppose my wife has been filling your head with stories of how much trouble Jake got into as a young lad, but don't you pay them any mind. No father was ever prouder of his son than I am of mine. We read that letter from Jake, so I know he went off searching for the woman that took his money. I can tell by looking into your eyes that you weren't that woman. You have honest eyes. So, I'm sure that there's a tale to be told. Let me get ready for dinner and we'll enjoy both of your cooking and you can tell us."

―――――

During the course of the lengthy dinner, Jake and Nora told the detailed story of how they had each been bilked, how they found each other, and what they had done to rectify the wrongs. They left out some of the more sexual aspects of the month-long trek around Kansas for obvious reasons. It wouldn't have mattered if they had included them anyway, as Jake's parents could see how much the couple was not only in love but completely connected in any way two people could be.

Rose was very pleased with his choice for a wife. Jake had always seemed to prefer the pretty girls that didn't have much in the way of substance. Nora may not be as pretty as most of them but wasn't as plain as she claimed to be, and she most surely had substance. Nora was a keeper.

When the narration was over, the astonished senior Fletchers sat back.

"That was an amazing story. Now, what will you do?" asked Arnold.

"We'll move back into my ranch and buy some more cattle."

"What about that woman, Lucy?" asked his father.

"That's the wild card in all this, Papa. We don't know if she's going to try to seek some sort of revenge or just go away. All we can do is be prepared."

"When are you going to leave?"

"Our train leaves tomorrow for Wichita. We'll pick up our horses and head back."

"You're not going to stay longer?" asked his mother.

"Not this time, Mama. We have too much of a mess still left to clean up, but we'll come and visit more often now that I have Nora. I'm enormously proud of her and I like to show her off."

Nora laughed, but at the same time realized that he meant it. His words weren't just meant to make her feel better. He really was proud of her and that meant a lot.

The rest of the evening was spent telling stories that didn't involve shooting or chases.

Jake and Nora finally retired to Jake's old room, and Jake thought it would be a bit risqué to make love in his old bed, so they did, just as quietly as they ever had.

Jake lay stretched out on the big bed with Nora in her standard, half on top of Jake position with her knee across his stomach and her head on his shoulder and chest as Jake was stroking her head and hair.

"You know, Nora, it's going to be great to be in our own home again. This keeping the noise down is a bit frustrating. It was different enough the first time to be interesting, but I do miss your enthusiasm."

"You'll see plenty of enthusiasm when we're alone in that ranch house," she said softly and smiled at the thought herself.

"When we leave Wichita, we're going to have to stop in Albert."

"I know. I've got to put the ranch up for sale and we need to find what we want to take with us."

"We'll just crate up what you want, and have it shipped with us on the same train."

"How much do you think we'll get for the ranch?" she asked.

"I don't know. How many acres is it?"

"It's only one section. Six hundred and forty acres."

"It may be a ranch, but it's still prime farmland. With the house and barn, I'm guessing around four thousand dollars."

"That much?"

"Yes, ma'am. When my Uncle Ernie died, a local rancher wanted to buy my place. With the 245 head that were on there at the time, he offered me ten thousand dollars. It's two sections and the cattle were worth around thirty-six hundred dollars at the time."

"Jake, we're going to have almost twenty-thousand dollars to do what you want to do. What do you think?"

"We could take advantage of the loss of all my cattle and yours to switch to the new shorthorns or Herefords rather than the longhorns. There's more beef per pound. I don't want to go crazy, though. I think about three hundred head will provide us with steady income over the years. That will cost us about seven thousand dollars. I won't hire a permanent ranch hand, but once a year, we'll bring in three men to round up the herd, brand the calves, and castrate the ones we want as steers. We can sell about fifty head a year and still have the herd grow."

She kissed him and said, "It sounds like a wonderful plan, Jake."

———

While Jake and Nora were enjoying married life, Lucy was on the train that they had missed and was heading west. Her blonde hair was washed out and she wasn't wearing a corset. Instead, she wrapped a towel around her chest and then added two shirts before putting on her most conservative dress. She carried her money-stuffed travel bag and had a trunk in the baggage car. She was heading for Denver.

———

Twenty-four hours later, Jake and Nora were on that same train, only they were going to Wichita to pick up their horses. They'd spend the day there and then head to Albert. When they finally walked into the livery to let the liveryman know that they'd be leaving tomorrow on the 10:40 train, he told them that the sheriff would like to talk to them.

When they entered the office, one of the two deputies who had been hit by buckshot was at the desk.

"Morning, deputy. How are you feeling these days?" Jake asked.

"As good as could be expected. Me and Lenny appreciate you getting us outta that fix and taking out those two."

"Wish I could've stopped them sooner. Is the sheriff in?"

"Nah. He's taking the day off 'cause he had to work double duty until we got back. Besides, it's me you want to talk to anyway."

"What about?"

"Now, I may be off my rocker, but yesterday, I was at the train station, checking out the passengers. We were looking for a wanted arsonist by the name of Willard Crenshaw. Well, anyway, I spotted this woman that looked a lot like Lucy Haskins sittin' on a bench on the platform. She had brown hair and not so well, um, developed, if you'll pardon the expression, ma'am."

Nora waved off his concern as Jake asked, "Did you look at her ticket to see where she was headed?"

"Nope. I didn't pay that much attention to the woman, but as I was steppin' off the platform, she turned and watched me leave. She had these bright blue eyes like Lucy Haskins did and looked so much like her, I'd swear it was her or a sister, maybe."

"She was an only child, so she wasn't a sister. It was probably her. When I asked about her in Chaffee, where she grew up, I was told she had brown hair. I imagine if she wanted to, she could hide her well-developed chest. So, if I had to guess, I'd say that you did see Lucy. She was heading west and trying not to be noticed. We kind of suspected she might come and pay us a visit. Now we're more positive about that possibility."

"Glad I could help. There was one other thing. She was sittin', on that bench with her travel bag on her lap, not on the floor like most folks."

"She probably has a good amount of cash in there. Thanks again. We're headed to the hotel and then we'll get some lunch."

They shook his hand before Jake and Nora left the office.

Once outside, Nora said, "Jake, this is getting more bizarre by the day. Why doesn't she just take the money, get away from here and start over again?"

"For normal folks, I guess that would be the way to go. But Lucy doesn't see herself as an average person. She sees herself as special. Just like you saw yourself as less than special for so long. How strange is that? She isn't special, except for her looks, and you are special in everything."

"I keep telling you to stop the compliments or I'll turn into a Lucy myself – without the bosom."

"You could no longer be a Lucy than I could," Jake replied bringing a light laugh from Nora.

They briefly returned to their room and then went down to the hotel restaurant for lunch.

As they were eating, Jake looked over at Nora and said, "Nora, when we finish lunch, let's go and visit the gun store."

"Jake, between what we have on the horses and at my ranch, we have a small armory."

"Small is the key word. I want to get a pair of derringers, and we'll each carry one from now on. The Remington is small, but it carries a significant punch at short range. If we get a pair and a box of cartridges, I'd feel better."

"That does sound like a good idea. Get two boxes so we can practice with them."

"That's my Nora," Jake said with a smile.

So, after lunch, Jake and Nora walked to Greenburg's Gun Shop and picked up the two Remington derringers and two boxes of .41 caliber ammunition.

———

The next morning, Jake and Nora checked out of the hotel after having breakfast, walked to the livery, and picked up their four horses. Each horse had a Winchester, and Coffee was still stuck with the pack saddle, already loaded with the panniers. They bought the tickets to Albert and brought the four horses to the railroad stock corral.

By mid-afternoon, they had disembarked from the train and ridden south from Albert and arrived at Nora's ranch a little over an hour later, pulled up to the house, and stepped down.

Nora went inside while Jake began unloading Coffee, carrying the panniers into the kitchen. When he walked in with the first pannier, he saw Nora just standing in the hallway, looking into her room. He knew that she was staring at the closet that had been her personal prison for two days, so he set down the pannier and walked to her side.

She turned to look at Jake and said, "One bullet wasn't enough for that bastard."

"We can't change what he did to you, Nora, but you are not only still alive, you're loved. If he hadn't done what he did to you, Nora, I never would have found you, and how much worse would both of our lives be?"

She turned, hugged him tightly, and with her head buried against his chest, said, "I'm glad I'm selling this place."

Jake asked, "We do have to spend a night here, or would you rather go back to town?"

"Can we leave? The train leaves for Colorado at eleven o'clock, and we have to go to the bank anyway."

"Of course, we can. Let's just pack what you want to take."

Nora smiled weakly and they began to walk around the house. The two extra Winchesters and Colts were packed along with some personal items, but Nora didn't take any of her clothes. They were all overly worn anyway. It was as she was walking through the house that she suddenly realized just how empty her life had been. There was nothing that she had from her previous twenty-seven years that even recognized her existence. She felt cold inside, despite the summer heat.

She turned her face toward Jake, who had never left her side, and said, "Jake, I had nothing that meant anything. You could walk through this house and not even know anything more than a woman lived here."

"Mine isn't too much different. I do have some things that my Uncle Ernie left that I treasure. Little things, like a pair of stirrups that I never wear, my first real boots that are too small, and an old Colt Dragoon that belonged to him. But that's all going to change now, Nora."

She smiled and said, "Yes, it surely will."

They packed the rest of her things that she wanted to take then reloaded Coffee and returned to Albert, leaving the horses with the liveryman before they checked into the hotel.

―――

The next morning, Nora and Jake went to the bank and Nora had her ranch put up for sale. She arranged for the proceeds from the sale to be sent to Nora Fletcher at the C-F connected ranch outside of Eureka, Colorado.

They boarded the train at eleven o'clock in the morning and a few minutes later were on their way home.

―――

In Denver, a still-brown-haired Lucy, but with her figure returned to its spectacular state, had arrived wondering what her next step would be. As big as Denver had become, she thought it might be a good idea to fatten her stash by finding someone who could provide her with sufficient income. She felt the best place to hunt would be where the money was. She'd go to a bank and find a single man, a single man with money.

While Jake and Nora were still in Albert, she was walking into the Cattleman's Bank with her travel bag in hand and wanted to impress someone. She looked at the clerks, but none seemed substantial. Then she figured that the one she might try is the man who handled real estate transactions. He gets a percentage of each sale, so he should have a healthy bank account. Now, all he needed was to be unmarried.

She approached a clerk and asked, "Excuse me, I just arrived in Denver and need to open an account and find a house to buy."

"Certainly, ma'am. I can help you with the account, and you can see Mister Barfield about the house."

She sat down, and the clerk efficiently started the paperwork to start the new account.

"And how much do you wish to deposit?" he asked as he smiled at the pretty young woman.

"I'll deposit some of my cash now, and when the sale of my ranch in Kansas goes through, I'll add that as well."

Lucy laid out a thousand dollars on the desk, leaving her $246 in her travel bag.

The clerk took the money and gave her a receipt. After the account work was complete, he showed her to Mister James Barfield's office where she took a seat.

Lucy quickly examined his hands for a sign of a ring, finding them bare. So far so good. She knew that many men didn't wear wedding rings, but she didn't see any photographs on his desk, either.

She sat demurely at the proffered seat and inspected the bank official. Mister Barfield wasn't a bad-looking man, although he wasn't in the best of condition. He was about forty with a receding hairline.

He smiled at Lucy and asked, "Now, Miss Johnson, I was told you'll be looking for a house in Denver. Is that correct?"

"Yes. My father left me our ranch outside of Chaffee, Kansas. I finally decided that I couldn't run the place and put it on the market. Jason Fletcher at the bank in Chaffee says that, with the cattle, it should fetch upwards of ten thousand dollars. I always wanted to live in a city, so I left the sale to him and came here."

"What are you looking for in a residence?"

"Nothing too large. I'm alone and don't want to spend all my time cleaning."

"No, of course not. Don't you have any family at all?"

"No. None at all."

James Barfield was already smitten. Here's this demure, extremely lovely woman sitting in front of him with not a soul in the world to care for her. Her shape hadn't escaped his attention, either.

"Do you have a place to stay?"

"I'm in a hotel right now. I may move into a boarding house, though."

"Well, I have a spare apartment that I haven't rented that you could use free of charge until we find you something."

"I couldn't take advantage of your kindness, Mister Barfield," Lucy said in her most alluring voice.

James Barfield was almost sweating as he replied, "No, it's no trouble at all. And please, call me James."

"Then, thank you so much, James. Please call me Lucy," she said as she smiled sweetly at him.

Mister James Barfield was hooked, Lucy knew it and she didn't have to reel him in. He was willing to jump into her boat if he had to.

CHAPTER 10

Nora and Jake stepped down onto the platform at Eureka, Colorado at 4:35 in the afternoon. They were tired but excited to be home at last.

Ten minutes later, Jake was riding Sandy, and Nora was mounted on Satin as they trailed Coffee and the still unnamed mare behind them.

Nora caught her first glimpse of her new home when they crossed a rise about a mile from the ranch.

"Is that it, Jake?" she asked, pointing.

"That's it, Nora. What do you think?"

"It's a lot nicer than my ranch. The house seems bigger."

"The house is bigger. I just hope it's been left alone this past month."

"It looks fine to me," she said as she grinned.

They turned onto the access road and Jake felt relieved that the long journey was finally at an end. He was coming home at last. He was coming home with Nora, and he knew that wherever Nora was would be home.

They reached the house and dismounted, wrapping the reins around the hitching rail.

They stepped onto the porch, Jake unlocked and opened the front door, and Nora started to go into the house when Jake grabbed her left arm.

"Wait! You can't just walk in there, Mrs. Fletcher."

He leaned over and literally swept her off her feet and walked her across the threshold of the ranch house. She was still smiling when he set her gently down on her feet and pulled her close and kissed her.

"Welcome home, Nora."

Nora just smiled up at him, then took his arm as Jake showed her around the house and Nora began immediately thinking of what she would have to change. First, she told Jake, they'd need a bigger bed.

"If I knew that I'd find the woman of my dreams when I left here, I would have done that, but you caught me by surprise."

Overall, Nora was very happy with the house. It had four bedrooms and a bathroom with a tub. The kitchen was larger than hers and she very much appreciated the large cookstove and oven. They'd need more dinnerware, though.

"You explore the house, Nora. I'm going to get the horses unsaddled and start bringing in the panniers."

"Okay."

Nora was more than just happy. She was content knowing that she and Jake were home and now they could just live like normal people. She had forgotten about Lucy, at least for the moment.

Jake hadn't forgotten about Lucy for a heartbeat. As he was unsaddling the horses and removing the Winchesters and the shotgun, he was thinking about potential places she could show up to exact her revenge. He knew the layout of the ranch almost to the individual shoots of grass, and there wasn't any place that could be used as an ambush site within a quarter of a mile around the fences, so they could forget about a Winchester shot. Besides, he didn't think that would be her style. Lucy would want a face-to-face confrontation but just didn't think she could pull it off.

Jake carried the weapons and the panniers into the main room, which took several trips. Then he had to fill up the troughs for the horses, spread some hay, and fill the feeding bins with oats. When he finally finished, it was growing dark and must have been close to eight o'clock.

Nora had prepared her Mexican dish for Jake, and he was deeply appreciative. When they finished and had cleaned up, Jake led Nora to his bedroom, their bedroom now.

"Nora, we can finally really let ourselves go. No restrictions tonight, my love. Just you and me."

"Then you'd better be ready, cowboy," Nora almost growled.

It was a long and loud night at the C-F connected. By midnight, they were totally exhausted as they lay on the bed bathed in sweat. It was a warm June night and Nora was almost glued to Jake.

"That was the most fun we've had in a while," she purred as she lay atop her husband.

"Lordy, you do keep surprising me, woman. I wonder if I can ever satisfy you."

"Oh, you satisfy me, sir. You do it many times over and each seems more satisfying than the last. I just can't get enough of you, Jake. You make me feel so alive, but it's more than that. I get so overwhelmed with how much you love me. I can tell. I know I've only been with one man, and will only ever be with that one man, but I don't think it would be possible for me to be any more satisfied."

Jake just kissed the top of her damp head, then let out a long breath.

————

The next morning after breakfast, they rode into Eureka, stopped at the bank where Jake had Nora added to their account, and added the $13,300 draft, the reward vouchers, and most of the cash. It gave them an impressive balance, which also meant they had a lot of flexibility in what they could do.

After the bank, they ordered the large bed and a new set of dinnerware that Nora liked and also ordered some new cookware. The orders would be delivered to the ranch in a week or so.

While they were there, Nora bought some more clothes for daily use. She had never had so much new clothing, and keeping with tradition, she included four new pairs of britches that she knew would inspire her husband, as if he needed it.

They bought all the other daily necessities for the house as well when they added food, soap, more towels, and personal hygiene items. The order was all loaded into the panniers and hung on Coffee, who seemed to have accepted his fate as a pack horse.

Before they left Eureka, they had lunch at the café and then returned to the ranch by late afternoon.

During their day in town, they were approached by many of the locals who'd heard the stories and their constant retelling of many of the events wound up adding almost three hours to the visit to Eureka, but they'd expected it and didn't mind answering all of their questions.

———

Lucy was surprised how quickly the anxious James Barfield had made his intentions known. He had her installed in her new apartment later that same day, and before he left, had asked if he could call on her. She smiled sweetly and said she'd be happy to have him visit.

He visited the next afternoon and after an hour of meandering conversation, he managed to coax a quick kiss from a blushing Lucy and was floating on clouds when he left the apartment.

After he was gone, Lucy smiled, wondering why she had ever even bothered with Charlie. This was easier than she'd imagined.

———

While Jake and Nora were setting up the ranch, Lucy continued setting up James Barfield. He had visited her twice more and had already told her that he loved her and would like to be part of her life. She let him get a quick grope in twice as well, but she held back to make him more anxious and to maintain her image as an innocent, helpless woman in need of a strong man.

Anxious wasn't quite descriptive of the state of Mister Barfield's mental state, it was closer to panicked desperation. He had never had luck with the ladies before, and here was this incredibly beautiful enchantress willing to let him touch her. He wanted her so much he was almost neglecting his duties at the bank.

Finally, when Jake and Nora were receiving their new furniture and kitchenware back at the C-F Connected, James Barfield made a formal proposal of marriage to Lucy Johnson.

Lucy kissed him and accepted his proposal graciously, realizing that this one had fallen faster than she had ever had with Charlie and Ralph.

She had spent some time in his big house too, and she knew that he must be worth a lot more than those others as well.

He was worth a lot more, but as Lucy was soon to find out, less than three thousand dollars was kept in his personal bank account. The rest was invested in his real estate holdings and in an account specifically assigned to his real estate business.

After she had accepted his proposal, she did some probing about his accounts by asking if she'd have to move her money into his account and what would happen when she sold her ranch. When he explained how his money was distributed, but she'd only have access to the personal account, she smiled and asked the critical question: what happened if he died?

James told her that she would be his only heir so everything would go to her. He didn't want Lucy to think that she wasn't important to him.

––––––––

Jake and Nora were settling into their new life as a ranching couple, and Nora was helping Jake out in the pastures preparing everything for the new cattle. They had agreed to make the purchase next spring so they could get everything set up.

Jake was in the barn sharpening tools when Nora walked in and asked, "Jake, now that we're starting with all new cattle, do you want to keep the C-F Connected brand?"

Jake put down the axe he was putting an edge on and looked at Nora.

"You're right, Nora. It'll be our chance to put our own brand on our cows. What are you thinking? I think J-N Connected would be pretty nice."

"I was going to push for N-J Connected, but it didn't sound right. Besides, the brand for J-N Connected works better," she said as she drew the brand on the floor, where the vertical bar of the J served as the left vertical bar on the N.

"I like that, Nora. We'll register the brand and order some irons the next time we're in Eureka. I'll make a new sign as soon as it's registered."

One of their favorite pastimes was to picnic near the large stream that crossed diagonally from the northeast corner to the middle of the southern fence. With no cattle, the water was clear and inviting. After the second picnic, Jake decided to take an impromptu swim in the still cold water and encouraged Nora to join him. She was hesitant, not because she'd be out there naked, but because of the water's temperature. But the adventurous part of her won out and she joined Jake in the water. It was cold going in, but when they were close together, they didn't notice.

On their fourth picnic, they were laying in the warm sun, stretched out on the blanket. Nora was snuggled in close, as they did when they used the more conventional bed.

"Jake, aren't we a little vulnerable out here like this?"

"You may think that, but no, my love, we aren't. I have my Colt within reach, and you have your derringer nearby."

"But if she has a rifle, we're in trouble."

"True, but that's not her style, Nora. She'll want to face us and tell us how we did her wrong. Plus, there's the whole jealousy aspect that I don't have a clue how she'll try to remedy."

"This is so nice, though," she said as she smiled.

When they returned to the house, what Nora had said gave Jake pause. Yes, he had his pistol, but it did leave them open to one other problem. What if Lucy had a new partner by now?

———

Lucy did have a new partner, but not the kind of partner that had given Jake pause. While Jake and Nora lay sunning themselves, Lucy Johnson was being joined in matrimony to James Barfield. He was so pleased with his good fortune that, like all her previous husbands, he couldn't see the faulty logic behind the union.

When he had mentioned the marriage to his few friends at the bank, they congratulated him but saw the obvious. *Why would this voluptuous young woman marry a man like James Barfield?* Normally, they would put it down to the woman being a gold digger, but his new wife was a woman of property, with a healthy bank account and a pending sale of a ranch, so they were mystified.

James Barfield couldn't wait to get his new wife home and to bed. Lucy wasn't looking forward to the prospect but had already conceded to herself that she'd have to give in this time.

She just planned on acting the part of the innocent young maid and was very hesitant when it came to carnal knowledge.

When her new husband brought her to the bedroom in their big house, she asked that the lights be turned off and the curtains drawn. He readily agreed to her request, as he thought that's the way it should be.

Once the room was properly darkened, he took off his clothes and expectantly waited for Lucy to do the same and join him under the quilts. Lucy took off her dress but left on her corset and bloomers when she slid next to him. He didn't seem to mind a bit. He pulled down her bloomers and consummated the marriage in ten minutes.

Lucy was disgusted as she lay under his now somnolent body. She rolled him to his side and let him sleep before she slid from the bed. She didn't even have to dress that much as she left the room and walked to the kitchen.

Once she was sitting at the kitchen table, she couldn't help but compare her recent experience with the wild three weeks she had enjoyed with Jake Fletcher. The thought of Nora enjoying that same experience fertilized the seed of hate and jealousy that had taken root in her soul. If she had known how close she had been to the timing of Jake and Nora enjoying themselves in the bright sunlight of a Colorado pasture, she would have marched out there before getting James Barfield's money. But for now, the money acted like a brake on her emotions.

———

Two days later, Jake and Nora were out in back, practicing with their Colts and the new Remington derringers. The small pistols were more powerful and accurate than Jake had expected. Nora was especially adept with the derringer. She could place both shots in a six-inch circle at twenty feet. The .41 caliber round had more punch than some of the smaller derringers Jake had played with in the past, too.

They had converted one of the bedrooms to a gun room and Jake had built a rifle rack for the stack of long guns. They had six Winchesters and two shotguns now. The extra Colts and gunbelts were stored in what used to be a bedside chest, along with the dozen boxes of various sorts of ammunition. They were a well-armed couple.

Their new brand had been registered and Jake had replaced the sign out front with a new J-N connected cross member. He had updated the deed at the land office and added Nora as an owner. Things were working out well.

Nora's ranch had quickly sold for $4350, and when the voucher arrived, they deposited it into their account giving them a balance of just under twenty thousand dollars.

After shooting, they returned to the house to clean the guns. Nora had insisted on caring for her weapons, so they were cleaning the guns when Nora turned to Jake.

"Jake, remember Amanda?" she asked.

"Of course, I remember Amanda. Joseph as well. Why do you ask?"

"I was wondering if we could name our daughter Amanda," she asked with a small smile.

Jake dropped his cleaning cloth, stood and trotted to her side of the table. She was rising as he reached her and scooped her from her feet.

"You're pregnant?" he asked excitedly.

She just nodded as she was too happy to say anything.

Jake kissed her and hugged her closer as he asked, "How do you know it's going to be a girl?"

"Just a feeling, but maybe more of a hope."

Jake kissed her a few more times as he whirled his wife in circles before finally setting her down in her chair.

"I suppose I should be a little less enthusiastic in how I treat you now."

"Don't you dare! Your mother mentioned it to me when we were talking in private. She told me that if I were to become pregnant, don't let it affect anything except when I got big enough to present problems with walking and *other exercises*," Nora said before she laughed when she used her mother-in-law's phrase.

"Then, I'll follow my mother's advice. You've made me even happier, Nora, and I didn't think it was possible. I know that you're going to be a wonderful mother."

"Jake, I wanted a baby so badly. A few months ago, before all this began, I was lying in bed one night and just felt so alone. I had no one. But what bothered me even more was that I knew I would never be a mother. It crushed me, Jake. Then, when Charlie showed up, I thought that would change, but we know what happened. I was almost as upset about not being given that opportunity as I was about being locked in the closet. But then, you arrived. Not only have you given me your love and respect, you've now given me my baby. I am as complete now as I could ever have hoped to be."

Jake kissed Nora gently. Not because he thought he had to be gentle, but because he wanted to be. His one last concern about his Nora was now gone. He knew that one last small hole in her heart was going to be filled and hadn't a doubt that it would be by their daughter, Amanda.

———

A week had passed since their marriage. Lucy had been able to forestall three advances by her husband on the excuse that she was new to all this and she was sore, but she had to give in twice more as well.

During that tedious week, Lucy had been setting up for another job. The previous day, when she had been going through his desk while he was at work, she had chanced upon a pistol. It was a five-shot percussion pistol with the name 'Cooper' stamped on the side. It was already loaded, and it was smaller than most pistols she had seen. She had picked it up, found that it was comfortable in her hand, and smiled.

Her new plan for her husband wouldn't require the pistol, though. She had decided to borrow Charlie's idea but modified and improved. She'd send him into the cold room and lock him inside. Then, she'd go to the bank and write a draft for five thousand dollars and tell them that James had gone to Eureka and found an excellent buy on a ranch but needed her to bring him cash because the old man would only take currency. It would mean that the clerk would have to transfer some of his business account money to their joint account, but if she worked her magic, she could do it. Any more than that would be difficult, she believed. Her own thousand dollars were still there, and she planned on taking it as well. Then, after satisfying her growing need for revenge and satisfaction, she'd return and find her new husband dead in the cold room…how sad.

So, Lucy prepared for James' cold imprisonment. She would do it tomorrow before he left for work, then just after noon, she'd go to the bank and tell her story, which would explain her husband's absence. The train going east left at 1:40 and once she arrived in Eureka, she'd rent a buggy.

But she wouldn't go down to the ranch during the day, she'd spend that day resting, and then, very early the next morning, she'd drive down to the ranch and when she saw smoke from the cooking chimney, she'd make her move.

CHAPTER 11

Tuesday, July 1, 1875, arrived as a typical midsummer day in Colorado. The sky was pale blue with a hint of high clouds. It wasn't going to be overly hot, and it was dry, so it was going to be a very pleasant day.

Lucy had kissed James as he went off to work, then returned to her room and began packing her clothes. She'd leave some of them here because they didn't matter. She had her travel bag which now had more money, as James had given her two hundred dollars to buy more clothes. She spent forty dollars and put the rest into her stash. She went into the desk and pulled out the revolver, verified that all five cylinders were loaded then slid it into her travel bag.

Now, she went about a normal day, waiting for her new husband to return happily from work, probably eagerly expecting another uninspiring romp. She smiled as she glanced at the door to the cold room.

———

Jake and Nora were enjoying the weather at the newly christened J-N Connected ranch. Jake had begun to convert the neighboring bedroom into a nursery and had already removed the existing bed and disassembled it for use later. He and Nora had ordered the crib for the baby from a catalog and Nora bought some other baby-related items. She knew it was very early in her pregnancy to do such things, but she was so excited about the prospect and Jake let her enjoy it. He smiled at seeing the joy on her face when she looked at the baby items in the catalog and hoped she got her wish for a daughter. He wondered if she really knew or if it was pure hope.

———

James returned home to a smiling Lucy, who gave him a welcoming kiss, which was different. James was just pleased to see her so happy. She had tried to cook and had failed, but James pretended that it was delicious and wolfed down her sad offering.

After dinner, for no real reason, she began to intimate that she was in the mood. James was excited and quickly led her into the bedroom, undressed, and slid under the quilts waiting for her to extinguish the lamp.

Lucy was enjoying herself as she played her game. She surprised him when she didn't turn down the lamp, but undressed in front of him, knowing it was driving him mad. Then she crawled into bed and let him have his way with her.

Twelve minutes later, a frustrated and angry Lucy lay next to her sleeping husband. *Why on earth had she done that?* She was going to be rid of him tomorrow and could have just made an excuse and gone to sleep. She slipped out of bed and pulled on her nightdress, having no desire to have him pawing her overnight.

After she returned to the mattress, she realized that she had been thinking too much about seeing Jake again and her own urges were pushing her.

———

The next morning was the day of reckoning for James Barfield. When he awakened, he found Lucy already in the kitchen making breakfast. She had intentionally left the biscuits in the cold room. It wasn't a big cold room, but it had a door that could be locked from the outside and not unlocked from the inside. She had already found an appropriate knife to slide into the handle to lock it. She had done a trial run while he was at work and knew it would get the job done. Now, just to get him into the cold room.

James walked into the kitchen and kissed Lucy, who reciprocated before asking coyly, "How are you this morning, my husband?"

"I slept well, and I'm sure you know why," he replied as he grinned.

"Well, you sit down and have your breakfast," she said as she returned to the stove. She could make scrambled eggs and ham without poisoning anyone but bought the biscuits at a local bakery.

James looked at the table and asked, "Do you have any more of your delicious biscuits, my dear?"

She looked over from the stove. "Oh, I'm sorry. I put them in the cold room to keep them fresh."

"I'll get them," he said, smiling as he stood and walked to the cold room.

Lucy already had the knife in her hand waiting for him to go inside. She had placed the biscuits under a cloth in the back of the cold room, knowing he'd have to spend a few precious seconds to find them.

He opened the door and walked inside, and just a few heartbeats later, Lucy stepped to the door and rammed it closed. Before James knew what was happening, Lucy slipped the knife into the latch, locking it. Inside the dark, cold room, James was confused. *What had just happened?*

"Lucy?" he shouted.

Lucy was already out of the kitchen. She exited through the back door, then crossed the porch, and walked to the carriage house where she quickly harnessed the buggy.

Satisfied that she was ready, she returned to the kitchen, and ignoring the repeated shouts and thumping from the cold room, she ate the scrambled eggs and ham and drank her husband's coffee. When she finished, Lucy left the dirty dishes on the table and walked to their bedroom, pulled her packed trunk from the bedroom closet and slid it out of the house, and managed to squeeze it into the buggy. She then returned to the house where she picked up her travel bag and then entered the parlor. She sat on the brocaded settee and took out her newspaper to spend a few hours until the grandfather clock's loud chimes told her it was time to drive to the bank.

Just after noon, Lucy rose, took her travel bag in hand, then after ensuring that the doors were locked, she strode from the house, stepped into the buggy, and drove to the bank, preparing to use her greatest skill, knowing that she could lie better than most people could tell the truth.

She walked into the bank and sought out a clerk that had shown interest that first day.

"Good morning, Mrs. Barfield. How can I help you?" he asked as he not-so-innocently gave her a long perusal.

Lucy let him have the full effect and replied, "When he got home yesterday, James received a letter about a property that he was very excited about. He took the train early this morning and I just got a wire from him that the old man would only accept cash, but it was an extraordinary bargain. He asked me to bring him five thousand dollars on the next train. I've written out a draft, and I know he keeps most of his money in his business account, but he knows I don't have access to that."

"I think he should have given you access, but as it is, I'll cash this for you and transfer the money. I'll give you a leather wallet for it as well."

"Why, thank you. And, while I think about it, could you close my account and just give me the money? James said there was no use for me to keep it separate any longer," she said as she smiled.

The clerk smiled back and said, "Of course, Mrs. Barfield. Anything I can do to make you happy. And I do mean anything."

Lucy dazzled him with her best smile and said, "I'll remember that. You're very nice."

The clerk accepted her response as an invitation, then walked quickly to the teller's cage.

He quickly got the cash and took one of the complimentary leather wallets for special customers. He returned to his desk and counted out the cash and then slid it into the wallet. When he returned, he counted the currency again, then slipped the wallet across the desk. She signed a receipt and smiled at him one more time before standing and giving the clerk the full Lucy view as she swayed across the lobby and out of the bank. The clerk had no idea that he'd just lost his job.

She left the bank, got into the buggy, and drove to the train station, her travel bag now loaded with well over six thousand dollars. She left the buggy, had the porter take her trunk, and then bought her ticket to Eureka, Colorado, took a seat on a bench, and just abandoned the buggy in the street outside the depot.

An hour and ten minutes later, she was on her way east out of Denver.

―――

Nora was hungry already. She'd never experienced being hungry so much and understood that being pregnant would have an impact on her body, but she didn't know about the hunger.

Jake did and told her it was expected and not to worry about it. The reason didn't matter to Nora though, she was hungry all the time already and as she tried to satisfy her need for food, she was just a little concerned about getting fat. She was worried that Jake would lose interest if she put on some unnecessary pounds.

"Will you tell me if my behind is getting bigger?" she asked.

"I'll have to inspect it more often," he replied as he grinned.

"I guess that you'll just have to enjoy yourself, but please be honest with me if it's getting too big. Would you do that?" she asked as she smiled back at him.

He slid his hand across her wonderful bottom, then said, "It's still perfect, Nora. I also noticed that you're trying to catch up to Lucy on the other end."

"I hope not. I still remember what you said about what would happen to her when she was older."

Jake laughed, then massaged her left breast before saying, "I was just kidding, Nora. They may be fuller now, but they'll never be anywhere as swollen as hers."

Nora put her hand over his to let him continue his well-appreciated comment and caress but hoped he wasn't telling her a white lie.

Nora had continued to wear pants until her stomach would get too big, which also gave her pockets where she kept her derringer.

It also gave Jake something to inspect.

Jake kept his derringer in his pocket as well, but he was also rarely without his Colt. Once she had the derringer, Nora stopped wearing her pistol. It had been two weeks since they had returned, and thoughts of Lucy were slipping into the past. They were happy and everything was good.

————

They were eating a late dinner when the train arrived from Denver. After checking into the hotel, Lucy had the trunk taken to her room, then went to the diner and had her dinner before returning to her room where she unpacked her dress for tomorrow's confrontation with that woman.

She was dressed as she'd been when she left Wichita, and no one had recognized her then either. But she'd been in this much smaller town longer and had to minimize her exposure, but only for one day.

————

Back in Denver, James Barfield was cold and despondent. He had food and water in the cold room, but it was dark, and he hadn't a clue what had happened. Just as Jake had done when he discovered Lucy missing, he imagined the worst. Someone had broken in and slammed the door closed and then taken Lucy. He was absolutely convinced that Lucy wouldn't do anything like this.

———

Lucy went to sleep early.

Jake and Nora went to bed early but didn't go to sleep.

James Barfield slept in the darkness and cold.

———

The next morning, Lucy dressed in one of her most provocative dresses before she left the hotel with her travel bag, headed to the livery, and rented a buggy, which the liveryman quickly prepared for her use. She had a shawl wrapped around her shoulders to hide her cleavage. Even though Lucy had been married in Eureka just a few months earlier, the lack of blonde hair did wonders for her being unrecognized. She climbed into the buggy without having any breakfast and drove south.

———

Nora and Jake slept in a little while, enjoying their time together in bed, even when they just spent time being close without talking. They finally stirred and dressed to begin their day.

Jake fired up the cookstove and began setting the table while Nora prepared breakfast, both of them unaware of the danger that was lurking just at the end of their access road.

Lucy had been waiting for the smoke to appear from the stove pipe, and once the first wisps began curling from the pipe at the back of the house, she waited longer to achieve perfect timing. Let them start eating and she would enter the house through the back door. She was very familiar with both the house's layout and where they would be when she stepped into the room. As she sat, waiting for the precise time, she seethed as she let her imagination fill with scenes of Jake satisfying that unworthy woman.

After fifteen minutes, she started the buggy toward the house, slowing it until she got within a hundred feet, brought the buggy to a stop, then reached inside the travel bag and pulled out the pistol. She stepped out of the buggy, tossed her shawl into the seat, then walked along the southern side of the house toward the kitchen.

Jake and Nora were eating breakfast and enjoying the morning as they always did. They were talking and laughing as Lucy approached the back door.

She quietly stepped onto the back porch and suddenly yanked the door open, slamming it into the side wall, and stepped inside with the pistol cocked.

Jake and Nora popped to their feet and stared with wide eyes at the expected, yet unexpected visitor.

"Hello, Jake and Nora," Lucy said with a smile as she pointed the gun at Nora.

Jake forced himself into a steeled countenance as he said calmly, "Good morning, Lucy. What's with the gun?"

"I never did thank you for shooting Charlie for me, Jake," she replied.

320

Before he could reply, Nora said, "Jake didn't do it, Lucy. I shot Charlie."

"Do you expect me to believe that?" she asked with a sneer.

Jake answered, "I could have killed him, but I let Nora take the shot. She had him under her Winchester and told him to drop his rifle. He turned thinking he could shoot her first, but she got him. Don't ever underestimate my wife, Lucy."

Lucy's eyes widened, then she laughed as she asked, "Your wife? You married her? Your standards have slipped, Jake."

"No. I've told you before, Lucy. You're nowhere near the woman my Nora is."

"Look at me, Jake! I'm a real woman. She's nothing. And now, we're going to prove it. I'm going to make you a widower, Jake, then I'll make you remember what you've obviously forgotten."

Jake and Nora were standing twelve feet from Lucy.

Nora was on Jake's left and Lucy had her pistol pointed at Nora's chest. Jake recognized the weapon she held in her hand. It was a Cooper Pocket, shot a .31 caliber ball, and didn't have a lot of penetrating power, but even if it had been a Colt .45, his decision would have been the same.

He suddenly rotated on his left foot and clung to Nora exposing his back to Lucy.

"You'll have to shoot me, Lucy," Jake said, facing the back wall.

"If that's what you want, Jake. I'll still shoot Nora after you're dead. I'll miss you after you're gone, but if it's what you want."

Jake whispered quickly to Nora, "If she shoots, shoot her."

Nora didn't weep, and she didn't panic. She slipped her hand into her pocket and fingered the derringer.

"Lucy, this isn't very smart. You've got some money. Why don't you just leave us in peace?" Jake asked.

"I've got more now. I pulled a Charlie on my latest husband. He's locked in a cold room right now. After I finish here, I'm going to take your advice and just disappear."

"You're never going to be able to disappear, Lucy. You'll have the law after you now. They were willing to let you walk after the other crimes, but not after you pull that trigger."

"Well, we'll just have to see about that," she snarled as she pointed the pistol at Jake and pulled the trigger.

The pistol boomed loudly in the enclosed space as Jake felt the projectile penetrate his back on his right side. It felt like a hard kick followed by a burn.

Nora didn't hesitate, and as Lucy was preparing for her second shot, Nora pulled the derringer and, while still holding Jake, cocked the hammer and pointed it at a shocked Lucy.

Nora fired, her .41 caliber bullet blasting into Lucy, who staggered backward dropping her pistol to the floor before she reached the back wall and slid to the floor.

"That's my Nora," Jake said softly as he smiled at his wife and felt his knees weaken.

Nora knew she had to be strong and slowly lowered Jake to the floor, then stepped over him to get to Lucy. Lucy had taken the shot in the left upper chest and would live with medical treatment. Nora picked up her pistol and looked down at Lucy as she slipped it into her waistband.

"I should just shoot you, you, stupid bitch. But I'm not as insane as you are."

Nora quickly turned to Jake, stooped down, and looked at his wound.

"Jake? How bad is it?"

"I think I need to see a doctor soon," he whispered as he grimaced.

Nora turned to the groaning and crying Lucy and asked, "Do you have a buggy outside?"

"Yes," she gasped.

Nora went to Jake, helped him to his feet, and began walking him to the buggy.

Lucy shouted hoarsely, "What about me? I'm dying!"

Nora didn't turn, but she shouted over her shoulder, "You're not dying, you, drama queen. I wish you were."

Nora got Jake into the buggy and then returned for the injured Lucy. She pulled Lucy up off the floor and as she groaned and sobbed, walked her to the buggy, managed to squeeze her into the buggy, then climbed inside and turned it toward Eureka. She had the horse at a fast trot, and they arrived in Eureka twenty minutes later.

Nora drove directly to the doctor's house, where he ran his clinic. After climbing past Lucy, she stepped out, then walked around to Jake's side and helped him out of the buggy. She could tell he was weak and kept talking to him as she helped him up the steps and onto the porch, then pounded on the door.

It was opened by the doctor twenty seconds later and Nora quickly said, "Doctor Mayfield, Jake has been shot. I have his shooter in the buggy. I shot her with a derringer before she could shoot again."

"I'll bring him in, you go and bring in the shooter."

Lucy let him take her husband and then walked slowly down the steps to the buggy.

She stood and glared at Lucy as she snarled, "Let's get you to the doctor, bitch. I hope it hurts when he fixes you up."

Lucy didn't respond. It already hurt.

Nora pulled her out of the buggy, then walked her up the steps to the porch, opened the door, and hauled her inside.

The doctor's wife had just come out of the examining room when she set Lucy down in a hardbacked chair near the door.

"That's the shooter?" she asked with wide eyes as she looked at Lucy.

"Yes, ma'am. She was going to shoot me, but Jake stepped in front of me to take the bullet. I shot her with a derringer when she was getting ready to shoot him again."

"Bring her into the second room on the right. We have another examining table in there."

Nora helped the still weeping Lucy into the second examining room and let her lay on the table.

Nora then left the room and opened the door to the examining room across the hall while the doctor's wife began pulling Lucy's dress away to check her wound. The doctor had Jake on the table and was cutting the bullet out.

She asked, "Doctor, I've got to go and see the sheriff. Will Jake be all right?"

"I think so. I'll get the bullet out. It didn't hit anything serious, and it's a small caliber, so he should be all right if there's no infection."

Nora nodded, then said, "I'll be back as soon as I can."

Nora turned and quickly left the house. She was calm on the outside but full of turmoil inside, furious with Lucy, and terrified for Jake.

She climbed into the buggy where she noticed the travel bag, then opened it and saw the bulging wallet with the cash. She closed it again, then drove the buggy to the sheriff's office, stepped out, and entered the jail. She knew the sheriff reasonably well. Jake had introduced him when they had returned and explained the circumstances of their meeting, as well as the events thereafter.

"Morning, Nora. What can I do for you?" he asked when she entered.

"Pete, Jake's been shot by that woman that stole all his money and cattle. She came back and was going to shoot me, but Jake stepped in front and she shot him. I shot her with my derringer. Both are over at the doctor's office now."

He was stunned for a few seconds then popped to his feet and hurriedly asked, "What can I do while he's getting fixed up?"

"She said that she left her latest husband in Denver locked in his cold room. I have her money that she stole from him here," she said as she put the travel bag on his desk.

"Did she tell you his name?"

"No. But we can go and ask. She's still awake."

"Let's do that."

The sheriff took the bag from his desk and locked it in a cell before following Nora to the doctor's office, then into the second examination room where they found Lucy still groaning as she lay on the table.

The sheriff didn't even have to threaten Lucy but simply asked the name of her new husband.

An almost despondent Lucy gave him the name even before he finished asking the question. She'd never been hurt before and having that bullet rip into her chest stunned her.

The sheriff then left and wired the sheriff in Denver, so he could free Mister Barfield and let him know that his wife had been shot and would be in custody after she was treated.

———

Nora was finally winding down after the surge of adrenalin left her body. She had been waiting in the doctor's office for more than an hour since bringing Jake in. The dread of possibly losing Jake finally hit her as she hung her head and the tears rolled from her eyes. Her beloved husband had taken a bullet for her. *Just how much more could he do for her?* He had rescued her from her lonely life and had given her confidence in herself. He had let her have justice and even given her a baby. And most of all, he loved her.

She cried for almost twenty minutes, leaving a growing pool on the floor when she heard footsteps, lifted her eyes, and saw the doctor approaching.

She wiped her eyes and asked, "How is Jake, Doctor?"

"He's resting now. He didn't lose as much blood as he could have. The bullet is out and now he just needs time to recuperate. He should be up and about in a week or so."

Nora felt an incredible sense of relief as she said, "Thank you so much, Doctor."

"Do you know what he kept talking about while I was fixing his wound?"

She shook her head.

"All he talked about was you. You and your baby. He's quite proud of you, Nora."

"I'm just as proud of him. I was so frightened about losing him."

"Well, you won't. If you want to go and stay with him, you can. I need to go and take care of the woman. I checked her wound and it wasn't bad at all. It was above her clavicle. I just need to clean it and then suture it."

"I'll be in with Jake," she said as she stood.

He nodded and walked to the second examination room to suture Lucy's wound while Nora quietly opened the door to Jake's examining room and walked inside, and then closed the door behind her.

She tried not to cry when she saw him, but it was hard seeing Jake swathed in linen around his chest. She sat in the chair near his head.

As she did, Jake opened his eyes, looked into those incredibly large brown eyes, and smiled.

"You're an amazing woman, Nora," he said hoarsely.

"You take a bullet for me and you call me amazing," she said as she laughed shakily.

"You took charge, Nora, as I knew you could."

"You're the one who made me believe I could, Jake."

"But it was always there, my love. You just needed to see it."

"Well, I need you to take charge again when you're better."

"Does this mean no more enthusiastic nights for a while?" he asked quietly with what could have passed as a grin.

"When you can ride a horse, then we can talk about enthusiastic nights."

"That sounds fair," he whispered.

"You get some sleep, Jake. I need to get you healthy enough to ride a horse."

He smiled and drifted off to sleep.

————

While Jake slept, the Denver sheriff released James Barfield from his cold prison and informed him of the shooting in Eureka. They also told him his money had been recovered.

It took almost two hours for it all to sink in as he sat in his kitchen with a blanket over his shoulders and a steaming cup of coffee in his hands. *His wife had locked him inside and then bilked him? Then she went to Eureka and shot a man?* It was a lot to absorb.

———

The next morning, Nora used the buggy to take Jake home. She helped him inside and got him tucked into bed, then she saddled Satin and trailed her to the livery to drop off the buggy. She checked with the sheriff and found that a deputy from Denver was coming to Eureka to pick up Lucy and the money. Lucy would be charged in Denver and would then be sent to Eureka to face charges of attempted murder. Jake told her that he was not going to drop the charges this time even before Nora could ask.

Jake was doing better after three days and was on his feet. Nora tried to convince him otherwise, and that he should continue to rest, but he insisted that he was doing better. She had been feeding him constantly to build his strength, so she knew it was a losing argument.

The trial for Lucy was held in Denver two days later. Her defense attorney had her dress conservatively, but it didn't matter, as the evidence was overwhelming. She was found guilty and sentenced to ten years.

As she stood in the docket, hearing the judge pronounce the sentence, Lucy was numb. *How could this have happened?* Everything had worked perfectly until that woman had shot her. She was nothing. *How could she have done this to her?*

She was returned to her cell and the sheriff sent a telegram to Eureka announcing the verdict and sentence. She would be returned to Eureka for her trial in two days.

———

Jake and Nora rode to Eureka for the trial. The prosecuting attorney had ridden out to their ranch the day before to go over their testimony. Nora had turned over the gun Lucy had used in the crime to the sheriff that first day and the prosecutor felt this was the easiest case he'd had in a long time. Everyone in town knew that this woman had been the one to scam Jake and the newlywed Fletchers were very popular, especially after hearing how Jake had taken the bullet for his real wife.

They were sitting in the courtroom waiting for the judge when Lucy was brought in. It was hard to associate the Lucy that they both knew with the woman being brought into the courtroom. She was dressed like a matron, but she also looked different. Her eyes were lifeless, and her face was drawn and tired. If she hadn't shot her husband, Nora might feel sympathetic.

The judge entered and was announced as he strode to his seat behind the bench. The trial of Lucy Barfield, which was now her true legal name, after the death of Charlie Haskins, began.

Nora had glanced at Jake who was already looking at her. Neither had realized that legally, Lucy was really married to James Barfield.

The prosecutor only had two witnesses. He called Nora first, and she explained in vivid detail what had happened the day of the shooting. She pointed at Lucy when asked to identify the shooter. The defense attorney didn't even ask her any questions. There was no point.

Then Jake took the stand. Again, he related the events of that morning, and the most insightful part of his testimony came when the prosecutor asked why he had stood against his wife to protect her rather than jumping at Lucy.

"She had a cocked pistol aimed at my wife. I couldn't risk it going off before I could deflect it. I saw that it was a lower caliber pistol, so I doubted if it could penetrate through me to hurt Nora. So, I held her close and covered her completely. I told Nora to shoot Lucy if she shot me, so when Lucy fired, I knew Nora would do what was necessary before she took her second shot. If she hadn't, I would be dead. I owe my life to my Nora."

He looked at Nora's expansive brown eyes as he testified. She smiled at him, knowing full well, as every man on the jury knew, that she would have been dead had he not taken the bullet. Only she knew that he meant every word of what he had just said.

The defense attorney tried to point Jake toward his marriage and harassment of Lucy across the state of Kansas as evidence of an obsession with Lucy. It was a losing argument, and he probably knew it before he started, but it was all he had.

The jury deliberated less than fifteen minutes. She was found guilty of attempted murder, and the judge sentenced her to twenty years to be served after her ten-year sentence from Denver.

Lucy had no reaction whatsoever as she was led from the courtroom. Neither Fletcher had any pity for her as she passed by, and she didn't glance their way as she shuffled along. Lucy was out of their lives forever.

———

Three days later, a buggy pulled up in front of the J-N connected house. James Barfield stepped out and knocked on the door.

Nora answered, asking, "May I help you?"

"My name is James Barfield. You are Mrs. Fletcher, I assume?"

"I am. Please come in, Mister Barfield," she replied, opening the door.

He entered the house and found Jake sitting in the main room. He was sitting after doing some work in the barn that had pushed him to his temporary physical limits.

He rose when he heard the visitor's name and asked, "Mister Barfield, how are you doing?"

"Probably better than you are," he replied as he smiled.

"Lucy did leave a path of damaged people in her wake. She got me twice. Have a seat."

He sat down, and Nora joined them, sitting next to Jake on the couch, the same spot she had occupied before the knock on the door.

"I felt like such a fool, Mister Fletcher. How could I have been duped by that woman?"

"You aren't alone. She duped six of us, from what I gathered. Please call me Jake, and my wife's name is Nora."

He looked over at Nora and smiled.

"We're just not honest with ourselves sometimes. If I had been, the first question I would have asked is why is this gorgeous young woman interested in me?"

"The same question we all should have asked, but it was a lesson we all survived. I was very fortunate to have found a real woman, the very best when I was trying to find Lucy to get my money back. She had been scammed by Lucy's first husband, so we went after Lucy with one goal in mind, to bring her and her husband to justice. But before long, that goal was secondary to another, more meaningful purpose. We found happiness together. It's out there, you know."

"Then I'll take that as good advice and keep looking. But the purpose of my visit was to drop this off with you," he said as he dropped the wallet on the table, "After I took out what she had stolen from me there was another $1540. They told me that I was entitled to the money because I was still legally her husband. I have no need for the money and felt that you both deserve it for what you did to get me free and bring her to justice."

"We don't need the money either. We're all right."

"You don't understand. I have sixteen properties in Denver and over a hundred thousand dollars in my business account. Thank God, I never let her have access to that money! Anyway, the extra money is more of an annoyance to me than anything else. Use it to buy a few more head of cattle for your ranch. It would make me feel better."

Nora replied, "Then, we'll do just that. We're going to repopulate the ranch with new cattle in the spring. That would add another seventy head."

"Wonderful. I read about your story in the Denver paper. It's a topic of conversation in all the barber shops and sewing circles. You took a bullet for your wife before Nora took over and got you and Lucy to the doctor. It's quite a tale. Maybe I'll find a woman I can love as much as you love your wife."

"It's possible. Spend more time listening and less time looking. The looking is secondary. I think my Nora is the most beautiful woman I have ever met," he said as he smiled at her.

"She is a special lady," James Barfield agreed.

He stayed for lunch and Nora made some of her Mexican-flavored mix that James raved about. He invited them to visit him whenever they came to Denver and left in his buggy at two o'clock to catch the train west.

After he had gone, Nora and Jake were in the main room. Jake had his hands on his wife's still thin waist, and she had her hands around his neck.

Nora smiled at him and said, "What was that line about my being the most beautiful woman that you've ever met? You're not being honest, Mister Fletcher."

"No, Nora. I'm being very honest. I look at you and see all of you. You, Nora Fletcher, really are the most beautiful woman I have ever met."

EPILOGUE

The following spring, Jake purchased four hundred head of prime Hereford cattle. They also added a few other improvements to the ranch, including expanding the barn and buying a buggy. Coffee was drafted into buggy duties, as they were not going to be requiring his services as a pack horse any longer.

The buggy was necessary because they couldn't travel anywhere as a family on horseback for a while. Because, on a cold February morning just three months earlier, Nora Fletcher gave birth to a six-pound, eight-ounce baby girl.

Nora adored her little Amanda Rose.

Nora Fletcher, the plain, skinny little girl who was the brunt of teasing and shunning her entire growing life and had lived a solitary early adult life now had it all. She had a perfect baby girl to love and cherish, a wonderful home, and above all, a caring and devoted husband who loved her more than life itself. There was no one more grateful or happy than the once-lonely Nora Fletcher.

———

Lucy Johnson died in prison eleven years later, never understanding how that plain-looking woman could have possibly been better than she was.

BOOK LIST

1	Rock Creek	12/26/2016
2	North of Denton	01/02/2017
3	Fort Selden	01/07/2017
4	Scotts Bluff	01/14/2017
5	South of Denver	01/22/2017
6	Miles City	01/28/2017
7	Hopewell	02/04/2017
8	Nueva Luz	02/12/2017
9	The Witch of Dakota	02/19/2017
10	Baker City	03/13/2017
11	The Gun Smith	03/21/2017
12	Gus	03/24/2017
13	Wilmore	04/06/2017
14	Mister Thor	04/20/2017
15	Nora	04/26/2017
16	Max	05/09/2017
17	Hunting Pearl	05/14/2017
18	Bessie	05/25/2017
19	The Last Four	05/29/2017
20	Zack	06/12/2017
21	Finding Bucky	06/21/2017
22	The Debt	06/30/2017
23	The Scalawags	07/11/2017
24	The Stampede	08/23/2019
25	The Wake of the Bertrand	07/31/2017
26	Cole	08/09/2017
27	Luke	09/05/2017
28	The Eclipse	09/21/2017
29	A.J. Smith	10/03/2017
30	Slow John	11/05/2017
31	The Second Star	11/15/2017
32	Tate	12/03/2017

33	Virgil's Herd	12/14/2017
34	Marsh's Valley	01/01/2018
35	Alex Paine	01/18/2018
36	Ben Gray	02/05/2018
37	War Adams	03/05/2018
38	Mac's Cabin	03/21/2018
39	Will Scott	04/13/2018
40	Sheriff Joe	04/22/2018
41	Chance	05/17/2018
42	Doc Holt	06/17/2018
43	Ted Shepard	07/16/2018
44	Haven	07/30/2018
45	Sam's County	08/19/2018
46	Matt Dunne	09/07/2018
47	Conn Jackson	10/06/2018
48	Gabe Owens	10/27/2018
49	Abandoned	11/18/2018
50	Retribution	12/21/2018
51	Inevitable	02/04/2019
52	Scandal in Topeka	03/18/2019
53	Return to Hardeman County	04/10/2019
54	Deception	06/02.2019
55	The Silver Widows	06/27/2019
56	Hitch	08/22/2018
57	Dylan's Journey	10/10/2019
58	Bryn's War	11/05/2019
59	Huw's Legacy	11/30/2019
60	Lynn's Search	12/24/2019
61	Bethan's Choice	02/12/2020
62	Rhody Jones	03/11/2020
63	Alwen's Dream	06/14/2020
64	The Nothing Man	06/30/2020
65	Cy Page	07/19/2020
66	Tabby Hayes	09/04/2020

NORA

C.J. PETIT

Made in United States
North Haven, CT
18 March 2023